BEAUTIFUL

By
Christine Zolendz
© 2013

Dedicated to the ones that are bruised and broken
Our voices are loud
Let us scream

Table of Contents

Author's Note:

The words I've strung together on these few pages are a world to many readers. These words carry so many different messages to every one of us. In fact, the world I saw in my head will be greatly different from the one you read in yours. That's the magic of the imagination. The story you read will be judged by your experiences, drenched with your history, your past, and your own pains. I began writing this story because the character of Samantha (which I strangely named after my dog, don't fucking ask) popped into my head as an image of a woman covered in blood sitting behind a steering wheel. It played in violent loops in my brain. Then Kade entered with his violent flashbacks and visions. I fell hard for both of them. They both have a brutality to their lives that not many people, thank God, have been touched with. Not every story is pretty, not every story is perfect, but this is their story; one that the characters dictated and I just sat back and typed. Their story is quite brutally beautiful. The situations that these two people are in are quite real. These are stories that are on the news. I hear them in my subconscious and I research them until I understand the psyche and reasons behind the actions and emotions. I have spent numerous hours, obsessing and reading victims' accounts, memoirs, police reports; you name it, I researched it. In real life, you can't control the story. You can't make your wishes appear and give everybody a happily-ever-after. Yet, as I was in Kade's mind, experiencing the chaos and pain, I couldn't think of anything I could give him other than hope and love.

So here is to victims and underdogs, may you find peace and calmness in your life. We are strong. Just because we've been under the hand of violence, it does not make us weak. It makes us see life clearer than others, and it makes us breathe harder.

All human actions have one or more of these seven causes: chance, nature, compulsion, habit, reason, passion, and desire.
Aristotle

Chapter 1

There was blood all over my hands and I knew I was losing control, because I was more desperate to find a drink, than a napkin to clean off the mess. A few *really strong drinks* to block out everything that happened. I needed something strong to jumpstart my terrified ass into breathing normally again. My fingers slid across my blood soaked steering wheel, while my body ached and pounded. Shaking with harsh violent tremors, I tried to catch my breath and focus on driving as fast as I could.

Icy chills from the cold night wracked through my shoulders, even though I had the heater turned up high and the windows closed. *Maybe the bitter coldness was coming from somewhere deep inside me.* The thought sent a quake of chills surging across my throbbing collarbone.

"Can you still drive? Lemme drive. Samantha, *pull over* and let me take the wheel!" Jennifer yelled in the passenger seat beside me. I turned my head to look at her. *Oh hell. Oh, no...she had blood all over her too.*

Her long, pale blonde hair was pulled back in a messy bun and a few wild loose strands stuck to the sweat soaked skin of her neck. Twisting in her seatbelt, she gripped one hand on the dashboard, leaving a smudge of dark fingerprints just beneath. Big, brown, unblinking eyes pleaded with me to stop the car and let her take over driving.

No way, no one drives as fast as I do.

And we had to get away.

Gunning the engine, I accelerated, trying to find the next rest stop, exit, or somewhere I could wash the drying blood from my skin. Jen was absolutely right. We needed to stop somewhere and assess our damage. "How bad do we look, Jen?" My eyes peeked a glance at her again, as I tried to focus on the dark empty road laid out in front of us.

"Well...you look like first degree murder, and me, I look like an assault with a deadly weapon. What the hell do you think we LOOK LIKE?" She rubbed her fingers over her face and smeared a streak of blood across her tanned cheeks. *Oh my...Oh my God, there's a lot of blood. What the hell did I do?* "Just pull over, Sam. You're going to freaking bleed out while driving. You're leaking like a sieve."

I gave her a little snort, "Don't worry, okay? They're just flesh wounds; nothing is internally bleeding. I'm just...I think we're in shock...that's all. And I don't think most of the blood is *mine*." I ran my hand through my auburn strands of hair and my fingers came away bloodier. Suddenly, I developed an acute case of Tourette's syndrome, "Fuck! That fucking-shit-son-of-an-ass-monkey-dick-weasel!" *I didn't remember getting hit in the head.* "I should have ripped his dick off!"

Shit! Shit. Shit, *just apply pressure...*

With almost seven straight hours of non-stop-adrenaline-fueled driving behind me, I pulled into the parking area of the first and *only* thing open on the long, empty stretch of road I found myself on.

Of course, it was a bar. God must have forgiven me already for my sins, since he was so kindly answering my prayers for a stiff drink. Although an all-night drug dealer with a special sale on *Vicodin* would have been more useful. But I wasn't going to complain. Alcohol was good enough.

"Oh, really? Samantha, this is a *strip bar*," she said, pointing her grimy finger towards my windshield. "That is a goddamn stripper club in the middle of a dark empty country road in the middle of North-Bumble-Fuck-Nowhere-New York; how much more horror movie cliché can we get? I'm not stepping foot in that shithole." My expression didn't change. "Come on, Sam. Let's not dive right into an episode of some B-rated slasher show, *please*?"

Shoving my gearshift into park, I clicked the interior light on. *Seven hours away. Seven hours away is good enough for now. Besides, I had to pee.* Sharp pains spiked all over my beaten body, as I climbed into the small back seat, streaking blood across the white leather interior of my last birthday present to myself, my gunmetal gray Porsche Panamera. "*Ughh...aghh...*I almost killed myself doing that. Can you get my first aid kit out of the trunk for me?"

"Crap, Sam, you're *serious*? You're going to walk into that bar looking like *that*? Someone is going to ask questions." With the new brightness of the dome light above us, I could see just how bad the bruises were that blossomed over her cheekbone. Just below her left eye, a deep purple and red discoloring from the ruptured capillaries beneath her skin fanned out, and the corner of her lip was a fat bloodied mess.

Thudding my head against the cool leather, I squeezed my swollen eyes tightly and tried hard to fight the tears that stung at their lids. I am stronger than *this*. I am stronger than *HIM*. I didn't want to waste tears on the pain, *or the reasons for it*. I should just be happy still to be alive. *That both of us were still alive.* "Jen, I need either a depressant or a potent analgesic so I can focus better. The pain is starting to scream at me. And, I need to clean out my wounds. Too many hours have passed, but it was more important to put miles between us and that *hell*."

The car door clicked and before I opened my eyes, the nearly muted thump of the trunk opening and slamming shut filled my ears. Then her soft whispers, "I got the bag with the clean clothes out, too. But, I swear, if any of those horny-ass bastards from that bar come stumbling on us changing in the car, we're going to have more blood on our hands, Sam."

Unclasping my first aid kit, I tore through the bag looking for anything that I could use.

Tearing off the cap of a bottle of peroxide, I poured it straight over my hands, letting it spill all over my lap. "DAMN, that HURTS!" I screamed out when the cold liquid flowed into my cuts, making my body explode with white-hot pain. I bit my teeth into the soft leather of the front seat headrest to silence my cries.

Jen pulled out a few butterfly bandages, and when the stinging of the peroxide settled to a dull ache, I began methodically cleaning and sealing my lacerations, biting down on my lip hard when the pain was too much. It was a freaking miracle that there were no deep puncture wounds, but still, this was enough. *It was all enough...I'd had enough.* I could feel how bruised and swollen both my eyes sockets were, and my lip felt as if it was split in half. *Thank God, it wasn't.* When the reality of the situation hit me, I looked up at her, "We need new names, don't we? And we need to get rid of my car."

We gave each other a measured stare. Without a doubt, we both knew there was no fixing this situation. We did what we had to do, and now we had to move on. There was no going back, and truthfully, I was so *relieved*. I inhaled deeply, and then slowly puffed out my breath. Even though it hurt like mad, I smiled. I was *free*.

Her lips curled into a smile to match mine. "I want to be Bree Masterson and I want to be at least five years younger than I really am. Think I can still pass for 28?"

My laughter made me grimace and moan in pain. "Sure, just clean off all the blood, that'll take at least two to three years off you." After scrubbing my face with a few scrunched up alcohol swabs I found, I slowly pulled on clean clothes. "I like the name Lainey. Lainey Nevaeh. I don't care about my age though. I'll stay 32." It was the only name that kept repeating itself in my head as I cleaned myself. It meant something to me, although I didn't think anybody else would have understood.

"Ah, yeah, because you never were like any normal teen and roasted yourself in the sun, you could still pass for twenty-one. Why the last name Never?" she asked slipping her legs into a clean pair of jeans in exchange for her bloodied ones.

"Not the word *never*. *N. E. V. A. E. H*, it's heaven spelled backwards. I don't know, maybe because, I'm not in *that* hell anymore. " Pulling a compact mirror out of my purse, I tried to cover up the redness of my swollen eyes as much as I could. "There's no use with the make-up, is there? Let's just get a few drinks and find a place to sleep. We are so deep in the Adirondacks that we should be fine here for a few days."

The bright pink neon light that flashed the bar's name read Mc*Smexymelts*, with a dancing neon ass-shaking animated sign next to it. "Holy crud, Sam...*ah damn*...I meant...*Lainey*, we're really doing this, aren't we?"

Trying not to limp too much with the burning sting from the cuts and scrapes on my legs as they rubbed against the material of my pants, I made my way to the entrance of the bar. "Yeah, *Bree*, we are really going to have a drink in a strip bar. I don't care how many lap dances I see or how many snail trails decorate the poles. We both need a drink after all of *that*." I waved my hands in the air in the direction of the dark patch of highway we had just come from.

She touched my elbow before I could reach for the door, a slow smile building on her battered face. "No, I meant, we're really done with it all. We're not going back, are we?"

"Freaking *LOOK* at me. I will never go back there. I don't care what I just gave up. None of that stuff is worth my freedom and my sanity. To hell with them all," I said, meaning every word. Then I laughed. I laughed and smiled for my freedom. *Hell, I wanted to break out into a cheer,* but I needed that drink first.

The cozy warmth of the bar was the first thing I noticed, the second was the sweet smells of cinnamon and vanilla. It was like a slutty Bed and Body store. The walls were painted a deep rich burgundy and the tables and chairs were a dark cherry wood. A long bar graced one whole side of the wall and a dimly lit stage decorated the backdrop.

Having never stepped foot in a strip joint before, Bree's eyes widened as they scanned around the room, taking it all in. Me, I'd been to tons of them when I was younger, the result of being stuck around so many guys and never having many girlfriends to relax with. It didn't faze me a bit.

Grabbing Bree's hand, I pulled her to the bar and settled myself on a tall elegant stool, complete with velvet cushion. The stage was empty, and just a few patrons, a mixture of male and female, sat at tables, eating and drinking.

"Well, this stinks. I thought I was going to see some strange cooch climbing up some poles," Bree chuckled, as she slid her body over a stool.

"Dancers don't come on 'til ten, love," a deep voice called out from nowhere. Bree and I both looked at each other, and then scanned the bar for the person who belonged to the voice that answered us. We came up empty. Her eyes met back up with mine, wearing a furrowed brow.

"Wow. Impressive. *Hairy McTittieBounce's Bar* has an invisible bartender," I chuckled. "Well, Mr. Invisible Bartender, we need the strongest drink you can make."

A head of thick sandy blond hair rose up from behind the bar in front of us, and the prettiest face you ever saw was attached to it, complete with a pair of clichéd baby blue eyes. No, not pretty, *beautiful.* Blah, like a damn Ken doll. God, men weren't supposed to be *that pretty.* Handsome, yes. Pretty, no. But, this guy? This guy was *beautiful.*

It kind of made me want to roll my eyes and gag. I might have, if my face didn't hurt so much.

The moment he laid eyes on us, the Ken doll's eyebrows arched up to his hairline and he made a little strangled gasp-like sound. "Are...Are you okay?" he asked me. A light British accent tinted his words. Well, wasn't that a bowl of *yum.* A beautiful man with an accent; it was going to be impossible to get Bree out of here.

I offered him my best smile, which caused one of the cuts on my lip to bleed again and he quickly handed me a wad of cocktail napkins. "Are you saying *I don't look okay*?" I gasped in mock horror, and then tried for a wink with my less swollen eye. "What? Do I have something hanging from my nose?" I asked, laughing absurdly and patting my lip with the napkins he had offered.

I had to crack jokes and laugh at myself, because the reality of the situation was too much for me otherwise. Life is tough; you have to endure the bad with the good, because the alternative is so...*final.*

I will endure this.

Next to me, Bree put her head down, covered her head with her arms and giggled into the wood. The bright purple welt across her cheek was darkening by the minute and didn't help her look any better.

The Ken doll paused to examine my face and reached out his hand, touching my chin lightly, while I tried not to flinch, "Well, it can't be too bad if you're both laughing about it, yeah? You need me to round up some boys and give somebody an arse kicking?" If my cheeks weren't so discolored with bruises, he probably would have noticed the hot blush that surged right under my skin.

"Um, no. Thank you, though. Just a few drinks, okay? Anything that will numb all this puffy loveliness we got going on," I said, slowly leaning my face away from his hand. *Why in the world would a man think it would be comfortable for a woman to be touched when she looked as battered as I did?*

"Sure, you bet, love," he mumbled, walking away to grab a bottle each of vodka, rum, and tequila off the top of the shelf. From the middle shelf, he pulled out some gin and another bottle of something I couldn't read and some lemon-lime soda. Then he just started pouring everything together. I was almost illegally above the limit of drunkenness just watching him make the damn drink. He placed two small cocktail napkins neatly in front of us and went back to mixing, I toyed with the idea of telling him to save his fancy little beverage linens, because I didn't intend on taking my drink from my lips long enough to set it down, but I didn't. Mostly because I didn't want anyone really to know the pain I was in.

"Dibs," Bree whispered softly next to me. As if I had a chance in hell with her around, me *Miss Plain Jane Smarty Pants* compared to her *Miss Lottie too Hottie*. Don't misunderstand me, I was attractive, but Bree fell into the *blonde-bombshell-outrageously gorgeous* adjective pile when people described her, and I got thrown aimlessly into the awkward-yet   averagely-decent-looking-brainiac pile.

Snorting out a laugh, I nudged her with my elbow. "Sure, he's all yours. He's way too pretty for my taste. Besides, I think I'm done with men for a while." Rubbing my clammy palms down the pant legs of my jeans, I bit at the one tiny part of my lip that didn't hurt, "I'm feeling kind of buzzed and I didn't even drink yet."

"Adrenaline. Loss of blood. Don't change the subject, I'm still calling dibs," she whispered.

Nope. I think it's freedom.

The bartender slid two glasses full of his dark concoction across the lacquered length of the bar, "Here you go, loves. This drink is called an *Adios, Motherfucker.* Which, I hope to God you both said to whomever the hell put their hands on you," he said, leveling a pair of serious-as-hell blue eyes at us.

Adios, Motherfucker.

Bree held up her drink to mine and clinked her glass against it. "To new beginnings," she whispered.

"To freedom," I whispered back.

Adios, Motherfucker.

I watched as the beautiful bartender walked away from us, moved around the bar talking to the other patrons and grabbing plates of food off their tables. He carried them through a door into a back area and reappeared with other steaming plates of food to serve. There were no other employees around.

We sipped our drinks in silence, both of us most likely trying to forget the last twenty-four hours of our lives. *But, man, I wanted to forget a lot more.*

Bree's eyes followed the bartender like a little lost dog, "So what do you think? Want to stay for a while? The scenery is nice."

"Oh, sure. Yeah. I always wondered what it would be like to live in a freezer."

"It's not that cold. And we're far enough."

"Jen...*dammit...Bree*....what the hell kind of name is Bree anyway? It's like twenty degrees and it's October. Across the damn world would not be far enough."

"Germs don't live in cold environments? We could dye your hair black. I could use a whole new hairstyle and look. It will be like playing hide and seek."

"Shut up."

"I'm serious. We have plenty of money and no one would ever look for you in the middle of the woods. They'd try looking in major cities and that's if anyone is even looking," she whispered.

I almost spit my drink all over her. "So you think nobody will be looking for me?"

"All I'm saying is that we could blend in here and the bartender is really gorgeous. What do you think? He seems nice, right?"

"Oh, yeah. I'm such a great judge of character. Please. I wouldn't know a sociopath if he tore off my arms and beat me with them."

"You ladies need anything over here?" The Ken doll asked a few minutes later, as he wiped down the top of the bar. My eyes zoned in on the sinewy muscles of his tanned arms as he dried off the condensation from our cool drinks in smooth circular motions.

"Oh, yes. Yes I do," Bree mumbled low.

"Yeah, actually," I said, as I nudged Bree under the counter of the bar to shut her up, "Do you know of any hotels or anything nearby?"

He offered me a small sad smile. "Love, you're in the middle of the Adirondacks. You have one campground with a trailer park, a few ranger posts and secluded houses, that's about it. You both look like you need a hospital, or a cop. Not a hotel. There's a small town about thirty minutes

18

drive north, where most of the people around these parts live, near the prisons, where the jobs are."

"Yeah? What kind of jobs can you find there?" Bree asked, completely ignoring the advice to visit a hospital and kicking me with her foot. *Oh God, she really wanted to set up camp here because of the pretty Ken Doll. Ugh.*

"Regular town jobs. There's the prison, a school, supermarket, library, and the local *POLICE*. There's also that *hospital* I mentioned, that you so sweetly ignored. Why are you asking about work? Are you girls looking for a job?" he asked, wrinkling his brow. *Crap, this did sound like the beginning of a bad horror movie...*

I knew if I didn't ask, Bree would. I could plainly see where her mind was going, *right into his bed*. "Think you could use two waitresses, just for a few days a week? My behind is way too big to jiggle up there," I pointed to the empty stage. "I'm Lainey, by the way. And, this is Bree."

"Lainey and Bree? Are you sure you don't want to dance? Those names are perfect for it," he laughed flirtatiously. "I'm Dylan Grayson and you're hired, but not until that, um, space alien thing you got growing on your face heals. It's not really working for you. I'm sure you're both very pretty under all that war paint." He flipped his bar towel over his shoulder and walked through the back door again.

"I've never waitressed before," Bree sighed next to me.

"I did, for a while in high school," I replied, finishing my drink. "Let's try to find a place to stay tomorrow, maybe at the trailer park, and try to get rid of that ostentatious Porsche." I held up my shaking hands and watched my fingers tremble. "Waitressing isn't so bad, pretty easy once you get the hang of it. I mean it's not like being a neurosurgeon or anything."

"Yeah," she whispered, as she leaned her head on my shoulder, "and living in a trailer sounds like loads of fun."

When our glasses were empty, Dylan walked over and slid over two refills. He leaned his elbows against the top of the bar and smiled at Bree, "So where is it that you come from?" *I had to hand it to her, even bruised up she could get a man's attention.* I hoped he wasn't married.

My head softly fell against my arms and I drifted away from their conversation. Heaviness spread across my shoulders and down both my arms, weighing me down, pulling me under like a fierce riptide drowning me, overcoming me; destroying me.

I stared blankly at Dylan's lips as he smiled at something Bree said. My vision blurred and I wrapped my arms tightly around my waist trying to focus on the way his accent lingered on each word, but he was just too pretty to watch. Too bright and shiny... "She just had a little run in with an old boyfriend, that's all...everything is fine now...She'll be fine...yeah, we need a place to stay..."

"Ladies room?" I asked, barely above a hoarse whisper. Dylan stared wide-eyed into my glazed expression and quickly pointed to a back hallway.

The bar stool crashed against the floor, making a horrible clanging and banging sound as I pushed off and rushed into the hallway. Racing into the bathroom, I locked myself into a stall and emptied my stomach into the toilet. A cold burst of sweat broke out across my forehead and I dropped hard against my knees on the cold tiled floor of the bathroom, trying to brace myself up with violently shaking arms.

I slid down against the vileness of the cold porcelain and squeezed my eyes tightly, swallowing down the hard knot of disgust. Panic tightened my chest into fast pounding explosions and desperation to stand up away from the dirty-filthy stench of my insides and the white watery bowl that held them was overwhelming.

Life as I knew it was over.

My life.

Over.

That woman I once was, Samantha Matthews, was gone. *Left for dead.*

Everything and everyone I ever knew...Everything I had ever worked for...gone. Just. Like. That.

Poof.

Gone.

What happened?

It was building like an unstoppable freight train in the pit of my stomach and I clenched my fists tight. I couldn't focus on clear thoughts. Frantic visions clouded my mind and my brain went off like a gunshot, fast and lethal. Thousands of images, words, and emotions fired out of my mind like a machine gun. Adrenaline surged through my body and my heart pounded unevenly. The dark gloves of panic gripped my entire body and squeezed. My head hit the floor with a wet *thwack,* and the edges of my vision blurred like reels of an old movie.

"Fuck you, Samantha," he says coldly, when he finds me in the living room with all my packed bags. I won't even face him. I can't look at him at all.

I choke out a laugh, "No thank you. I don't want to catch anything." Jen will be here any minute; I hope there's no traffic.

"Samantha, you're sick, baby. You should have taken all your medicine," his monotone voice drolls.

"You're the one that's sick..." I spin on him as he's clamping his heavy hands around my throat, cutting off my words. Thick fingers press into the skin of my neck, crushing my esophagus. I kick and thrash wildly, frantically clawing my way to break free. Pure panic rushes through my throat as I gag and gasp for the air he is stealing from me. Lifting me easily off the ground, he slams my back against the bookcase, my head and shoulders landing on the spines of all my books. Pain explodes across my body; bursts of light blurs my vision.

He's yanking me by my hair, dragging me along the coarse carpet of the floor, burning my palms and the skin on my knees. I pull away, digging my heels into the plush rug, but his fists just twist my hair tighter around his hand and my body lifts off the ground. Swinging my fists out, I fiercely try to connect with his flesh, clawing and punching.

I stopped loving him.

When I knew what he did, it was instant.

This, this is him just getting rid of the evidence.

Images of *that monster* clawed their way into my skull, how could they not? It was because of him my hands trembled so much. It was because of him that there was death all around me. *Monster.* A fucking vicious troll; a beast who I once loved, like an evil mythical creature that lied and waited until he thought I was powerless and struck me hard and fast, like the poisonous bite of a cobra. Deadly.

Me. Unknowing. Foolish.

My panic turned into hysterics. Tears streaked down my cheeks, raining down on my lap. I let myself breakdown in the solace of the small closed off room, where no one would be witness to my weakness. Even strong people needed to break sometimes.

I didn't cry from fear, or hurt, or pain.

I cried for Samantha Matthews, the woman that they forced me not to be.

For everything I lost.

There are only a few words I have left in my mind for them:

You never should have underestimated me.

Chapter 2
Kade

The puddle of blood that lies beneath the limp bodies of my friends is quickly spreading thickly across the floor. There's a heavy pool of blood in my mouth that spills out over the corner of my lips to mix with the seeping blood bath along the cold slabs of tile. My breaths are noisy, raspy and there's no oxygen in the room. Did someone turn the oxygen off? Why can't I breathe? Why can't I get enough air? I want my mum.

My math notebook is lying near my head and pages of my algebra equations are scattered around the room. All at once, they absorb a swell of thick red blotches that cause the ink to blur and disappear. The pungent smell of some sort of acrid odor lingers thickly in the air, weighing heavily on my stomach.

Haunting, mumbled singsong crooning, whispers through the room. "Did you ever think, when a hearse drove by...that you might be the next to die...they'll cover you with a big white sheet...after I splash through the puddles of life beneath my feet..."

I can hear the clip clop of footsteps. The squish-squash of two boots squeaking and sliding over the bloodied tiles. "Pl...ple...ease. Please, don't." I hear a shaky voice whimper. I can't tell if it's a female or a male's voice, but I know it's an older voice, so it can't be one of my classmates. I know it's not Mrs. Turner's voice, because Mrs. Turner is lying *in front of me with her dead glazed eyes staring at me. She tried to shield me from what was happening, but I don't think it made a difference, something still got through. My body trembles with the coldness that is drifting up through the tiles. "Please! NONONO!" The voice begs as a loud click echoes across the room. Then POP! POP! POP! POP! Click! Click! Click! Click!*

Click!
Click!
Click!
Click!

CLICK! I jerked against the steering wheel, my pulse pounding against my temple as I pulled up to the parking lot of the bar with heavy anxiety. Yanking the gearshift into park, I ran my hands over my face to focus back on reality, trying to bury the flashback in my head. My mind was heavy with thick red images as I tried to rub the blur of them from my eyes.

Focus.

I told my brother I would stop at the bar.

I have to go in.

I hated going there. I hated the long day I'd been through already and I just wanted to be alone, but I promised my brother. So I stepped out, still dressed in my tuxedo, the one my agent said I had to wear to the prior day's festivities, and I dragged myself into my brother's den of hell.

I knew I was being irrational about everything, especially about the awards dinner the night before. Any normal man would have been rattled with pride receiving the highly coveted

Bram Stoker Award, but I was far from normal. I was barely able to sit next to Gary, my editor, and his wife Mable with her glazed over eyes that reminded me of a corpse staring vacantly into the nothingness. Every time she spoke to me, her whiny voice clawed at my self-control, which I had very little of to begin with. It took just about all my energy not to shove my napkin down her throat, and watch her gasp and flail about for breath.

When I was finally introduced, I tried to shake off my fury, but the twisted tension that followed me everywhere gripped deep in my muscles and seeped into my bones. My speech consisted of a wave and a whispered thank you. I wanted to flip my audience the finger, but I held myself back. I always held myself back, but I was always one bullet shy of self-destruction. The prize was thrown in the bottom of my suitcase awaiting its poor fate of being shoved in the back of the extra closet in my guest bedroom, never to see the light of day again. I hadn't even stayed the night in the hotel my assistant booked. I just jumped right back on the next available flight and headed home. Now I have to pretend to be sane and normal and visit my brother.

I just needed to focus on *now*. I'll have one drink then leave. Leave society for as many months as I possibly could. The bloody images of my flashbacks faded from my thoughts slowly as I walked through the door, but they always lingered in the outskirts of my mind, waiting for the most inappropriate times to peek out.

Stepping my foot in, I instantly scanned the room, taking inventory of the number of bodies, exits, lighting, and furniture. Then I watched the patrons in their various states of expression. It is a subconscious action now, as thought provoking as breathing is to me, but it's ingrained in me nonetheless.

My brother's place was packed, of course, it was, and there was a bloody tart gyrating on a glittery pole in the middle of the stage shaking her ass to the sounds of Lady *Blah Blah* or whatever the hell her name was. I didn't see my brother, Dylan, anywhere as I sat myself at the back, farthest away from everyone, back to the wall, nearest table to the exit. Looking at my watch, I saw it was almost eleven.

I'm staying exactly one minute.
No more than sixty seconds.
Screw it, time's up.

I was just about to sneak out and hide from my brother and the rest of humanity for the next damn six months, when I glanced up and froze. A small fluid movement caught my eye. A flutter of something, someone, who shouldn't belong, grace and poise, yet strong and vicious. It pinned me to my seat.

The deep throb in my temple that always accompanied my flashbacks disappeared instantly.

Thirty feet away from my dark corner stood some sort of *angel*. Backlit as she stood in front of the illuminated bar, I had a perfect view of her silhouette. Dark black hair tumbled wildly over her creamy white neck, falling to her tiny waist as if it were liquid silk. Petite, yet voluptuous, with soft curves that had me instantly, thinking about sinking inside deeply and riding her hard. She was wearing a high collared, tight black long-sleeved t-shirt, which hugged her shape but was covered by a torn up apron that coincided with the *idiotic* name of the bar. She was dressed excessively conservative for being inside a strip club; it was as if she didn't want anyone to see *her* flesh. Like she was hiding. The sounds of the bar seemed to fade into low murmurs and Lady RahBlahGah, *whatever*, was now quietly whispering that she was born some stupid certain way, as I watched the woman move.

That's what I'm extremely good at, watching people. Reading them. I was always more of a voyeur when it came to social situations. Notoriously introverted, I have mastered the art of hiding myself and detaching from *everything*. I learned an invaluable lesson once. If I stayed silent for long enough, and just watched long enough, people and life would pass by me, as if I were invisible. *Or dead.*

Her nails were short, just a bit longer than the pads of her fingers, and were devoid of any colored polish. She leaned on one of the tables in the middle of the bar and tapped them on the table, waiting for a bunch of drunken guys to make their orders. She wrote *nothing* down, wasn't even holding a pad. She was listening intently as the men seemed to banter back and forth in their blatant inebriated states. Her lips smiled at them, full and lush, the kind of lips that when they speak to you all you hear is *sex*. Any man could look at those lips and think *sex*. Hell, her whole mouth would be any man's fantasy. I shifted in my seat to ease the pressure those thoughts brought against the zipper of my pants. It wasn't even that she was beautiful, though she was in my eyes. It was the way the features on her face melted together in a delicate balance of strength, intelligence, and sensuality that had me intrigued. And the fascinating way she tried to disguise it, working in a strip club and looking as plain as if she didn't think anything about her lack of *attention-grabbing appearance*. Yet, she stood confident and hard, like she knew her hidden attributes were better than showing her tits to the patrons.

She wore no wedding band, no jewelry of any kind and not a stitch of make-up. Then, one of the men placed his hand on her ass and I waited for what always happened in shitholes like this, the worst of humanity. My lust immediately ceased to exist for the woman. *She'll move her ass against his hand and flirt with him to try to make a few dollars extra tip from him. Maybe she'll give him a lap dance, suck his cock in the back of his pickup truck for twenty bucks or for a line of blow in the bathroom.* I've seen it a dozen times here already. I fucking hated visiting my brother. Although, *I must admit*, I wouldn't mind witnessing the sucking cock part, which might be *mildly entertaining*, especially with those lips. I slumped back in my seat, already gutted that I wasted time thinking the whore looked like an angel.

I was caught off guard, though, when the woman in front of me froze. The second the guy squeezed his fat fingers over her ass, she went completely rigid, and *pretended to* spill an entire drink in his lap accidently. I chuckled out loud. *I guess she didn't need the tip.* Another waitress was there in an instant, a gorgeous blonde one with her tits almost bursting out of her shirt. She stepped in between the raven-haired waitress and the drunk. I leaned forward in my seat to watch how this would play out. The dark-haired waitress moved her blonde friend out of the way, protectively. The show of courage and safeguard for her friend interested me.

It took him a few trips and falls, but the drunken guy eventually jumped out of his seat and stood up, puffing his chest and enormous beer gut at the girl. She had to be about half his size and he was leaning his face down into hers threateningly. I scooted forward in my seat a bit to hear the conversation, but couldn't make out anything that was being said.

The drunk raised his hand, pointing at her. I pushed out of my seat in a flash, aching to rip the skin off his face if he touched the girl in front of me. With my teeth grinding hard, a heat flushed through my entire body, my fingers itched to grab the beer-gutted moronic imbecile and choke him dead blue. But, then the dark-haired waitress leaned in closer to him, reached into her apron and jabbed the man in the gut, *as if she had a concealed weapon*, poking it at him. She whispered something, *calmly and very controlled*, in the man's ear that made him freeze, lean back and lift his hands in surrender.

What?

How?

What the hell did she say to him?

The fact that she was almost attacked by some drunken dolt didn't show in her expression. As a matter of fact, nothing showed in her expression, *nothing at all*. She was calm and in full control of her composure; it was almost unnatural. Then the woman *smiled* tightly, walked away backwards from the table, and moved back behind the bar. The blonde followed her and rubbed her back in a friendly way. I had no idea what I had just witnessed, but that little-bit-of-a-wisp waitress seemed to have put that wanker in his place with her presence and words. Unafraid and confident. Fearless. Impressive and deadly sexy.

Beyond sexy.

That was the sexiest thing I'd ever witnessed outside of porn.

When I sat back in my seat, Dylan was leaning over me; chuckling and holding a brandy out for me. "Hey bro, how was your day out with the humans?" He sat down next to me, slid my drink over and sighed.

"Overrated." I sipped my brandy and enjoyed the soft smooth burn at the back of my throat.

"Congrats on the award," he chuckled.

"Sod off," I said, still watching the waitress *liquefy* herself around the bar.

He looked at me and then back to the scene in front of us. The drunken guys were back to gawking at the dancer on stage and completely ignoring the one dark-haired waitress that was behind the bar, who was now glaring at a bottle of whiskey as if it personally offended her in someway.

"Does she dance here?" I asked.

"No. Neither of them do," Dylan answered me, but his eyes were still watching her.

"I wasn't asking about the blonde," I stated.

"I knew exactly who you were asking about, Kade," he murmured. "She's not your classical beauty, yet stunning in her own way, yeah?"

I just nodded. Then...silence.

Shit...I wanted to know more about her. Just keep your damn mouth shut. How do you think getting to know more about her is going to end? Ugly. Fuckin' ugly...

"They don't look like the kind of women who would work here. What the hell are they doing here?" I snapped.

"Intriguing situation. They both showed up here about two months ago, beaten to bloody hell. The one you asked about is Lainey and the blonde is Bree. They work here a few nights a week. Both are really sweet. Both are the most intelligent women I've ever had the pleasure to meet, and the blonde is *sexy as hell, yeah*? Both of them have tried to change their appearance as if they're hiding from something. That's all I know."

Lainey looked up from where she was standing behind the bar. Her eyes collided with mine for a few *gut-twisting* moments before she darted them to Dylan. I wondered if he was sleeping with her. It angered me just thinking about it.

On one side of her face, her long hair was pinned back with a soft lilac ribbon that made her look indecently innocent. Shiny waves were cascading down from the little clip and fell around her face framing soft porcelain features. She wore a familiar emotion on her face that I knew all too well, *haunted*. The plain raw intelligence of her face was utterly breathtaking and for the first time in my life, I couldn't find the correct adjectives to describe something. No mere words would have done her natural beauty justice or could have described the way she moved.

It was like...*liquid*.

That's the only word I had for her.

Flowing, fluid, melting into everything with a precision that seemed naturally calculated. I felt like Adam looking at Eve for the first time, having never seen another woman before her.

What the hell did I just let myself think? I just need to drown myself at the bottom of my damn brandy.

Fucking...hell... I caught myself leaning forward, almost falling off my daft chair trying to watch her move around. Brilliant.

"Jesus, Kade. I never saw you look at anybody like that. You want me to tell her to come over here?" he asked.

"Fuck off," I laughed, angrily. "You know I don't play well with others." I forced my fingers to relax their tight grip on my drink before it shattered under all the pressure. I didn't clearly understand why I was unable to keep my eyes off the woman, or why my body reacted the way it did to her, or why my gut feeling told me she was more than she appeared. I took another pull on my brandy.

My brother's mouth opened to say something but thought better of it. He raked his hand through his hair and hung his head in his hands. "How have you been, really?" He mumbled into his hands.

I dropped my head from my line of vision of her. *That's it for the next six months*, no, year...I was already fed up with people. And talking. Talking with people. Stupid people.

And who the hell cared about a freaking waitress?

Yeah, she was pretty in such a different way, and intriguing, *so damn what.*

Dealing with thoughts about her would end up like all my thoughts did, in *sickening violence.* I would need to find more words to match her beauty and somehow mar her *fictional* existence in my head with the exquisite release of her last breath, or possess her with demons, slaughter her by the hands of a delusional lover, disfigure her in a gruesome accident or something equally horrifying.

That's how I deal with my *issues*. That's how I deal with my anger and my rage. I live in a world of lies, fictitious characters I dream up and breathe life into, just to break, for the enjoyment of horror readers throughout the world. I wondered what lies this woman had told; what her story was, not that it mattered if she had one, I'd gladly make one up for her. Everyone was just a character to me. Each person was just another empty name I would put to paper and control with my whims, develop into people I wanted them to be. Complete and unconditional control.

I glanced my eyes over the waitress again.

For a small second, she looked fragile, a tilt forward of the head, the small slump of her shoulders and I wanted to protect her. But the thought was nonsense in my head. I wiped it away as fast as I thought it. *Who would protect her from me?*

Guzzling down the rest of my brandy like it was a cheap shot, I left the bar without even saying goodbye to my brother. He was used to my idiosyncrasies. I drove home wondering what color her eyes were, which is the single most asinine thought ever to cross my mind, so I cancelled any more thoughts of the woman. It wasn't like I would ever see her again.

I stormed into my empty house, slamming the heavy wooden door behind me, locking myself away from the rest of the world and bring new meaning to the word recluse. I won't lie to myself as others do and pretend I have any control over things. It's easier to find and gain control if you stay in a very small space and let no one else in.

Yanking off my tie and jacket, I threw them over one of the leather chairs in my den and sat myself in front of my computer. I poured myself another brandy and sat it beside my keyboard, sipping at it slowly every so often to cherish the thick warm burn.

I brought up the screen to my work in progress and the last scene I was working on.

Words had always come easily to me. Violence and hate were in my veins. I was *rage personified*, and horror and malice were my only friends. We had lived together peacefully since I came to terms with being *me*. Yet, as I sat before my desk, with a bright white empty screen in front of me, cursor blinking and mocking me, I didn't see the red of an award winning horror writer. All I saw was silky black liquid hair and pale pink lips.

Temptation.

Damn, this wasn't going to be good for me.

Chapter 3
Lainey

An unexpected warm rush of heat spread across my chest as soon as I looked up from concentrating on the bottle of whiskey. I was trying to calm the nausea down from that drunken degenerate's attempt at manhandling me, counting to twenty in my head and taking deep breaths.

Mother-effin' twenty.

Son-of-a-bitch nineteen.

Eighteen, seventeen... Calmly closing my eyes, my brain was still screeching at the pot-bellied piss infected Neanderthal. My insides wanted to claw his eyes out and *dickkick* him for touching me.

Three.

Two, *just breathe*...one.

My eyes fluttered open and all thoughts about drunken men touching me vanished. Actually, *all my thoughts* completely faded into oblivion when I noticed a strange man watching me. I heard myself gasp when I saw him. The air just sort of sucked itself right out of my lungs. Not only was he devastatingly handsome, he was *staring at me.*

Me.

Not Natalie, aka *Lace*, who was up on the stage wearing only her sparkly little thong and humping a pole.

Not Bree, the blonde bombshell who every man drools over.

Me.

I'm just going to put it out there, right now. I've *never* seen a man watch me like *that* before. It was personal. Intimate. I mean...I was one of those women who got acknowledged for their brains more often than their looks. And I took pride in myself for that. I liked being intelligent and confident, but that *look*...

My cheeks heated at the severity of the stare; his gaze was unnerving. It was animalistic and primal. Hot-as-hell; it made me tingle with a damp warmth between my thighs and against the cotton material of my panties.

I was completely embarrassed. Fully flushed and blushing, I was literally reacting like some silly virgin from a cheesy romance novel. *Then*...then to make matters worse, I started to fan myself a bit with one of the laminated menus.

But, *damn*, it felt good to be looked at like that, you know? It was a look that made you *want* to swing your hips a bit more, smile a little wider for, because you *knew* this man was enjoying the view, appreciating the way you looked. I felt *wanted*. Desired. Hungered for. *Lusted*. Preyed on. *Was this what Lace was feeling right now on stage with all the men watching her?*

I fanned myself faster.

He was leaning back against the red velvet of the booth chair, dressed in an expensive looking tuxedo. His hair was as black as mine, deep inky black, and wildly arranged on his head. His *face*...all hard angles. His skin was light, pale against the silky darkness of his hair. A jaw carved out of stone, strong cheekbones and full perfect lips. But those *weren't* the attractive features of him. *Well, they were, but it was more than that.* He seemed to wear a deep intelligence and life experience in his expression. Strength and pain. Knowledge, endurance, and raw danger were blatant on the planes and hollows of his skin. Dangerous and unfriendly, an angry outsider looking into the world from some far distant places in his mind. The sort of man that didn't fit in. The one you would always pick out of the crowd as different, uncomfortable and on edge. *Kind of like me.*

I stared at him a little too long, holding his gaze, which made my senses, all of them, kick into overdrive. The exchange was maddening and arousing, and like nothing I'd ever felt before, primal and visceral in texture. It was purely mouthwatering.

My eyes diverted to Dylan, who had just sat down next to him and without a doubt, I knew they were brothers. Where Dylan's features were soft and blond, this man was a chiseled, harder, darker version of him. Serious trouble.

The man's dark eyebrows were pulled together and light pale-gray, almost colorless eyes, stared fiercely into mine. Raw and primal, as if I was being hunted.

Hunted? For a moment, terror surged through my body. Could this man have been sent to hurt me? *Did they find me?* As quickly as the thought came, I debunked it. No one was going to be coming after me. There was no way of knowing where I was or that I survived.

No, this man who was staring at me like that *wanted me.*

Squeezing my thighs together against my moist panties, I shivered uncomfortably. I wanted to gag at the pathetic nature of my discomfort. Whenever I had listened to other women say silly things like, "*Oh, it was love at first sight,*" or "*I felt sparks right away,*" I always laughed. I guess I just never felt that. There were other things, more important things than men in my life. There wasn't such a thing as love at first sight. I didn't even believe in lust at first sight. I was a true believer of *hotness* at first sight, but that's about it. I've felt love and lust before. But this, what I felt while this dangerous man fucked me vigorously with his eyes, it was *insane.* Intense. It might have been the first time in my life that being a woman had made me feel *good.* Okay, it made me feel like a porn star, and no man had ever made me feel like that. There, I said it. We're all adults here, right? I mean, I shouldn't be ashamed. I've already told you my panties were wet, so my dignity was out the window.

He was still staring at me. Even though I quickly looked away, I could feel his eyes on me, as if they were burning an impression against my memory. Touching every one of my nerve endings with the rough dangerous caress of his eyes.

Then he just dropped his head down low, spoke to Dylan for another few minutes, ran both his hands through his hair, drained his drink, and stalked out of the bar. My insides ached to run after him and just pretend to bump into him, just to see him up close, and to see those eyes stare at me like that again.

Just watching him walk to the door had my pulse beating harder. His gait and long, strong strides had me biting down on my lip. I smiled to myself thinking that, maybe for the first time in my life, I might have been acting like a *normal* healthy sexual woman. I shook the thoughts from my head. It was nice to feel good, to feel confident, and to believe in myself again, but I wasn't ready to deal with men any time soon, especially one that looked like he should have a triple X rating tattooed on his forehead. This was one of those men a woman would probably shrink in heartbreak from, weeping loud and bitterly into their extra-large-super-sized apple martini glasses. *What am I talking about?* It was silly and immature of me to think I could judge a man by his likeness and not by his character, foolish and naive. I was not by any means a foolish girl, who fluttered away on whims and heady needs. *Heady needs?* Maybe I needed a vibrator; it had been way too long.

"Hey, Lainey," Dylan said, as he slid behind the bar and grabbed a bottle of tequila. "What put that smile on your face?"

"Oh, nothing," I said as I wiped down the bottle of whiskey I was stupidly smiling at. "That gentleman you were sitting next to, just now, that was a relative, right?" *Oh Lord, why was I asking questions about him?*

Dylan rubbed the back of his neck and sighed. "Yeah, he's my brother, Kade."

"It's sort of eerie how you look the same, yet completely opposite. He's like the darker version of you," I laughed, playfully. *Is he married? What does he do? Is he intelligent? Is he playful? Does he like long walks on the beach and can you give him my number? Shut up and don't ask! Being in the woods this long is making me crazy, and I'm definitely buying a vibrator. That should have been the first thing I packed when I left!*

Dylan didn't laugh with me.

His eyebrows furrowed and his lips tightened into a small scowl. "He's definitely a dark version of something. Listen, stay away from him if he ever comes in here again. He probably won't anyway, but if he does, just ignore him. He's tainted with a ton of issues. He's a loner anyway, doesn't date, and doesn't enjoy being around people, sorry love. He's pretty *savage*."

Okay, he's not making any sense. I was just asking if they were brothers, not to set me up with him. *I didn't ask any of those questions out loud.*

"I wasn't saying I was interested in him or anything, I had just noticed the resemblance, that's all. What's wrong with him?"

Dylan chuckled, full out laughed, and then all the seriousness drained away from his features as his eyes fixed on mine. "Nothing, love. He's like a *living-breathing-yet-emotionally-dead* J. D. Salinger, but with more secrets. I think he just finds his own mind so much more interesting than anyone else's, that he locks himself away because he doesn't like distractions.   And he's got major trust issues. Savage."

"J. D. Salinger? So, he's a writer?" I asked.

"Yeah, but he's more of an arsehole, so just steer clear of him. He could be intentionally hostile to people most of the time just to keep everyone at a distance. Vicious and savage."

Third time. That was the third time he said *savage.* Dylan walked away, leaving me standing there, even more curious than before our talk. I wondered if he had drunk too much tonight. Obviously, Dylan knew nothing about women, because he just intrigued the hell out of me with his warning. Men were so clueless sometimes.

I spent the rest of that night wondering about Kade, and the reasons Dylan gave me to stay away from him. However, I ended up wasting my time wondering if I'd ever see him again, because within twelve hours, he was sitting in his dark corner, alone, watching me, *again.*   Dressed in a crisp white button up shirt with the sleeves rolled up, his suit jacket flung neatly over the back of the booth, he looked like he was waiting for an important business meeting, yet his attention was all on *me.*

I was hoping not to see him again.

Not anytime soon anyway, and especially not *that* night. Dylan spent that entire morning grumbling about Kade and how screwed up in the head he was, repeatedly telling me to stay away from him. Why he didn't mention anything to Bree, was beyond me. That in itself made me feel extremely uncomfortable. Why wouldn't he be warning Bree about him? Bree was the one that he should care about, *not me.*

I chanced a small peek at him from behind the bar. His jaw was clenched and his eyes looked so dangerous, they made my heart hammer in my chest and echo in my ears. A muscle twitched in his jaw as he leaned back against the red leather cushion of his seat. Crossing his arms over his broad chest, he *ferociously* stared at me, like a caged animal, and I was his prey. The common sense in me knew women shouldn't like being objectified, like the way his eyes roamed my body, but I did. I liked it. *A lot.* It stirred an emotion in me as if I had just found out I had some sort of super power; it was powerful, raw, and dirty. It was intensely sexy as hell and my stomach fluttered with the excitement of it. *God, I needed to get a grip and a life. I definitely needed to get a life.* Quickly, I backed into the kitchen door, pushed it open with a swing of my hip, and ran in.

I found Dylan with his phone to his ear, smiling like an idiot. He pointed his index finger to the phone and mouthed, *Bree.* Covering the mouthpiece, he whispered, "I'm picking her up in a few. Are you sure you're okay for a few hours?"

Nodding a smile in return, I calmly said, "Your brother is sitting at the back table."

His face went pale, and then an enormous smile brightened his features. "Twice in two days, that's a record. Maybe he's returned to the human race. Take his order, let's see what he does." Then he reached his hand out to touch my shoulder. "Just...if he says anything nasty to you, don't take it personally. Just give it right back to him and I'll handle him if you can't. Then I'll go get Bree." His hands were completely covering his phone now, and I laughed, knowing full well that Bree was still talking to him on the other end.

"Dylan, trust me. I can handle people. Just go take Bree out. You guys have been flirting like two sheltered teenagers with me as the third wheel for the last two months, so go have fun. She deserves a nice date." Before I reached the door, I tapped my hand on the frame to make sure I had his attention, "Oh, and be romantic. She likes romance and all those girly things. She loves when a man brings her flowers."

I walked out and around the bar, across the floor and stood right next to Kade's table. Heat flamed across my body and I forced myself to take a deep breath before speaking. "Hello, I'm Lainey. What may I get for you today?"

Kade looked up, but his glare didn't reach my eyes. He just looked at my shoulder, or just above it. His dark brows furrowed together and his lips turned down like he was appalled at my question, his face as hard as granite. "Another waitress," he growled darkly.

"Well, then," I smiled brightly trying not to show my complete mortification. *I was confused. Wasn't he just looking at me as if I was the last woman on earth?* The sexy man was supposed to flirt with me and ask me for my number. I was supposed to decline kindly and walk away, feeling a little more confident in myself, like I could still *pull off* being sexy. He was ruining my fantasy. "I hope you enjoy the next few hours without a drink then, because I'm the only waitress here tonight."

"Where's Dylan?" he barked.

"He has a date tonight and since there's never anyone here on a Monday, he's taking a few hours off and I'm here." *All right then, that was enough, hop on out of here, jerk. Bye. Off you go now.* I bent forward and spoke lower, "I guess that means you should leave?" I know I shouldn't have said that, but I was angry. He made me feel like a goddess and now he didn't even want to speak to me.

Intense stormy gray eyes flickered up to mine. There was a strange silence that traveled between us in the empty bar. His stare was dark and hostile. Antagonistic. *Murderous.* His whole demeanor was tense. "Fuck. Are your eyes green?" he asked, venomously. His fierce eyes maintained complete unwavering contact with mine, the kind of look that makes you want to back down.

I sure as fuck didn't back down from anyone. I've eaten boys bigger than him for a snack.

I was surprised though. That wasn't what I was expecting to come out of his mouth. "Yes. Scandalous isn't it? Maybe I should poke them out for you and insert a color of your choice? Are you against all green-eyed waitresses taking your orders, or am I the only lucky one?"

His posture instantly changed. He leaned his body away from me, a look of complete fury falling across his features, as if he just watched me kick a newborn baby clear across the room and do a touchdown dance. What the hell is wrong with *him?* We had never even spoken before today. Maybe he had some mental issues going on.

From the corner of my eye, I watched as his right hand clenched into a tight fist, the tendons of his arms twisting and straining against his skin. His left hand gripped the edge of the table, knuckles turning white, as if he were holding on for dear life.

His dark eyebrows pinched together and his gaze averted to the stage behind me. His eye narrowed and with a curled lip, he muttered dryly, "Why don't you just make yourself useful and lose your clothes and dance."

Was he trying to piss me off? I stood frozen, blinking my eyes blankly at him. "I'm not a stripper."

"I'll pay you," he smiled tightly, still looking beyond me at the stage.

"I. Am. Not. A. Stripper."

"I bet you would be for ten grand," he smirked, meeting his eyes to mine.

The urge to smack him tingled through my hand, but I didn't. I couldn't. Forcing myself to detach from the situation, which was something I was trained to do, I smiled wider. "So, you think because you offered me ten thousand dollars, I would gladly jump on that stage and dance for you?" *Was I on camera? Was he serious?*

For a few slow heartbeats, he glared at me. Leaning forward, his voice dropped into a low raspy whisper, "For ten grand, I'm betting you'd do a hell of a lot for me." He was dead serious.

I pulled out the chair across the table from him and sat down, clasping my hands together and plopped them under my chin. This conversation was not going to end well. I didn't want to screw up anything for Bree by attacking my boss's brother. I certainly couldn't afford to cause any attention to where we were hiding by beating him to a bloody pulp either, so I had to calmly figure out how to deal with this animal.

"Please, Kade. Do tell me what makes you come to this conclusion of me, having never met me before."

He stood up, and I immediately regretted thinking I could sit down and talk this out with him. Obviously, he needed to be taken to a psych ward, the freaking *Freud Squad*, for *immediate evaluation*. He was glaring down at me, raging gray eyes full of disgust. "You're just like all the other sheep around here. Maybe a tad bit prettier than the rest of them, and I'm certain you *will* use it to your bloody advantage, people always do." He flattened down his shirt and backed away from the table. "Now go make yourself useful, shake your pretty little ass up there for me and earn yourself a year's salary. Maybe you could buy yourself something pretty with the money. And, don't call me Kade. It's Mr. Grayson, since it's your job here to serve *me*." His slight English accent becoming more pronounced the angrier he got.

Again, I gave him a sweet smile, but damn, my hands were clenched into sweaty fists that were aching to knock a few of his perfect teeth out. "Wow. Big head, small mind, huh? I wouldn't have pegged you as mentally incompetent, but I guess you really can't judge a book by its cover." I stood up slowly and leaned both hands down on the table. "I won't dance for your money, Mr. Grayson. Sorry to shatter your clichéd stereotypical expectations of me." He had no idea who I was or what things I had accomplished in my lifetime. Then again, look at what he was seeing; a pale faced woman, wearing ripped jeans, worn sneakers with holes in them, and hustling tables in a strip joint in the middle of nowhere, so maybe he's right to assume things. I didn't know. I didn't care. I spun on my heels and walked away. Screw him. I knew this was the part I had to play now, *but GOD, did it twist me up inside not being able to be myself in front of everyone.*

"So why are you here then? If you're not this clichéd version of a sheep I believe you are? Why not do something better with your life?" He barked. *Oh, what now? Was he trying to save the poor waitress with his Prince Charming complex or was it an ignorant attempt at continuing the conversation with me?*

Looking back, I met my eyes to his challenging ones. "How do you know I haven't? And how do you know that this, right here, isn't better than someplace else I've been?"

His mouth snapped shut. His dangerous dark features softened for a mere second before I turned my back to him and left him alone in the bar. This was his brother's bar, I was sure if he wanted a drink bad enough, he'd know how to pour it, or snap his fingers to get some magical fairy that could. I sat behind the bar, pulled out my phone and pulled up some online newspapers to read figuring it was going to be a long night with him staring at me from his back table, fuming like a toddler for not getting under my skin. To hell with him, my skin was way too tough for some pathetic gorilla in a Gucci suit to break through.

Within ten minutes, I was blissfully comfortable reading the *New York Times* on the small screen of my phone, no longer thinking about *Mr. Grayson*. The next twenty minutes passed without incident, until a cold wind blew in from two older men coming through the front doors. The gentlemen, who were regulars, greeted me with a warm wave and before I could even get to their table, they called for two beers and two plates of burgers and fries.

Peeking my head into the kitchen, I whistled for Trevor, who was cooking that night and had to wake him up off one of the cots in the back room to cook. He groaned and muttered profanities at me playfully all the way back into the bar area, and I came out of the back laughing. My eyes went directly to the table Kade had sat in before, and to my relief, it was empty. But, when I grabbed two cold beers from the coolers behind the bar, I heard the slide of one of the bar stools across the wooden floors right next to me.

"Have a drink with me," Kade's husky voice said.

I looked up, stunned by his demand. He was leaning against the stool, which he had pulled up next to mine and was pouring an enormous glass of brandy for himself. There was no malice in his expression, no disgust from before, but his eyes were suspicious and cautious. *Maybe he has multiple personalities?*

Without giving him an answer, I turned and walked towards the two customers with their beers, telling them their food would be out in a few minutes. Walking back behind the bar, I pulled my stool as far as I possibly could from him and sat down, ignoring his glare.

"Did you not hear me or are you just ignoring me? Maybe you're too simpleminded to understand me?" he demanded. *Nope, not multiple personalities, just one big egotistical shitty one.*

I laughed a small soft laugh and gave him a sad smile. I was too old to play games. I was too messed up with my own issues to care about his, and I didn't do drama, not even on TV. "No, thank you, Mr. Grayson. Trying to intimidate me and putting me down might make you feel like more of a man in your small world, but it does nothing for me. I'll enjoy sitting here alone a lot more." I turned my back on him and continued reading my phone, in my mind betting that was the first time anyone told him no. I'm sure Kade Grayson had a long line of interested women offering their dancing services or doormat services to him for his money, but I wasn't going to be one of them.

From the corner of my eye, I could still see the intensity of his stare. The man made me want to turn my head and stick out my tongue at him, and kick him hard in the shin. I didn't though. I just watched him drain his drink, quietly place it back on the bar, push off from the stool, and walk to the exit as he whispered, "Goodnight, Lainey."

"Goodnight, Mr. Grayson."

After a while, when the men that were sitting alone finished their meal, they waved goodbye, leaving me with a generous tip, and I was alone. I didn't want to let myself wonder about the mental state of Dylan's brother, but I found myself analyzing what I might have done to cause such hostility in a man that had, only moments before, looked at me with such intense desire in his eyes that it made *my* knees weak. I came to no conclusions.

After a few quiet hours, Dylan and Bree came back from their date, followed by a friend of Dylan's they had met up with along the way. Dylan jumped behind the bar, had us sit around a table, and brought out some beers for us. I just sipped at mine, feeling more and more uncomfortable with the events that occurred with Kade a few hours before. I wished I understood where his anger stemmed from; it could not have truly been from me, so I wondered where the misplaced anger was born. Being the person I was, I couldn't walk away from a puzzle, no matter how complicated it presented itself to be. Especially if it took my mind off of the situation I was in.

"You are certainly as nice looking as Dylan said you were," a male voice murmured at the table. *Hmm. Nice looking...I hated that adjective used on me...*

I shook the thoughts about Kade out of my head and looked up to see Dylan's friend. Short brown hair, angular features, and a long Roman nose. A nose, which he held up in the air and constantly wrinkled as though criticizing a nasty odor that no one else could detect. He had a handsome smile; a right as rain *Mr. Perfect*. He was nowhere near as shockingly handsome as Kade and his dangerous dark features. With *that thought,* I gulped down my beer and had the strong desire to punch myself in the face. Why the hell would I compare him to Kade? Kade was a mean piece of work, and someone I would never allow myself to spend time with, no matter how attractive he was. I learned my lessons well about good-looking, dangerous, powerful men and believe me, Kade needed to be the last thing on my mind.

"I'm Francis, by the way."

"Lainey. Pleasure to meet you," I smiled.

Bree giggled next to me, obviously happy about this little set up. She wanted me to be happy here, and I understood her wanting to stay and make a home here. I just didn't know what my plans were yet.

Francis talked with me for the rest of the night. He was a yapper and a gossipmonger, talking about everything and everyone. I let him dominate most of our conversations, which he fell into easily and I found him witty and kind. And *so freaking boring*. But right then, boring was good and the lack of effect and attraction was good for me, helped me to keep a distance. He was some sort of Environmental Scientist that specialized in something or other and had just returned home from somewhere in the Artic, and some other things that I really couldn't stand to keep up with, but he was thrilled about telling me, so I just listened as much as humanly possible. He was born and raised in Oregon; married then divorced, backpacked across Europe for a few years while studying abroad, and thankfully was too narcissistic and self-absorbed to ask any personal questions about me.

He was sweet and nice, overly friendly and attentive; the complete opposite of most men I'd known. And, when the night was winding down, he asked, "Since you're relatively new to this town, how about you let me take you out and show you around? I would really love a chance to get to know you."

"That sounds nice," I said, wanting to *want* to go, but honestly cringing at the thought of listening to his nonstop blabbering. Maybe he was just nervous and he'd be better on a date?

"How about tomorrow night? Can I steal you away from the bar for a while?"

Eager, are we?

"That sounds lovely," I smiled. Then I told him where the trailer was that Bree and I lived in. He didn't look down on me and he didn't make me feel like I was just a lowly waitress or some stripper he could buy a lap dance from and then throw away. I looked forward to the date, if just for the fact that he was the complete opposite of Kade Grayson.

After Dylan drove Bree and I home, he came in for a while and they eyed each other as if they were ready to pounce, making me feel like the ugly redheaded stepchild that follows you around the playground, humming to herself. The three of us were standing in the small kitchen and she batted her eyelashes towards him in that flirtatious way I could never attempt for fear of looking like I was having an epileptic attack. Suddenly, my phone seemed really interesting to me and I uploaded every stupid app I'd heard about in the last month. *Scrabble, sure! Bejeweled? Why Not. Word-With-Friends? Bring it! Singles support group? Hell yeah.*

Dylan and Bree started peeking at the bedroom, obviously wondering how to go about dealing with the issue that was *me*. Let me translate: small trailer, one bedroom with two single beds and *I don't cherish watching live porn.* Or having threesomes, for that matter. I would think that they took way too much coordination, way too much thought on where to put my elbows, and one more wet spot to worry about. Oh, and I am way too competitive, because if I didn't score *the winning shot,* I'd be pissed off.

"Hey," I waved at both of them. "Hi...how are you? Remember me? Lainey? Yeah... So... Um, why don't you move this potential slumber party you're both having in your heads to, let's say, Dylan's place, so I don't have to be scarred for life, sound good?"

"Will you be okay here alone?" Bree whispered.

"Yes, of course, go have fun," I laughed.

Dylan's shoulders relaxed and he nodded his head like a dork.

Bree clapped her hands as if she won the lottery and skipped into our bedroom yelling about packing a bag of things she'd need. *Oh Lord*, he's in for a wild ride. "Dylan, prepare to be boarded...and don't forget to fasten your seatbelt," I giggled.

Raising his eyebrows, the man looked downright giddy. God, they belonged together.

"So, Lainey, I forgot to ask, how was my brother tonight?"

"Fine," I said, because that was the only four-letter f-word *I wasn't thinking of*.

"Fine is never a word that comes to mind when I think of Kade," he said, raking his hands through his hair. Then he ran one hand over his face and sighed, "I wish I knew how to help him, but he's chosen such a solitary life. I think he loves his misery." I said nothing, and he looked at me and shrugged, continuing. "But, something brought him out tonight, yeah? I wonder what it was. I've never seen him two nights in a row."

"Has he been evaluated? Seen by a medical professional? Is he manic?" I slapped my hand over my mouth. Hell, when am I going to learn to keep my mouth shut?

Dylan scoffed and offered me a sad smile. "No, love. Believe me, my brother is doing a public service being the recluse he is. He's got demons to work through, but nothing medical."

Bree came running out of the bedroom with an overstuffed messenger bag slung off one of her shoulders. The expression plastered on her face was almost euphoric, like she'd already started having sex without him. I couldn't even think past that thought. I just smiled at her, shook my head, and looked down at my sneakers.

I desperately needed a new pair.

Bree hugged me tightly, and kissed my cheek. I knew this was big for her, so I gave her a firm squeeze in return, slapped her on the ass, and told her to have fun. She bounced to the door like a twelve year old and waved goodbye to me.

Dylan was right behind her, smiling. He reached out and softly touched my elbow, "Thanks again for taking over the bar tonight. And for putting up with Kade, I'm sure fine wasn't the word you wanted to say."

I shrugged, and held the door open for him.

"He's damaged. And he's just grown very attached to all his demons." He jogged down the front wooden steps, and they moaned and creaked with complaints. I wrapped my arms around my chest to shield myself from the cold air that blew through the door and watched them walk to Dylan's car.

When they drove off, I closed the door, locked it, and climbed right into my bed without even changing my clothes. I was beyond exhausted, but sleep didn't come easily, tossing, turning, and wondering if Kade Grayson's demons were as violent and terrifying as mine.

Sleep played a nasty game of laser tag with me all night. Each time I thought I was about to fall under, I'd be zapped awake from a noise, or a nightmare, or the strange whistling sounds of the wind and the rain drizzling against the tin roof of the trailer. I ended up playing on my phone most of the night, searching through any news stories concerning me from the city, wondering what was happening back home and how I was going to plan the rest of my life as somebody completely opposite of who I really was.

My alarm startled me at ten the next morning, causing me to fling my phone across the room and fall right out of bed, almost strangling myself with my covers. I wasn't used to sleeping on such a narrow mattress. Still half-asleep, I showered, dressed, and started my walk to the bar for an afternoon shift, already dreading my long day *and a* date with Francis. But, this was my ordinary life now.

Taking off my coat and smoothing down my shirt, I made my way into the bar. It was noon, and a handful of people were seated at tables eating lunch and talking. I walked behind the bar, threw my coat and purse in the small locker just underneath, and met Dylan in the back.

"Hey, you," Dylan called, popping his head out of one of the freezers.

I held my hand up to him. "Stop. I can't hold a realistic conversation with anyone right now. Not until I inhale a whole pot of coffee." I ran to the coffeemaker and fumbled with a huge Styrofoam to-go cup until Dylan came to my side to help me hold it steady. I felt the slight tremors in my hands from my exhaustion as I held up the steaming coffee to my lips and sipped, moaning delightfully. "We are definitely going to need an IV drip in here. I'm sure we could hook that up straight to the back of the coffee machine and pump it right into my veins."

"Rough night? I thought we left you *alone*," Dylan chuckled next to me.

"Yeah, well. I slept in a tin can and it was raining. That's like being front row at a rock concert to me. Where's Bree, anyway? You didn't chop her up into little pieces and bury her in the yard, did you?" I looked up to see Dylan frowning at something behind me. Deep creases settled in the middle of his brows and his eyes widened.

"Burying bodies in the backyard again, Dylan? I thought that was my job," a deep voice rasped behind me, lightly sprinkled with an accent matching Dylan's. *Shit.*

Taking a deep breath, I turned around, narrowing my eyes at Kade, standing in front of us, for the third time in three days.

Dylan echoed my thoughts, "Third time in three days."

The three of us stood there silent. Dylan gaped, open mouthed at Kade. And Kade? Well, Kade seemed to find something intensely interesting in my eyes. His gaze roamed my face as if looking upon a piece of fine art...gazing at each little piece of me...my eyes, my nose, my neck, and landing intensely on my lips.

Raising my cup up to cover my mouth, I drank my coffee and casually ignored him. There were hundreds of emotions zipping through my head, warring with one another; hate, curiosity, shock, embarrassment, need and...*God, I wanted to kick myself for it*...lust. You could feel the energy surrounding us shift and tighten as his eyes met back up with mine, daring me, fiercely challenging me to look away, or cower, or whatever game he was playing.

I sure as shit wasn't going to play any game by his rules.

"I forgot my jacket here last night," he mumbled, still gawking at me.

"It's on Dylan's desk in the back," I said coolly, turning my back on him and walking away indifferent to his plight. And yes, I did swing my hips and walk straighter when I did. *With my chin held high*.

Walking out into the bar, I spoke with a few tables full of people asking if they needed anything. A few orders later, I was leaning behind the bar with my ankles crossed and back against the counter.

"Offer still stands," Kade's voice murmured in a low gravelly tone. A masculine hand leaned next to me on the bar, which my eyes followed up, along his thick arms and across his chest to meet his eyes. He raised a dark eyebrow at me and smirked.

"Are you *that desperate*, Mr. Grayson? Tell me, what *do* you get from trying to belittle me?" I asked, with the best poker face I could muster.

"Most girls would jump at the chance to make that kind of money, for such a little thing." He licked his lips *purposely* and seemed to move closer to me than what was socially acceptable in my book. *And, dear God, his lips? Seriously, why did he have to have such great lips?* "Most girls don't even ask for the money."   His eyes flickered down my neck, giving me a whole once over before returning to my stare.

"See, there's your problem," I began to explain, stepping away. "You're talking about *girls*. I'm *a grown woman*. Big difference."

"Hey, there you are," Dylan came behind the counter of the bar stepping between us. "Lainey, you're exhausted, so go home so you can have a good night. Bree will be in later. And Kade? Can you drive Lainey home?"

"No," I replied calmly, before Kade could answer. "Thanks for the day off, but I could walk myself home. I definitely like the company more."

Without another glance or word to either of them, I grabbed my belongings from the locker and walked out of the bar.   Relief flooded my belly, thinking I was getting away from that idiot.

"Lainey, wait! Wait," his voice called after me, closing the door behind him.   "I'll drive you home."

"No thank you, Mr. Grayson."

The expression on his face was hard to read, but I didn't care to figure it out. Kade Grayson wasn't much to figure out, he was just a complete dick.

"Why? What's your problem?" he asked, *like this would be a surprise to him.*

"What's my problem? You're acting like a bitch, and if I wanted a bitch, I would have adopted a dog." I walked away from him as he mumbled something about writer's block and stupid green eyes.

Fucking sociopath.

All the way back to the trailer, I walked through the woods, not wanting to be anywhere near the road, just in case Kade Grayson lost his last marble and decided to do a drive by on the way home.

By the time I reach my empty trailer, my hands were cut up from catching on bushes. I was emotionally drained and so confused my head was spinning. The man looked at me one way, yet wanted to humiliate me and degrade me into hating him with his words. I thought I already had the market on meeting the most screwed up men before I came *here.*

Throwing myself on my bed, I closed my eyes and tried to unwind from being emotionally sideswiped by the freight train that was Kade. Immediately, I was asleep, and I awoke hours later when someone was pounding on my trailer door.

I stumbled out of the bedroom and made my way to the front door, and was completely embarrassed when I saw Francis standing on the top step holding a beautiful bouquet of white roses.

Shit. I'm already messing up this date.

But it's okay. I'll gloss over our date for you, only highlighting the GOOD parts. He showed up wearing a shirt that read, *I recycled this shirt from yesterday!* I'll let you savor that tidbit of information for a minute. *Yeah.*

He was easy. Careful. Nice. Safe. He held doors open for me. Paid for dinner. Talked about himself constantly and his field of whatever the hell he was interested in while I played word with friends on my phone. I won, by the way, with the word bracketed (triple word score) for 54 points. Woot! And no, I don't feel guilty for it, because throughout the entire time he was with me, he continuously instagrammed, facebook-statused, and twittered everything that he thought was status worthy. I swear, during dessert his tweet was, *'There IS no organic soymilk in the ENTIRE RESTAURANT! How do they expect me to drink my tea? WHOLE night is RUINED!'*

He was nice, don't get me wrong, but I really couldn't have a *relationship*. I didn't want to. I told Fran exactly how I felt and was as honest as I could have been with him. Getting to know one another and becoming friends was fine, but more than that, I didn't want to deal with, especially with someone who was so *Fran*. I mean, come on, Fran had a five-year plan and at the end, I was his goal. No one should ever have a goal of another person. You can't be someone else. Your goals should be to strive for better things in yourself, not depending on other people. Besides all that, I couldn't do another relationship; I couldn't trust anyone, not after what happened to me this last year. The only person I put my trust in was Bree, and I was just staying here for her, because I hadn't seen her this happy since the day my brother asked her to marry him.

Chapter 4
Kade

It was getting closer to Dylan's 30th birthday.

I sent him an eCard. *What? That's good enough.*

He called and screamed at me.

He's having a party. Of course. A small dinner party and he asked me to come. And, to come with a date. *A date?* Grand. Now the woman I have casual sex with will think we could date now.

Best part: Dylan's girlfriend is hosting it for him, along with her *roommate.* In her trailer. Trailer. *Trail...Errrr. Great, tonight's dining experience: Ramen fucking noodles.* I called Morgan, my casual *friend*, and she agreed; her husband won't be in town, so she can make it.

Clutching a bottle of $500 wine, I climbed out of my *Land Rover Range Rover* and walked through the yard crunching over the cold hard dirt and gravel that led to the doublewide, cringing with every step. I took inventory of the small wooden steps that led up to the front screened door to the dilapidated mess my brother's girlfriend calls a home and find a few muddied pair of converse sneakers, an industrial size gallon of bleach, and a box of generic latex medical gloves. A half burned out car from the 1950s was in the yard and a white picket fence that surrounded a dead tree. A small wooden crucifix was staked in the ground around its roots. *White-fucking-trash.* It was like a scene from one of my books. My skin crawled thinking about stepping a foot inside the trailer. I strategized on focusing solely on Morgan and the suction of her mouth on my cock after this dinner debacle. I really didn't understand how I was going to make it through the night.

I knocked on the screen door, which was ripped to fucking shreds, like an animal had tried to claw its way inside, *or out,* and the images of the massacre in my head left me a bit breathless. *It very well could be the beginning of a new book...the opening scene already writing itself in my subconscious.*

Behind the screen, the scratched-to-shit wooden door opened before I could compose my thoughts back to reality. Lainey was standing in the doorway, framed from the light within the tin trashcan impersonating a house. I hadn't seen her since I chased her out of the bar two weeks ago, when Dylan asked me to give her a ride home. She looked out of place. She looked awkward and suspicious. Stunning me with her raw beauty, she looked like a fucking dark angel. And sexy as fucking sin. *Shit.*

I had no clue she was going to be here.

She tucked a wavy lock of hair behind her ear and offered me a tight smile. "Mr. Grayson." Her greeting was curt and short. I hated it. I loved it. *I'm fucking insane.*

She stepped to the side to allow me to walk in. The smell of her soap or shampoo or whatever the hell it was that filled my nose left me hungry.

No, not *hungry*. Fucking hell, *ravenous*. I blinked my eyes rapidly, focused on the inside of the tin box, and swallowed a small gasp. I had never seen the inside of a trailer before, other than the idiotic movies I watched, but I would have never assumed one could look so...*homey*. The walls were a warm chocolate color and everything from the clean comfortable looking couches to the small yet elegantly decorated table and chairs were in earth tones and warm soft colors. It made me want to lay down and surround myself with its calmness, take some away with me. Steal it for myself. Morgan was already there, sitting at a small counter that separated the kitchen area with the living room area, a blood-red goblet of wine held tightly in her hand and she smiled at me like I was the second coming of Christ on a platter, just for her. She was dressed up like it was her fucking high school prom, make-up caked on her face and dark brown eyes weighed down heavily with mascara. Flecks of red dotted the whites of her eyes, as if her capillaries were bursting from strangulation, making me think of someone wrapping their hands tightly around her neck and squeezing tight.

Then my eyes locked on Lainey as she stepped in front of me to the counter, and a tall lanky man moved up behind her, hesitantly placing a hand on her ass to ask her if she needed any help. If I hadn't been staring at her form, the curve of her hips and flatness of her belly, I would have missed the minute flinch that happened just as his hand made contact with her body. She was uncomfortable under his fingers, and for some ungodly reason that made me feel ecstatic. I scanned up the slope of her body to the swell of her chest, the smooth ivory of her neck and then to the wide smile she offered him with her lips. I wanted to fucking crush his heart. A strange stab of jealousy coursed through me, and I could distinctly visualize in my head the blood splatters and the trajectory of the spray of brain matter after I slammed him with my $500 bottle of wine on the side of his head. I placed the stupid pathetic bottle down on the counter in front of them a little too hard, just really itching for the chance to swing it at him.

"Would you like a glass of wine?" she asked me softly, tossing her hair over her shoulder, slicing the bloodstained scenes from my mind with the smell of *motherfucking* cinnamon apples.

"Yes. Thank you," I found myself saying. Her eyes found mine. Her lashes looked incredibly long against her ivory cheeks, and a small darkening of shadows graced her skin, as if she'd been having trouble sleeping. Those green irises were like gentle pools of brilliant meadows of sage and green-envy coneflowers swaying in a warm breeze.

HOLY fuck. *What the hell sort of poetry was that dribbling out of my twisted brain?*

Her brows knitted together as she stood in front of me, handing me a full glass of the blood-red wine. I tried to imagine it splattering across her face, trying to think of the words that I could twist onto a clean crisp white paper, words that would slice the life from those eyes, but I could think of none. *None.*

This bitch was giving me writer's block.

The man who pawed her ass held out his hand to me and smiled. "So, you're Dylan's infamous brother? Glad to finally meet you, I'm Fran," he said, shaking my hand weakly.

The only thoughts in my mind were at that very moment were first, that hand was just touching Lainey's ass, second, what the fuck kind of name was Fran? And third, his fucking hand was just *touching Lainey's ass.* I squeezed his hand more than I should have. He grimaced.

"Fran?" I asked, curious to the femininity of the name and why a parent would hate their child so heinously that they would name him that.

"Short for Francis," Lainey uttered, a little above a whisper.

"Ah," I chuckled darkly, "*that* makes it *so* much better."

She rolled her eyes at me. Fuck, it was as if I was in high school again. *No, high school was bloodier.* Francis smiled then, a full mouth of white shiny teeth and I wanted to knock each and every last bright ivory enamel-coated structure out, maybe the whole damn jaw too. That would be a *great scene*; my fingers began curling into tight hard fists.

My brother strutted in then. Man of the hour. Wearing *thirty* like it was some sort of trophy he competed for and won. His eyebrows shot straight up, as if he was actually shocked to see me. I guess he might very well have been, since

I had only seen him a handful of times in the last few years.

"You actually came?" he asked, stunned.

"Nope. Not here at all," I replied, a bit too harshly. Dealing with people wasn't my thing. "Happy birthday."

A blonde woman, whom I recognized as the other waitress, and could only assume was my brother's new girlfriend, Bree, bounced out from the back of the trailer and she and Lainey pushed us to sit as they placed food on the small table. Morgan didn't help, I noticed. She sat herself down next to me, tall and regal, waiting to be served. For some reason, that messed with my head. I wanted it the other way around, with Morgan serving Lainey, and *that* messed with my head even more. I drank my wine in one enormous gulp, almost embarrassingly vomiting it right back up. When Morgan's French manicured hand reached down into my lap and cupped my balls, I pushed away from the table to get the bottle of wine I had left on the counter. *I was going to need a few more bottles to get through the night.*

Lainey was standing next to the tiny sink holding a steaming bowl of something. My mind tried to make it a bowl of wiggling maggots, but all I saw was fluffy delicate curls of pasta. Her eyes traveled over me and landed on mine. One beautiful soft eyebrow arched up at me questioningly.

"So, *Francine* seems *sweet*," I said. I was incapable of having a healthy normal conversation, wasn't I? *I wanted to goad her, and to bicker and fight with her.* I wanted to get her angry and outraged. To offend her so harshly that her beautiful sweet features would show some sort of fucking expression other than the complete control that I lacked.

Her eyes remained soft and delicate. *Fuck, was that pity? Was that fucking pity she was looking at me with?* "I wouldn't know, Mr. Grayson. I haven't tasted him yet. However, if I do get the pleasure of that, I will let you know how sweet it is."

I wanted her to be one of those characters I killed off in the first chapter; the stupid innocent beauty that follows the clichéd killer down his rabbit hole. I held the scene in my head for a mere second, before it blurred and changed into me bending her over my knee and spanking her bare creamy ass until she was pink and wet.

The thought made me dizzy with want.

Dinner was deplorable. Not only was the food absolutely unnaturally the most delicious thing I had ever eaten, I could not stop myself from staring at Lainey's mouth the entire time she ate. The pure shade of pink was the natural hue of her lips. The full flesh of them as they pressed against her glass of wine. I tried to focus on a figurine that was sitting alone on one of the shelves. It was a sculpture of a human brain. *Who the hell would keep that in their home?* The need to walk over to it and crush it in my hands was so strong that I could taste the dust of the ceramic pieces as they floated past my own lips in my mind.

Lainey's green eyes kept meeting mine. Each time, her eyes would narrow and hold my stare. She didn't fear me, didn't back down. She was a complete contradiction to anyone I had ever met before. I smirked to myself thinking of her underneath me, the smooth skin of her legs wrapped around me, the burn of her nails as she clawed them down my back. Climbing over my body, riding me deep and fast, until my body convulsed inside her.

My hand gripped my fork so firmly against the plate it bent at an awkward angle. *Fuck.* How was I going to explain *that*?

Lainey gently pushed her chair back from the table and dabbed a napkin to her lips, "Anyone need more wine?" she asked, walking into the kitchen area, swaying her hips so sensually it could have killed me. Maybe it did, maybe it did kill me and this was my hell. My brain fogged up, hearing everyone around the dinner table talking but not being able to understand a word of it. My focus was completely concentrated on Lainey's subtle movements as she went about pouring more wine. With her back to her guests, she filled her goblet and pressed the edge of it against her lips, sipping softly. Placing her glass back down, she reached up and swept all of her thick dark hair into a wild sexy bun at the nape of her neck. I was drowning, lost in a twisted sea of darkness.

The smooth creamy curve of her neck against her dark skin made me clench my fists tighter, almost snapping the damn fork in half.

Jesus H. Christ, what the hell is wrong with me?

Then the darkness of her hair slipped over her shoulder as she turned her head, laughing at something somebody had said. And there, against the nape of her neck, hidden beneath the tumble of her hair was a dark tattoo. *Give me your hurt.* The tattoo above the elegant dress, against her ivory skin was an erotic mix of good and bad, heaven and hell, and I wondered what her story truly was. *How had she come here? Why? Who hurt her? What was she running from?* And, why the hell do I care?

I wanted to hate her, break her, and keep her the hell away from my sick, twisted mind. But, there was no point in lying to myself, was there? Because I wanted a taste of her even more. I wanted *her.*

I didn't like not being in control. That wasn't me. *I needed out of here.*

I grabbed Morgan's hand and yanked her up from the chair she was sitting on, still eating, apparently. She gave a little choked yelp as I tugged her to the door. "Well, thank you for a lovely evening. We have to be off now. Happy fucking birthday." I slammed the ridiculous excuse for a door behind me and walked through the icy night to my truck.

"Finally," Morgan breathed behind me, her hands reaching out to grab mine. "I can't believe we had to sit through that."

Ignoring her, I clicked open the locks on the truck, opened the driver's side door and shoved her in past the steering wheel climbing in after her. Ramming the key in the ignition, I blasted the heat and grabbed for her waist, placing her on my lap, her dress hiked up to her bare thighs as they straddled mine. "Don't talk, unless you're telling me how hard to fuck you."

Morgan clawed at my face and kissed me hard. My hands were on her bare hips and I chuckled deep into her mouth; leave it to Morgan not to wear any panties so I would have easy access. I should have fucked her right at that dinner table. I should have done it just to see the look on Lainey's innocent face while I fucked like an animal in front of her. The thought got me harder than I had ever been in my life.

Morgan slid off me and unzipped my suit pants; my cock sprung free slapping against her hands. I wasn't wearing underwear either.

She fisted my cock with both hands, wrapped her lips around the head and started to pump and suck. "Fuck. That's good," I whispered, pressing the back of her head into me, gagging her. She hummed and moaned, vibrating her approval against my skin. I lessened the pressure of my hand and moved her head to the rhythm I wanted and rocked into her. Images of Lainey looking out the window, finding me fucking Morgan's mouth in the front seat of my truck, almost pushed me over the edge. Pulling her mouth off me, I spun her around to face the windshield. She steadied herself against the dashboard and lifted her ass into my face as I yanked a condom out of my pocket, ripped through the foil with my teeth and rolled the fucker on. Then I slammed into her, making her yelp in surprise, then giggle and moan. I made her ride me fast and hard, pushing and pulling at her ass to get her to move fast enough for the feral fuck I wanted. I knew Morgan liked it hard anyway. That was why we played. She needed a man that wasn't afraid to fuck her and I needed a woman that I could break if I needed to. I never thought about Morgan as I fucked her. She wasn't *real* to me. It was like there wasn't a woman attached to the pussy I pounded. All I thought about were the sensations around my cock. I felt her pulse and tighten around me when a small ivory hand pushed back the curtains to one of the windows in the trailer, and the thought of Lainey had me surging forward and coming so hard I saw spots before my eyes. *Holy shit.*

"Get off me," I grunted.

Lainey's big green eyes were in my head.

"That little girl in there got you twisted up or something, Kade? You were staring at her like you wanted to devour her."

Rolling the condom off, I still felt the tremors in my cock, but fuck me if they were from Morgan. "Get out. I want to be alone."

She stepped out with pursed lips and slammed the door. I didn't wait to see if she got in her car safely, she wasn't mine to worry about, so I rolled out over the gravel drive and pulled onto the main road, tossing the full condom out of the window. Out of guilt, I'd end up texting an apology later, but she knew how messed up I was and she expected me to be a detached piece of shit to her, she got off on it.

I tried focusing my eyes on the painted traffic lines that glided quickly beneath the hood of my truck as I drove purposefully in the middle of the street. Chuckling to myself, I turned off my headlights and sailed into the darkness, taunting death to meet me head on. Pressing my foot down lower, I increased my speed, wondering to myself if other people ever did *this*. Played with death, such as I did. I'm sure there's a fucking fetish club for it that I could find online.

Unfortunately, I got home unscathed.

I ran right to my computer, opened a new document, and thoughtlessly titled it *Green-Eyed Woman*. My blood and soul poured through my fingers as they moved across the keyboard, raw and angry, chilling. The setting is a dinner party in a small quaint mobile home. Sprays and splashes of red wine and blood crashed violently against its cream colored walls as the massacre begins. The beautiful girl stared with wide green eyes as the world turned crimson around her, but she's not scared. She's *fearless*. Blood dripped from my fingertips as her pure unscathed lips touched mine, pulling the hate and anger away from my soul.

Pure unadulterated raw sex emerged from the pages. Erotic touches, words, and violence twisted together to form an epic story of horrific proportions, with a sick tangled web of obsession and passion.

I had never been afraid of anything in my life with the exception of one violent day from my youth, which completely changed the person I was then, to the empty shell, I was today. Since that day, I've kept everyone and everything away from me so I don't hurt anyone with my wrath and my belligerence. But this girl, this *woman,* she was slowly captivating me, slipping the fear, the hate, and the rage away from me with her mysterious poise and calmness in my world.

When the sun rose over the evergreens that surrounded my home, I had over fifty thousand words to my next book. I didn't stop either, I couldn't. My muse would not shut the fuck up. The obsession consumed me for days. The girl, I knew would be an obsession for longer. I wanted to scrape the words I've written off the white of the screen, grab them tightly in my hand and smash them against her face. Have her feel my words against her flesh, smear them into her pores, and have them seep into her skin.

I needed to see her again. I needed her to hate me and to stay far away from me, because I wanted to consume her completely.

Chapter 5

Lainey

Empty wine bottles and burgundy bottom stained glasses littered the trailer. Fran had tried to be a gentleman and attempted to help me clean after Dylan's birthday dinner last night, but we didn't get too far. From the moment Bree and Dylan slipped out of the door to *sleep* back at Dylan's place, Fran's hands were all over me.

When his lips met mine, I felt like I was watching myself from a distance, trying to find some sort of feelings or something…some glimmer of *want*. But all I could think of was the life I'd run away from. How I thought I'd be able to delude myself into thinking that I could possibly date a man after what I'd been through was laughable to me. My body tensed up, a small whimper escaped from my mouth and I simply pushed myself away from Fran's pawing limbs. *My past was going to haunt my every kiss from now on, wasn't it? Every time another man places his lips or hands on me, I'm going to cringe and wonder what it is he really wants to take from me, aren't I?*

I did my best to compose myself and offered a silly excuse about getting to know one another better and cleaning, I had to clean. Fran, the gentlemen he was, understood and helped clean a bit, but I just called it a night, and when he gently asked me, I agreed to another date out of guilt.

After he left, I had another miserable night of sleep, tossing and turning, nightmares pecking at my grey matter. Nightmares about blood and fists, hospital ceilings, dark shadows on city streets and moonless desert nights listening to explosions like music in the air. Nightmares about my brother. Nightmares about Kade and the way his dangerous eyes watched me during dinner, and the way I *liked it*.

At eight in the morning, right in the middle of gulping coffee straight from the *coffee pot*, my phone buzzed and I groaned out loud. "I'm cleaning it up. I don't need help, go back and snuggle with your Bucket of Yum, and relax," I laughed into the phone, not even bothering with any hellos.

Bree sighed on the other end and whispered, "The guilt is killing me."

"This isn't about the cleaning, huh?" I asked, knowing full well it had everything to do with *not cleaning*.

She whimpered into the phone.

"My brother loved you more than anything, *Jen*. He'd want to see you move on and be happy. Michael's been gone over a year and you deserve a little bit of fun and happiness. Please, just enjoy yourself." I laughed loudly, "I mean don't enjoy *yourself*, enjoy Dylan. Go. Have fun. And sex. Have lots of hot, dirty, nasty sex."

"I know you're right, but...God, I have felt numb for so long. My body just shut down when he died, and now with Dylan I feel alive again." She sobbed quietly into the phone and sniffled. "*But*, I feel like I'm cheating on Michael," she whispered.

"Honey, you're not going to be able to have a future with anyone if you keep yourself in the past. What you and Michael had was beautiful, but he's gone and you need to let yourself live. You never know what's going to happen, just be happy and live for *you, live for today*. I'm not asking you to forget him, just let some other people in, that's all."

"Michael and Dylan would have been friends. Great friends," she whispered.

"And, I bet he wouldn't be able to pick a better guy for you to date," I said.

"You always say just what I need to hear. I'm glad we stayed close because I wouldn't have been able to deal with losing Michael without you. I would have been all fucking alone."

"You're like my sister. No, you *are* my sister, look at what you did for me. You ran away with me! You wouldn't let me do any of this alone," I replied.

"I couldn't, because you didn't leave me. You're the only family I have," she sniffed softly.

"I love you, sweets. I really do, and you deserve to be happy. Dylan makes you smile again. He's a nice guy. Go and enjoy yourself for a little while. I'm not telling you to marry the guy, just have fun. No excuses; continue with your love fest please."

"Shut up," she laughed. "I'll be by later to get my bag for work. I forgot it last night. Love you and thanks, *Sam*...for everything."

Hanging up, I smiled at the state of chaos in the trailer. "Prepare to be cleaned, O-C-fucking-D style," I laughed out loud, swallowing back the last remnants of coffee from the bottom of the pot.

So, dressed in only my sleepwear, which consisted of a tiny black tank top that ended above my navel and a tight pair of boy shorts, I armed myself with a pair of latex gloves, broke out the bleach, my iPod and speakers.

An hour later, the pungent smell of bleach and lemons filled the air and the place was literally *sparkling*. All of the dishes were washed, everything that was ever touched by human hands was disinfected and I felt brand new. I threw my gloves off and looked around. The only thing left to clean was the floors, *one last time*, so I raised the volume of the music and mopped to the beat of *Raise Your Glass* by Pink. Dancing around, I sang the words into the mop handle and tried to bust out some moves like I watched the girls do on stage at the bar. In front of the stove, I did one of those sexy stripper stomps in my white beat up chucks on my tippy toes, pretending they were stilettos. When I got to the couch, I flipped my hair around, squatted down into one of those spread eagle moves and slid myself back up, laughing, shaking my backside and spinning around the mop.

"Um...Lainey," Bree's voice stammered, pulling my eyes up to hers at the door. She'd caught me doing a hell of a lot worse, so I felt no shame. Hell, we usually giggled and practiced these moves together. However, when I saw who was standing next to her, my stomach dropped and I yelped out a squeal of mortification.

Kade fucking Grayson.

Kade fucking Grayson got to watch me dance after all. Well, universe, you seem to be desperately trying to rain all sorts of shit down my neck, what next?

Bree's voice interrupted my arguments in the case of Universe vs. My Shitty Life. "I just came back to pick up my uniform and I came upon Kade here, looking at something very interesting to him through one of our windows," she laughed. "I have to get to the bar, or should I stay here?" she asked, eyeing me and grabbing her workbag off the hanger on the door.

Wait. What? He was watching me freaking dance while I cleaned?

My mouth wanted to drop open. I was beyond humiliated, but there was no way I would let him know it bothered me. "I'm fine, Bree," I answered, indifferently.

"*Ooookay* then, enjoy whatever the hell you got going on here..." she said awkwardly, and walked out of the trailer.

Slowly, I moved myself behind the small kitchen counter that separated the kitchen and other rooms, trying to block his view from me. "What are you doing here, Mr. Grayson?" A slow burn spread across my cheeks and heated my scalp as I stood, waiting for his explanation. *He watched me dance?*

He moved around the counter closer to me. His intense stare lowered from my flushed cheeks down to my breasts, across my stomach, and lingered with heat on my bare legs before it traveled slowly back over my entire body again to my eyes. His look was dark. *Sexy.* Oh. My. God. It felt as if he licked me in one long slow stroke, up and down my entire body. Thanks universe, just crank the sexual tension up a few notches, *whydon'tcha?*

I stood there trembling, uncertain as to what I should do. Uncertain as to how I felt about his eyes on me. Okay. Fine. I. Liked. It. *There, I admitted it.*

"Uh...I...I forgot my jacket again. Last night. Here," he choked out.

Was I making that man stutter? Because of what I was wearing? Was barely wearing. Small beads of sweat broke out across my forehead.

I seriously wanted to cross my arms over my chest. Even though I *was* wearing clothes, the small amount of them combined with his lusty stare made me feel completely naked. And those dark dangerous eyes of his made me want to move closer to him. *Shit.* "You know what I think? I think you forget a lot of shit when I'm around."

"You're beautiful," he whispered hoarsely, eyes still fixed on mine.

I lost all rational thought. Lost the use of my limbs and I was melting fast.

The mop slipped from my hands and clinked against the counter, averting my eyes from his. I tried pretending that those two pathetically simple words didn't just cause my panties to leak a drip down my legs. "Beautiful," I repeated flatly. That was the first time in my life a man called me that and it had to come from an asshole.

He moved toward me with intense purpose and power, dipping his head, forcing me...challenging me to keep eye contact with him.

Well, too bad. I turned my head away from his, looking past him, beyond him, as if he didn't matter. Heat crept over my skin as he slowly inched closer to me and I turned to face him again, my eyes locked on his. There was something unnerving in his gaze, something dark, cold and alive there, begging to be warmed. His steel eyes fluttered slowly down to my lips and my pulse instantly started hammering through my veins. The closer he moved, the faster it pounded. Both his hands reached up and gently cupped my face, and he leaned forward laying his forehead tenderly against mine. "Yes. Beautiful. Stunning. Bewitching. Ravishing. *Fucking angelic.*" He smelled like the most expensive brandy money could buy, it was dizzying. I had no personal space left. He took it all, absorbed every last breath of it, almost knocking me to my knees.

One strong hand cupped the back of my head, his long fingers doing something to the nape of my neck that sent chills down my spine. His expression was dark, intent, lusty, making heat scorch up my neck. His heather grey eyes bore down on mine, making my heart pound violently in hopes of escaping from my rib cage.

My mouth opened to speak, but our breath just mingled and he growled a low rumbly groan as he fiercely crushed his lips against mine, drowning out my words, capturing my breath. A relentless flood of warmth swelled in my whole body. His lips were soft and unyielding, moving against me in slow passionate circles. The heat of his mouth made me gasp for air, and the taste of the dark brandy that flavored his mouth was delicious. Hard and rough, his mouth raked over mine. I swayed back against the sink, hands leaning back. I needed something to hold on to – something that would keep me here on earth, because his lips on mine, his hands, fingertips cupping my face, my head, made me *feel...everything.* My heart pounded erratically in my chest. The heat of his fingertips singed into my skin, and my insides thawed, softened, liquefied into a wet hot mess. Every spot where his skin touched mine, I felt a powerful staggering heat. The squeeze of his fingers over my flesh sent a rush of need through my belly. *Where was this coming from? Why the hell was I standing here letting him TOUCH ME? WHY the hell WAS I KISSING HIM BACK?*

I pushed him away, covering my mouth, breathing heavy, unable to catch my breath. *I had no words.* I could tell everything by the way this man kissed me. I could tell how rough, hard, and erotically passionate this man was and how *I was losing the ability to breathe because of his kiss.* He stumbled back a step, breathing just as hard as I was, eyes blazing into mine, savage, wild and hungry. This stolen kiss, this theft of lips, this *claim* on my mouth was the most erotic sexual kiss in my life. My knees were so weak; I leaned back heavily against the counter again to stop my body from melting into thick sweet syrup at his feet.

"I didn't think... I didn't think you'd taste...*so good*," he whispered, dragging his hands roughly through his hair and back down over his face.

He had to ruin the moment, right? A dark laugh bubbled out of my throat, "What? You thought waitress flavored kisses were too sour for you?" Shoving myself off the counter, I walked away to the opposite side of the trailer, putting as much distance as I could between the both of us, and wanting to scream at him. I paced back and forth trying to regain my composure. *Hell, just trying to stop panting like a dog in heat would be helpful.* A thick dense knot settled in the pit of my stomach. *I just let him kiss me and I loved it.* I had no control over it, not a damn ounce. *Now he's going to degrade and belittle me and be all Kade-like again. Why? Why did he have to kiss me like that, yet be the biggest asshole I'd ever met?*

For a moment, he looked as dazed as I felt, then his arrogant lip quirked up in a cocky smile. Look at that...the man had a playful dimple that introduced itself, mocking me on one of his cheeks. I wanted to smack the offensive boyish charmer right off his mean face.

Narrowing my eyes at him, I stopped my pacing. "Don't. Don't say anything else. You'd be perfect if you just kept your arrogant mouth closed. Your intimidation skills are lacking and I'm not the kind of woman who would actually believe that you are superior to me just because you're a man. You think you're better than me and you're not Kade." Anger at his stupid pompous smirk made me want to burst his narcissistic bubble and tell him that I was a hell of a lot more than a waitress in a strip club, but I clenched my mouth closed. *This wasn't like me to let someone get under my skin*.

He raised his eyebrows and stalked towards me with purpose. "That's what you think?"

"What I think is that you're a disgusting, demeaning, lonely man who looks good in an expensive suit."

By the time I ended my sentence, he was seething. He lowered his face to mine and looked straight into my eyes, viciously. "Let's get everything out, yeah? I'm the first person to acknowledge that I am 100% fucked up in my head. That's why I stay away from everyone. When I first laid eyes on you, God forgive me for my stupidity, I thought you were a fucking *angel*. But, I've met people like *you*, you're just like everybody else I've ever known," he sneered, disturbingly. "I think people should strive to be more than what *you* are. Look at what I saw when I first saw you; a waitress, poor as shit, working in a strip club where men *pay her for the way she makes them feel*, living in a fucking trailer. Then you came up to me, swaying those perfect hips, and you asked me what I wanted to drink. I made my assumption on what you gave me, love. And I offered you a job."

Stunned, furious and explosive, I held my chin up to him, "That's all there is, just the black and white cover of a book? Never even opening it up to see the inside. So I'm just a waitress or, as you explained so eloquently, a whore?" I closed the small distance between us, wanting the confrontation, wanting to fight with him. "Then all you are is a pathetic storyteller who lives in a world full of *make-believe.* You're like *Mister Fucking Rogers!*"

Without warning, he hauled me up by the waist onto the counter, gripping my skin tightly. His fingers splayed out over the bare skin of my legs, the tips of his fingers pressing against the edge of my cotton boy shorts. Holding a steady gaze, his thumb lightly brushed across the skin of my inner thigh, before gripping me tighter.

"Get your hands off me, Grayson. Don't make the mistake of underestimating me," I whispered, our faces less than an inch away from each other. "I'm more than what I do for a living. I'm a friend, a lover, a sister. I'm *ANYTHING* I want to fucking be. I pity you for defining yourself because of the four walls you box yourself into. And stop looking at me like you're going to kiss me again, because it's not going to happen. If I'm not good enough because I'm a waitress, don't settle for me, don't sink down to my level. You don't deserve anything I have to offer. Let that shit hurt for a hot minute, simmer in it then leave me the fuck alone. Repeat that shit to yourself in your head when you walk out of here, rinse and repeat."

His expression darkened, "You can still feel my lips on yours, can't you?"

"Shut up, Kade, and get your hands off me."

"*Tell me* I'm wrong," he hissed.

I pushed forward, moving him away with my body, "You're wrong."

"*Prove* me wrong," he hissed again, louder.

Jumping off the counter edge, I walked past him and scowled, "You kissed me, not the other way around. I think you need to look into therapy."

He laughed darkly and shook his head, "I don't want proof about the kiss; I know you still feel my lips on yours. We both knew the truth after that kiss. I wasn't moaning all by myself in here. You kissed back just as hard. We both want to fuck each other until we can't walk straight. I want you to prove me wrong that you're not like every other person on this planet." A minute or two passed as we stared at each other. Ardent slate eyes bore into mine, waiting; wanting. *He didn't want me to prove him wrong. He wanted me to be like whatever it was that had hurt him; that was plain to see on his face.* What the hell happened to him?

"You don't want me to prove anything to you. You want me to be just like everybody else."

Kade was silent for a few long moments, and then he slowly moved past me to the door. His eyes gave everything away, but he said the words anyway, "You're right," he whispered, "because then, I'd have a tangible reason to stop thinking about you."

Clearly not thinking, I stepped in front of him, blocking his way to the door. "Kade?" *This man has to be suffering from dissociative identity disorder.*

He lifted his head up to meet my eyes, "Don't, Lainey. Don't listen to anything I'm saying. I'm drunk as hell and I liked what I saw through your window, that's it."

I nodded my head sharply, "Right, because I'm only good for a dance. Well, you got what you wanted, so no charge either. I guess you were right about how easy I was to label into your lap-dancing-gold-digging-uneducated-waitress-trailer-trash file," I smiled. "Oh, wait. Hold on," I said, pulling my aid-bag off the hook by the door and rummaging through it. When my hands felt the small-foiled package I was looking for, I grinned wider at him, flicking the condom right into his face.

Kade caught the condom with a quick flick of his hand. *Yeah, great reflexes for a drunk, right?* He arched his eyebrows up at me.

"It's a condom, Kade, because if you're going to act like a dick, you might as well dress like one," I explained, smiling so wide my cheeks actually hurt. Then I grabbed his jacket from the hook I hung it on last night and tossed it at him. "Thanks for the pleasant visit."

"Well, love, maybe you are one step above trailer trash," he smiled sadly.

"Well, *fuck me gently with a chainsaw* and no lube. Thank you for the compliment!" My head started to ache from all this crazy. *This man needs an array of meds.*

A knock at the door silenced our immature conversation. Both of us realized we were mere inches away from each other, and ready to either claw each other's eyes out or lick each other silly.

I swung the door open to find Fran standing behind the screen with a dozen red roses. He's eyes bulged out of his sockets when he looked at me, and I felt the deep flush of embarrassment across my cheeks when I realized I had not gotten dressed the whole time I was fighting with Kade.

"Excuse me," I snapped, shoving past a sneering Kade as I stalked through the trailer, straight to my closet to make myself look decent.

Through the thin slats of the trailer blinds, I looked out in time to see Kade kick a huge dent into the side of his truck, swing open the door and furiously climb into it, slamming the door shut so harshly that his jacket got caught in it. I hoped to God, he wasn't drunk, then felt guilty as hell for not making sure before letting him drive. I've seen the results of too many drunk-driving accidents, and my stomach knotted. I yanked a sweatshirt over my head, slid my legs into a pair of yoga pants and ran back into the kitchen to my phone on the counter. I typed out a quick text to Dylan telling him his brother just left here and that he was drunk, and to maybe check on him to make sure he got home and didn't kill any innocent people. Slamming the phone back down on the counter, I tore my hands through my hair and almost jumped clear out of my skin when I heard a throat clear behind me.

I completely forgot that Fran had come over.

"So...is there anything that I should know?" he asked sadly, placing the beautiful flowers across the counter and gripping his long fingers on the edge to lean forward.

"Not at all."

He cocked his head at me, and offered me a sarcastic chuckle under his breath, "Last night that man couldn't keep his eyes off you and today I come here at 9:30 in the morning and you're half dressed with him, looking quite *flushed*." He tapped one hand on the counter, and continued, "Lainey, I know we've just met, but I really would like to know if you're having any sexual relationships elsewhere."

I burst out laughing.

Poor Francis looked heartbroken.

"Trust me; I am not having any sort of relationship with that idiot. He came here this morning because he forgot his jacket last night and all we did was to go at each other's throats." I picked up the bouquet of flowers with my trembling hands and pulled out a plastic dollar store vase Bree had bought the first week we were here, and placed the flowers inside. "And for your information, I haven't been sexually active for a very long time." *But, seriously, what I would give to be fucked until I couldn't walk straight. Just to see what the hell I've been missing.*

My stomach coiled up into thousands of little hard knots, because I knew my next sentence would be a lie. "Kade is not even a thought in my mind." *I still felt his lips on me and I knew he was pushing me away from him because he was just as attracted to me as I was to him. He said he pushed people away on purpose.* But, let's break this down right now, shall we? I will not fool myself. Kade would never be healthy for me. He's too wrapped up in whatever it is that consumes him. *He's sick.* I let that shit seep into my brain the minute Kade came here throwing his invisible demons at me. It pissed me off for a minute, and then I moved on. The man had dangerously glaring-in-your-face character flaws, and I knew there was no such thing as believing love will conquer all and change everything. If it did, I wouldn't have a missing person's file out on me in the tri-state area, and the police probably wouldn't want to take me in for questioning. I'm not surprised, nor could I bring myself to give any fucks about the situation. Seriously, my fucks had been all used up already.

Fran cautiously shifted his body in front of mine and tenderly lifted my chin with his finger, attempting to make me look him in the eyes. "What do you think of being in an exclusive relationship with me?" His eyes scanned my face, searching for an answer he wanted to hear.

"I just ended a long monogamous relationship, Francis. I explained that to you. I don't want to be part of another relationship right now."

He leaned closer to me, his breath hot on my face, "I would like getting to know you though."

My stomach churned as he brought his other hand to my cheek and dipped his head closer to me, kissing me slowly and softly with closed lips. I opened my lips against his and he pulled in a sharp breath. I wanted desperately to feel a spark, or a flutter of something, but all I thought about was how different his lips were from Kade, or how Fran kissed just as softly, robotically and clinically as the man, I had once been married to did.

I pushed the thoughts out of my head. I wasn't Samantha Matthews any longer.

Fran buried his face in my hair and pulled me in tighter for a hug. "Okay, I will take this as slowly as you need me too." Raising his head, he slowly ran his nose along my cheek and kissed me on the forehead.

Breaking away from his embrace, I moved along the counter, grabbing my phone to find no new messages. My stomach ached a little, worrying about anyone in the path of Kade's truck.

"Anyway, I came over early to help you clean, but I see that you stayed up all night and scrubbed this place raw," he said, looking around in amazement.

I laughed. "It only took me an hour, Fran. I like cleanliness, what can I tell you? I have this thing for sterile environments." I walked over to the coffeepot I used as a mug earlier and placed it in the sink, running soap and water over it. "Would you like some coffee?" I asked.

"I have a better idea," he said running his hand down my arm. "Why don't you go put something nicer on and I will take you to the quaintest street festival you've ever seen. Then, I want to take you to an early dinner and then to the best little book store on earth." The man bounced a little on his heels, "Bree told me last night how you love reading."

"A street festival? It's the middle of winter. Isn't it too cold to be outside at a festival?"

"Not for this one. It's under enormous tents and has outdoor heat lamps that line the streets. You will love it, I promise. Artisans line the streets and sell their wares. There are antiques you could buy, and up-and-coming artists selling their paintings; it's lovely."

"Okay, but I need a huge cup of some sort of sugary caramel coffee to get me through the rest of this morning, maybe even more than one."

"You *do know* how unhealthy caffeine is for your body, right? I've read that if you drink more than a cup a day that you can suffer from insomnia, upset stomach, jitters, and a rise in your blood pressure. It will lead to heart attacks, tooth decay, slower metabolism and has..."

"Okay. Thank you," I said cutting him off. I walked into my room and tried to find *something nice to wear* for a day outside. "I guess coffee is my vice then," I called from my bedroom. "I used to drink only one cup a day, but for the last few months, I find that I need to make up for the time I spent refraining from it."

Dressing quickly in a pair of jeans, a form fitting turtleneck sweater and a pair of boots, I walked out to Fran still assaulting me with statistics of the nine rings of hell that you allow your body to go through when drinking coffee.

I practically shoved him out of my door; desperate for the coffee he was trying to forbid me from.

We hopped into his brand spanking new hybrid car and drove for a good forty-five minutes with Fran discussing *with himself* the benefits of driving a fully hybrid electric car. I wished I owned a pair of earplugs. *Maybe I could find some at the festival.*

"...Some people argue that it seems like an odd dichotomy that a hybrid car that has *two energy sources* could be better for our environment as opposed to a traditional car that has just one. Now the facts about the hybrid are..."

"STOP! Stop the car!" I yelped gleefully, making Fran swerve into the shoulder of the road. "A STARBUCKS!" I pointed happily, bouncing in his tiny electrical shit box of a car.

Driving into the parking lot, he pulled into the first empty space he saw and placed his hand over his heart. "You almost gave me a heart attack," he chuckled. "I really thought something was wrong."

"Something *is* wrong," I winked at him. "I haven't had enough caffeine yet." Opening the car door, I smiled at him, "Would you like a cup?"

"No, thank you." He touched his hand to mine, "Didn't you understand what I said before about drinking too much coffee."

I stared at him, confused. "Yes, I did." I blinked my eyes rapidly, trying not to burst out laughing. "I guess I'm just too far gone into my addiction. There's just no saving me."

I came back into the car with three coffees, putting my lips to each one in turn, and slurping them loudly. Fran slowly dragged his eyes from me back to his windshield and continued his drive to the street festival he promised to take me to.

Fran was correct about one thing; the street fair was lovely. Antique shops, small novelty stores and a few bed and breakfasts lined the small cobblestoned main street of the quaint nameless town. Old, yet well-maintained Victorian homes littered the twisting back roads and when you drove by, the inhabitants offered you a big wave and a friendly smile. Covered bridges crossed over flowing streams and tents were set up for blocks along the main road of the town, and people milled around laughing and drinking *coffee*, warm cider, or hot chocolate.

The two of us roamed around the booths. Every once in a while, Fran's hand made it to the small of my back or his lips found my temple. Every ten minutes, Fran would stop and take a picture with his phone and post it on instagram and twitter like an obsessed teenager. I cut him off after he posed me in front of a booth that sold organic clothing and tweeted a picture of me to his 459 followers that said, "Organic socks rock!"

We found a small intimate restaurant and we were just sitting down to grab a drink at the bar before an early dinner or late lunch, whatever you wanted to call it, when in walked Morgan and an extremely distinguished looking older gentleman. Fran waved them over and offered to share a drink with them, while we waited for our tables since the place was packed. Her faced blanched as the gentlemen she was with agreed, and I looked at her curiously.

He pulled out a chair at the bar for her and she offered a tight smile to us, and a curt serious nod. "This is my *husband*, Jeremy." She looked at him with flushed cheeks and continued with her introductions, "Jeremy, dear, this is Francis and Lainey. I met them at a small dinner party I was invited to last night, while you were still away on your business trip."

Well now, wasn't that just a dick-slap right there?

Morgan gave a brilliantly flirtatious grin at Fran and batted her lashes at him, "Francis, darling, would you mind if I stole your *treasure* here to accompany me to the restroom?"

Really? Really now? She just asked a man for permission to have me accompany her to the bathroom? Oh, this ought to be *awesome.*

Fran just waved us away, as he dove into an intense conversation with a seemingly already intoxicated Jeremy about the degradation of our ozone layer and how without its protection, we would all fry up like little eggs on a hot stove. Then he proceeded to list off all the *Organohalogen* compounds that we use daily, and which ones were the worst global environmental pollutants for our beloved layer of ozone.

Yes, I think I rather stay in the bathroom with Morgan, instead of listening to his next debate with himself. *Masterdebation.* He should go tweet that.

Once inside the bathroom, she slumped against the wall and covered her face, "Please. Please don't say anything to Jeremy. I know how bad I look, but he's never home, always away on business, and God, I mean have you seen Kade Grayson? He's a perfect specimen of a man."

I giggled next to her. "Yeah, a perfect sociopath. Don't worry, I won't say anything and I'm no one to judge." I opened my purse, took out my lip-gloss, and dabbed a bit on my lips. "How long have you been married?"

"I've been imprisoned for fourteen years," she laughed. "Married me right out of high school and promised me the world. He's got loads of money and I live in the lap of luxury, but it's a lonely world." She lathered her own lips with a bright fire engine red lipstick, which I would never have the courage to wear. "So how about you and Francis?"

"We've only been on a few dates. I'm not looking for anything serious, and he's way too serious," I answered.

"Kade seemed really taken by you last night. His eyes were on you all night. He hardly ate his food."

"Grayson is an ass," I stated.

"He's so damaged and dark. *Intense.* I think I like the danger of it," she said softly.

"Oh, I can definitely see him as one of those dangerous bad ass types," I laughed.

She gave me a measured stare and giggled, "Don't knock the alpha male types, they're delicious."

"Oh sure," I laughed. "There is nothing wrong with bad boys, unless you have self-esteem and confidence. Then you're fucked, *and* you're smart enough to know you're fucked. I know, because I've fallen down *that* dark hole before."

"Yeah, but, I've always loved those dangerous damaged men. I wonder why, you know?"

"Daddy issues?" I laughed at my reflection in the mirror, "Mine was mommy issues, really." I glanced over at Morgan who was sniffing and staring down at her hands. I nudged her and smiled. "I think the truth is that we are in love with the fantasy of being that *one* person who could inspire, arouse, or *affect* someone who is so untouchable to the rest of the world. It makes us *feel* special; like we're the diamond in the rough, the one in a million, the one that everyone else couldn't be, and do what everyone else couldn't do. Imagine being *that* significant to someone? To never have to doubt that he loves you, or needs you, or more importantly, *wants* you more than any other."

"I totally agree with you," a strange small voice said from behind me.

"Yeah, me too. I'd give a limb to feel like that," said another voice.

Lifting my eyes to the mirror, I noticed the group of women behind me, nodding their heads in agreement. I smiled at all of them; we were all striving for that same desire, weren't we?

"The question is," a tall, older brunette began, "is that a *reality*? Does love like that, desire and passions like that exist?"

Morgan shook her head next to me, "I don't think so. If it does, I've never felt it."

Some of the women agreed, some didn't. I just shrugged and sighed, "For me, I've learned the hard way that I can't ever expect a man to make me feel that way. I have to make myself feel that way. I want to be the *one* person who could inspire, arouse, and *affect me*. Because, let's be honest, no one is going to be with me longer than *me*."

The way those women reacted to what I said, I thought I was going to be carried out of that bathroom on their shoulders with them chanting my name. I had never been more proud of my ovaries and uterus for all of womankind.

Morgan and I walked back to our table laughing with our arms hooked like teenage best friends. Fran was still on his soapbox, while a slanted Jeremy hovered over a dark amber drink, smiling at the table, and nodding his head. Fran stopped mid-rant and smiled at me, "There you are. I ordered a red wine for you. I hope that's okay."

Smiling at him, I nodded and sat in the seat next to him. The four of us ordered dinner together and our dinner discussions went from one extreme to another, never touching on anything personal. Throughout the dinner, I couldn't help but feel as if I was separated off from the three of them, even though we all shared in the conversations. They seemed so far removed from my life and my experiences that I felt as if I were from another universe. Of course, my mind wandered to Kade and that kiss. What made it so earthshattering? Was it my attraction to him? Was it because he was mean and degrading, and I wanted to prove to him what and who I really was? I always did have a big issue with people who underestimated me. I loved to prove them wrong. Then I wondered what was it that made Kade so damaged. Was he just as damaged as me?

After dinner, Fran, as promised, took me to the best bookstore I'd ever been to. *Well Red* was a bookstore/wine house, where you could buy books, sit and read them over a glass of wine; a little spin on the bookstore/coffee houses of the city. We sat there for two hours, sipping a glass of red wine and read. I left with a stack of new books, and he left with a smug, proud smile on his face. Nevertheless, I let him keep it there, since the bookstore was perfect and I guess I was thawing a little towards him.

Chapter 6
Kade

Kicking my foot through the pile of clothes on the floor, I watched them fly up until I spotted my pants and pulled them on. The rest of the material belonged to the naked woman sleeping on my bed, the one that still had my reddened handprints on her ass. I'd already let her sleep fifteen minutes past the time I would let anyone stay in this room (incidentally, that's usually fifteen minutes), and that's only because I left her to search my house for the strongest whiskey I had. A fifth of the bottle was gone already. Do you know how many shots are in a fifth of whiskey? About twenty-drunken-five shots, so I should have been out cold.

I kicked my foot against the bed, the mattress moved about half a foot off my box springs, and I took another swig. "It's time to go, um..." I'd completely forgotten her name. "Hello, love?"

The body stirred quietly on the bed and the woman's eyes peeked out from under the covering of my sheets. I scooped up the clothes that belonged to her and dropped them right in front of her face. "I've got work to do, so you have to shove off now."

She sat up, and the sheets fell away revealing a pair of large breasts that I didn't even bother to look at, let alone touch, thirty minutes ago. I tossed her purse onto the bed and leaned against the far wall where I'd already opened the door for her highly anticipated (only by me it seemed) departure. Resting my body against the frame of the door, I gestured my hands for her to move along and hurry.

The whites of her eyes became bigger, but I didn't feel remorse. I felt completely nothing. *All right*, I lied. I felt like throwing her body out of the window, because she wasn't moving fast enough.

The woman dressed quickly, trying to do so seductively, but I was too busy pretending to look at my phone and the empty inbox of messages I had, to watch her. I'd already had my fun with her, *well* just one certain part of her, and that's all I needed. She was the one that propositioned me, at the grocery store, no less. I was just a willing dick. The only reason I said yes was because of her dark black hair that allowed me to pretend she was someone else. Sick, yes? Yeah, and that was why I was holding said bottle of whiskey to my lips. *Open. Insert liquor. Forget. Repeat until you could look in the mirror again.*

"Will you call me? Maybe we could go out some time," she smiled, walking to my front door.

"Love, I don't even remember your name, and I don't plan on asking you for it again."

"You're an asshole, you know that?"

"Yes, and you're the whore who let me stick my dick in you and spank your ass," I said, closing the door on her surprised expression. I would say I cared, but I hated lying.

Anything other than sex is off limits. Out of bounds. Most women (read as every fucking last one of them) have wanted something from me that I couldn't give them. It was not the typical excuse of me wanting to fuck without strings either. I would give an organ away for one fucking normal day, where I could pretend to be right in the fucking head and whole enough to be in a healthy relationship with someone. I would love to find one person I could be comfortable to be myself with, but I was lost and I couldn't. I didn't cherish taking someone along with me through my hell, skipping along, clueless to my madness. Even Lainey, which was why I wanted her to hate me; she would anyway if she ever got the chance to know me. I was one *sick fuck*.

I took another swig of the whiskey and found myself in front of my writing desk staring at my two newest manuscripts, one titled *Behind Green Doors* and its sequel, *Accepting Darkness*. I had emailed them both to my editor a few days before. Eight hundred, twenty-three pages altogether. Two hundred, eighty-two thousand, six hundred fifty-nine words. Two weeks, three days, nine hours and change. That was all the same amount of pages, words, and time since I last saw Lainey dance around with a mop, cleaning her kitchen and knocked at the door to my soul almost punching my heart right out of my chest. I didn't want to let her in. I wanted nothing to do with her, but the words that poured from my fingers across my keyboard stated otherwise. So I locked myself in my office and wrote straight through until the entire story was told. My way of trying to purge myself of the obsessive thoughts of Lainey that ran loops in my brain.

Personally, I hated the story. It flowed from the first page to the very last and shocked the hell out of you with a terrorizing mindfuck that I'd never seen written before. I loved it. I hated it. It was everything I was. My entire being was in those words. Everything I had ever felt was there for the entire world to read. Pure insanity, horror at its finest. Just plain *me*.

And, let's up the insanity here for a minute…if I believed in it, if there was a possibility of it being actually able to happen, I would have said I might have fallen in *love* with my character. She consumed every thought I had. I felt the need to protect her from everything and everyone. I could feel her silken skin under my fingertips when I wrote about touching her, and I could smell the spiced apples of her soap when I wrote that she was near. And, the fucking way she tasted? It wasn't *waitress flavored*, but completely Lainey, and my God, did I taste her in my book. Over and over again, like a goddamn addict I slid my tongue against the unique sweetness of her body, outside and in. It wasn't just these physical things that I obsessed with, either. This character's mind possessed me. Her words tore through my heart like bullets. I had written the perfect woman for me; the perfect lover, the perfect friend and companion, based on a fucking waitress that I couldn't stop thinking about.

Do you want to hear something else that has twisted my dick right the fuck around? For the first time EVER, I wrote a *happy ending*. CAN YOU BELIEVE THAT? A happily-ever-fucking after that would leave a Disney princess with tears and slit wrists from the jealousy of it. For her. And *me*.

I clawed at my hair as my stomach rolled. I'm...I'm...fucking...insane. I always knew I'd snap completely one day. Never thought it would be over a woman I hardly knew.

And that kiss? The kiss in that little trailer of hers... *Still burned my lips*. Since that kiss, there was this unloosened feeling in my limbs, as if I could float away, as if gravity had just given up on me and I could hurtle into space at anytime.

I grabbed both manuscripts and stormed onto my back deck. It was freezing outside, matching the mess of my insides, frozen, alone, and empty. Ice had lined the stones beneath my feet, causing me to slip and fall right on my ass. The pain as I hit the ground was welcomed, and I laughed into the cold dark night, emitting a thick cloud of mist from my lips. My bottle of whiskey was unhurt, and truly, that was all that mattered.

Lying there on the wet ice for a moment, looking up at the stars, I wished I had cracked my head right open and died on the spot. By the time the maid would find me, a year would probably have passed and I'd be nothing more than a skeleton with an expensive pair of designer slacks on. I'd finally be free of the hold that Lainey had on my mind.

I crawled to the fire pit I kept on my patio and threw both my manuscripts in, and from the stone shelves under it, I pulled out the igniter and set them on fire.

I watched my books go up in flames and drank the rest of my whiskey, wishing my fucked up feelings would burn along with my words.

Lainey.

Lainey.

Lainey.

I could barely see straight as I staggered into my office. I had to shake this need, this desire to know her. I felt cursed. Possessed. Her face haunted me. Her laughter echoed in my brain. Her smile plagued my thoughts. But mostly it was her calmness that affected me. Soothed me. Mollified the rage.

Who was she really?

Where did she come from?

What happened that she ended up bloody beaten at my brother's bar?

My obsession continued; I was spinning out of control. I googled her. I read everything I could find on Lainey Nevaeh, which was about a gram of information. Facebook, blogs, MySpace, that ancestry site, and various forums stated she was either a twelve-year-old girl from Bessemer, Alabama, or a stay-at-home mom from somewhere in Colorado. I gorged myself on information, anything I could find. I tried to put together the pieces of her life from the tiny bits I found, the rush of it made me high. However, after hours of searching, I was more intrigued with the fact that no trace of any Lainey Nevaeh that matched the mysterious waitress from the bar could be found.

It was as if she wasn't real. I mean, really, you could find almost anyone on Google nowadays. Try it. Google yourself and see what happens. You'll probably find some sorry ass picture of that one time you fell asleep drunk at a friend's party in college and they drew a mustache on your face, and then snapped a photo of you. That's your legacy. Google is the largest database of people and pictures that can pinpoint your exact fucking location on earth, especially when everybody in the fucking world had turned on their geo coding on their phones and tablets. Don't people know how dangerous it is for the world to see exactly where you are at the exact moments you're there? It's a great resource for criminals. With Lainey though, it was as if she had no past. Like Lainey Nevaeh never existed. She didn't even have a social security number.

A thick unsettling feeling washed over me; like some sort of darker shadow over my soul than the one that was already there. I hadn't had one flashback since the night I met Lainey. Somehow, without me knowing, my uncontrollable compulsive thoughts of her brought a splash of color into my dark world. Like the colors of the rainbow, bleeding and seeping out of the darkened night sky. My obsessive behavior towards her filled that gaping hole that contained all my deep rage. She was like a medicine to me. She was like the fire I had just set on my books; her flames engulfed me and brought me to ashes. Charred.

Was it as simple as the way she looked, or, as simple as just wanting to unravel the mystery of

Lainey? And what would I want to do with her after all my needs were fulfilled and my questions answered? *What would I do to her when my darkness wanted a piece of her too?*

I awoke almost a whole day later, on the floor of my kitchen with dried blood all over my hands and chest. Brilliant sunlight was filtering in through my French doors, harshly lighting my cold skin. I was shirtless. Across the palm of my hand was a deep gash that looked red, angry, and still *slick with slowly clotting fluids*. Thick shards of bloodied crimson stained glass lay across the floor, under me, across from me, inside of me. The strong urge to rub the blood between my fingers was maddening. To touch the life flowing out of my skin, the thick red liquid that once surged through my heart; *this is how I cope now*. Reliving my nightmares. Reliving my past. Touching my thumb to the rest of my fingers, I swirled the congealing mess around, pain hit me instantly as the sharp bit of glass still embedded under the skin of my palm dug itself deeper. It throbbed a fiery burn up my wrist and arm, making me clench my teeth in anger. My throat was parched, blood pounded in my ears and my body felt coiled tight; ready to spring.

I looked down enraged, wondering what the hell was happening to me. Did somebody steal my cock to sell on the black market? Leaving me a pussy. What the hell was I letting my own mind conjure up for me? I needed to get over this insanity. I pulled the piece of glass out of my palm and smeared my bloody hand against my pants, ignoring the bite of pain.

Throwing a shirt on, I stumbled blindly out of the house. Bright sunlight hit my eyes like a prizefighter and almost, *almost* knocked me on my ass. Lumbering to my truck, I climbed in vaguely, wondering if I might have still been drunk from the previous binge I accomplished undertaking the night before. I highly doubted it.

I had one thought in my mind.

Bagels.

Fresh bagels from a bakery, with butter and coffee. Maybe a few pots full. My stomach lurched and rumbled as I drove a good twenty-five minutes from my house to the nearest place to eat.

Like a grade-A jackoff, I parked in two spaces, not wanting anyone near my truck, and stormed into the diner, fists clenched. Sitting in the booth nearest the exit, *always nearest the exit, with...3 waitresses, 11 faceless customers and 2 exits*, I nodded at the waitress who in turn gave me bulging eyes and a downturned mouth. Getting a fucking bagel should be easy, but not here, not with me. These people knew of me, heard of me, and they were *terrified* of me. *The dangerous recluse that never comes out in the daytime*, isn't he crazy? Didn't he kill people? Didn't he die? Didn't he go insane? Isn't he horribly disfigured like that *Mel Gibson* character in that movie? Didn't he spend years in jail or an asylum, *blah-blah-blah*, just give me a fucking bagel and coffee, and no one will get hurt.

The waitress actually snorted loudly, walked over to my table, and crossed her arms.

Before she could form a simple thought in her most likely one-celled simple mind I growled out, "Coffee. Toasted Bagel. Butter."

The twit clucked her teeth like a monkey and walked away.

My head started pounding. People walked in and out of the front door letting a cold draft breeze against my arms. My eyes attacked each and every person who walked in.

This was a fucking bad idea.

The rattle and clink of a coffee cup against its saucer brought my attention to the presence of the waitress spreading my order out on the table in front of me. "Can I get you anything else, *sir*?" she said with a sneer.

"Solitude," I snapped back.

The waitress narrowed her eyes at me and snapped a piece of gum in my face. Then she walked away, leaving me to my solitude. Grabbing my knife and opening the little pat of wrapped butter, I began buttering my bagel.

"So, I'm not the only waitress you snap at, good to know," a whispered voice said. The strong smell of apples, cinnamon, spices, and *sexy* hit me right in the chest. The butter knife slipped from my fingers, and clanged and clunked against the plate as Lainey slid into the seat across from me.

I had to take a deep breath before I could look at her. When I lifted my eyes to meet hers, she almost blinded me with her beauty. *Ah, shit.*

"Are you okay?" she asked. The brilliant green of her eyes and the kindness of her question overwhelmed me. It knotted itself in my chest and throbbed.

It took me a moment of staring at her to answer. "Yes." She had a serene calmness about her, like the lapping waters off a tranquil Caribbean beach. I fucking wanted to dive in. "Why do you ask?"

Her smile was soft and gracious, but her brows wrinkled as she looked down at my hand. I followed the trail of her eyes, and then realized I hadn't bandaged up my cut, or cleaned the blood off my hands and arms. At that particular moment, my throat lost the ability to remember how to swallow correctly and I ended up choking and hacking on my own saliva. Very becoming. Normally, at this point in a conversation with someone where I see blood, this would have caused me to crumple into a heap of trembling anxiety, rage and self-hatred, lashing out with whomever I was speaking. But for a few moments, I had been staring into those calm green eyes and the panic and rage *didn't come*. It was as if Lainey had some sort of superhuman secret ability to help me hold the door to my skeleton-bloody-carcass filled closet closed.

"I cut myself," I explained.

"I can see that," she said. Her eyes scanned my face, my hair, my clothes, and then journeyed back down to my hand. Softly clearing her throat, she said, "Do you need anything? Would you like me to get some bandages or something?"

"Fuck no, why?" *Did I have the word pussy written across my head?*

"Have you looked at yourself in the mirror this morning?" she asked.

Grabbing the aluminum napkin holder, I held it up to my face. Wide blood-shot grey eyes stared back; dried blood was caked across my cheeks and forehead. My hair, God, it looked like I had gotten into a fight and lost. I slammed down the napkin holder on the table and the clasp popped, sending napkins flying across the table. *Fuck my life.*

Lainey freaking giggled. I watched her, she tried not to, but the napkins and me being an idiot and everything, she couldn't stop it, and she giggled. The sound of it was jarring, and I found myself wanting more of it, needing more of it.

"It's too early to laugh," I mumbled, which was probably the most unintelligent thing I could have responded with, but hey, there I was sitting in a diner with the woman I had been obsessing over for two weeks, wrote two books about, and had blood smeared all over my body. Intelligent conversation eluded me.

"Why? Do you hate morning people?" she asked, smiling.

"It has nothing to do with mornings...it's the people part," I retorted, smiling a bit myself. I ran my fingers through my hair, trying to alleviate the mess, but then gave up. "I had a rough night. I didn't even think to clean myself up," I smiled wider.

HOLY CRAP. I. WAS. SMILING.

"Mr. Grayson, your charm is showing. You might want to tuck it back in," she said, standing up. "You seem okay, so, I should go. Enjoy your breakfast." She started to turn away. I wanted her to stay, but I knew it would be healthier for us both if she kept on walking. Leaning her hand against my table, she stopped and faced me again. "You should really clean that cut, though, Mr. Grayson. It looks deep and you could get an infection or something..."

I watched her smooth ivory fingers tremble against the dark cherry wood of the tabletop. My gaze traveled up her creamy arms across her shoulder and along her neck to her face; to her eyes. For a second, the thought of spending time with her overwhelmed me with a strange emotion. I didn't know what it was; hope maybe? *She wasn't like anyone I'd ever met before, was she?* "I apologize for offending you the other day. Please, call me Kade," I croaked.

She stopped moving away and looked curiously at me. Then a man walked up behind her and placed his hand on her arm, causing her to look away from me and into the man's face.

Francine, the man-girl.

"Hello there, Kade." He glossed his eyes over my state and cringed. Instantly turning his eyes back to Lainey, "I've paid the check. Are you ready?"

Lainey's lips pressed together tightly and her narrowed eyes moved from him to me, and back again. She shook her head as if to say she didn't quite understand what he was going on about, then locked eyes with me again. "You're sure you'll get that looked at?" she asked pointing to my hand.

"I'll meet you in the car, sweetheart," Francis interrupted tightly, stomping away like a child. Lainey bit her lip to stifle another laugh and shrugged her shoulders.

Sipping my coffee I looked up at her and nodded, "I'll be fine."

Her lips opened as if she was about to say more, then she just pinched them together, nodded a goodbye, and walked out the door.

Dropping my head in my hands, *which hurt like hell*, I squeezed my eyes tight. I needed to stay away from her. I *needed* to stay away from her.

I needed to stay away from her.

Rummaging in my pocket, I took out my wallet and threw a fifty down on the table, grabbed my bagel and walked out of the diner. Fran's smart little car was just pulling out of the parking area and onto the main road.

Yeah, I was going to follow her. Staying away from her was not an option. I would have to staple myself to the damn seat to stop myself from running after her.

Tearing out of the lot, I trailed them for a few miles, hiding myself behind a few other cars.

Fran dropped her off at a grocery store. Psycho me followed her in.

I hid in aisle five, grabbing a box of Band-Aids and a giant box of double stuffed Oreos; she got coffee. She caught me near the cash registers when a group of local elderly jackasses nodded my way and started grunting loudly about the *hermit being out of his lair.*

"Oh my goodness, is that *him*?" One ancient fossil hissed. "Dear God, it's the Devil himself!" To add to the disgust, she made the sign of the cross over herself. That made me laugh. Out loud.

The mother next to her, actually covered her daughter's eyes from looking at me. "Don't look at him, Becca. Just ignore him and he'll go away."

"Is he really the devil, Mom? But, he was holding a bag of cookies!"

Goddamn small town bullshit. I growled at them and bared my teeth; I mean I might as well let them believe all the shit that's said about me, right? "The cookies are for all the monsters I keep in my basement," I whispered and winked at the little girl.

Laughing, Lainey shoved me past the harrumphing townies. Pulling me by my coat sleeve, she dragged me to the first aid aisle and loaded my basket with peroxide, gauze and other shit I didn't need. I stared at her as she looked thoughtfully at the items. "That should be enough to help you." Her thick dark lashes swept up and her green gaze met mine. The beginning of a small smile played on her lips and a faint blush covered her cheeks, "Stop making these people afraid of you. You're just fanning the flames. You're no more the devil than I am Mickey Mouse."

Glancing at the crowd of people still gawking at me, I blew them a kiss. "Sorry. Momentary lapse in judgment."

Chuckling and shaking her head, she left me standing there staring after her, my eyes hungrily eating her swaying form.

Jetting after her, I walked through the group of rubberneckers and loudly greeted them all a *devilish* good morning. I promised myself to buy a pair of horns online for the next visit to town. Placing my basket near the cash register in the line behind Lainey, I watched as she bit back her laughter, paid for her coffee, then walked out of the store.

I threw a hundred dollar bill at the cashier and threw my shit in one of those irritating plastic bags that you could never find the freaking opening to, and have to lick your fingers and use friction and the *Jaws of Life* to open. Telling the cashier to keep the change, I ran out of the store as Fran was driving down the road.

I followed them back to her trailer park and waited. Exiting my car, hidden behind another trailer, I stood on the threshold of the woods that surrounded her little home. Watching, transfixed, I could barely breathe, thinking that lanky bugger might have his lips on hers. The thought tore me apart. Then Fran walked out. Sweet relief flooded my body as she stood by the door and waved to him. No kiss goodbye. When his car was out of view, she leaned the back of her head on the doorframe and dragged her hands over her face. Within seconds, she let her hands fall limply to her sides and she looked out into the shadows of the trees. She looked as lost as I did. I blew breath into my hands, trying to find warmth, and watching her slowly close the door, robbing me of my view.

Convincing myself it wouldn't be a good idea to knock on her door, and would probably creep the hell out of her, I trailed back through the woods to the place I hid my truck and drove back to my house.

It was the first time, except for that pompous awards dinner, that I had been out in the daytime for that long in months. I drove home in a daze. *Fucking bloody hell, welcome to the world of crazy.* I had lost all control.

I was well aware that my behavior was stalker-like and beyond inappropriate, yet I could not demonstrate a reason to stop. I wanted to know all about her, everything she did; everything she was. I sat in my den with none of the lights on, staring into the dimness of the room, scrutinizing my thoughts. Trying desperately to find order in the jumbled chaos of my mind.

I wanted to *pursue* her, make her laugh again, and get to know her.

My brain was well aware that she would undoubtedly have no intention of returning any attention to me after the way I treated her.

Was her skin as soft as I wrote it to be?

Showering and cleaning my hand was a chore, as my delusional mind had me being a normal undamaged man, ready and willing for a relationship with this person I truly knew nothing about. I tried to focus on the facts. I tried to concentrate on the reality that I was not in a healthy place to offer even the remotest of friendships with her. Was I truly this sick and twisted inside? Was I really trying to talk myself into believing I could trust and offer something other than my written words and ideas to someone?

When dusk softly overshadowed the sky, my hand was neatly bandaged and I was dressed impeccably. Swallowing the hard knot in my throat, I walked out of my house and climbed into my truck. All my sick tangled thoughts of the day came to one conclusion: I just wanted to get to know Lainey. Let her make her own choices about me, because my mind would not rest until I understood the strange spell she had over me and why since the day I'd met her, I had not suffered one uncontrollable flashback.

Driving to my brother's bar, I cringed at facing my actions. How will she view me? *Let's get my mind clear.* First, I belittled and degraded her. Terrific beginning. Second, I did more of the same shit, but I added some staring and gawking at her lips over a dinner party. I was pretty close to humping her leg that night, and everybody seemed aware of that fact. Next, I was caught peeking into her window as she cleaned her house and performed a dance that I can't even think about for fear of busting a nut where I sit. Then came the kiss that I attacked her with, which was right after I criticized her yet again, because I was in total awe of her lips. After that, I write two books, each with the main character based on her. Lastly, I followed her; stalking the shit out of her.

Fuuuck, I'm twisted.

The thoughts about my behavior were even creepy *to me*. By this time, my truck was idling in the parking lot of the bar and I decided just to go home. My infatuation with her was completely one-sided, unhealthy, and without a doubt, would end ugly.

Before I could pull out, Fran's car turned into the lot.

I blinked as his red taillights flickered through the darkness, and the parking brake light reflected against the bark of the trees surrounding the lot. Slithering down in my seat, I could hear that wanker's voice laughing loudly as he slammed the car door shut. Straining my ears, I couldn't hear anything from Lainey. I just watched as she quickly walked toward the bar, probably trying to get out of the frigid night air. When she reached the door, she glanced questioningly towards my truck, then smiled, and slipped into the warmth of the bar.

She *smiled*?

For twenty-minutes, I listened to the heater fan as it warmed the air in my cab, sitting and contemplating what to do. There was no talking myself out of going in.

She smiled at my truck. So in I went. Seemed like good logic at the time.

I slowly made my way over to my back table. It was almost five, and there was a small crowd for a Thursday night, but my table was empty. My table was always empty, even when *I* occupied it.

Lainey was behind the bar pouring a beer, when her eyes collided with mine. They stayed on mine for so long that the beer overflowed the cup and spilled thick white foam over the edges and her fingers. It made my body pulse with arousal. Twisted, yeah?

Placing my case on the table, I slid out my laptop and opened it up. My goal was to watch her and get some research down for my next book. Keying in the Wi-Fi password, I checked my email and opened one from my editor.

Kade,

These were impressive; I wouldn't dream of changing a thing. Just scan through my notes and make any necessary corrections.

Gary

There were only three corrections for both books? Usually Gary had more to say. I quickly typed him a short email, explaining that I wanted to keep the manuscripts out of the publishing house, and self-publish. I did this with my books every so often, especially if I wrote a book that wasn't scheduled for publication, which these weren't. My publisher hated me for doing it, but I told them they could find another me if they wanted to place rules on the things I did. Being somebody's bitch was not in my nature; it went completely against my DNA makeup.

A soft clink of glass against the wood tabletop caused me to look up from my screen. Delicate fingers slid a drink closer to me and a smooth voice asked, "How's the hand?" My lungs found trouble with the task of inhaling.

All my senses were heightened as soon as I looked up. I tried to ignore the overwhelming emotions, but it was of no use. Spiced apples and cinnamons twirled in the air around me. Five shades of green danced in her eyes as my focused gaze caught hers and my chest just *surged*. *What the hell was that about?* As I laced my fingers around the brandy, her fingers brushed gently against mine with the slightest touch of almost infinitesimal tremors. "Just a little scratch," I answered her hoarsely.

She slid her hands away from mine and pushed them deeply into the pockets of her apron. Her cheeks started to flare with a deep blush. I tried, but couldn't stop the slow smile it brought to my lips. "I'm surprised you still want to be friends, after such an arsehole I've been towards you."

"Friends?" She asked, composed, unsmiling.

"Yes."

"Yep. Just wait. Our friendship bracelets are in the mail," she said sarcastically. "Please don't mistake my being a naturally caring person for wanting to be friends. Is there anything else I can get for you?"

"A smile?" I whispered.

"That's not on the menu, is it?" Calm. Cool. Emotionless.

"Fuck." I took a pull from my brandy, letting the flavor smoothly fill my mouth and burn its fire down my throat. It didn't quench my thirst though. I wanted a taste of the woman standing before me. I laughed and looked down, shaking my head. I cleared my throat, "So being friends is an impossibility? You'd be missing out."

"Yep. I guess I will just have to live with never knowing how great a friend you could be. It'll be difficult, I'm sure. But, with years of therapy and psychoanalysis, I bet I'll be able to overcome the heartbreak of not getting to know you." Her eyes never left mine. Curt, yet nice and emotionless. She just completely handed me my own order of sublime indifference and I could have buried myself in it. "Will there be anything else?"

"No, thank you," I said, and watched her walk away, smiling at the other customers and going on with her life, with not one ounce of effect from me.

All that night, I watched her work the floor, mesmerized. She never let anyone touch her; it was as if she would melt away right before their hands went to touch her. No one touched her but Bree. Always keeping a distance from everyone like she was more comfortable with being alone than with other people. She smiled politely and answered when asked questions, but there was *something* missing. It was as if *she* was missing. Every time my glass was empty, she would bring over another one, but I never caught her looking over at me. I stayed there until closing. I stayed there while she and Bree sat with that dolt Fran, and ate dinner after the bar closed. My brother gave me strange looks, but I just flipped him the finger and ignored him.

I didn't care how sick I looked. I couldn't stop myself; I didn't want to look away from her.

Lainey leaned against the back of her chair swirling a French fry around her plate drowning it in ketchup, but not eating a bite. Very prim and proper, she sat back rigid and ladylike. It made me see images of her on her knees in front of me, seeing how dirty I could get her to be.

Bree was laughing at something Fran had said, but Lainey wasn't. She didn't seem to be listening, not even looking at anyone around her, she just stared out across the bar. Bree touched her hand to get her attention, but she just planted a robotic smile on her face that never reached her eyes. Then she turned her attention back out across the bar again and her gaze collided with mine. She didn't look away.

Seconds.

Minutes.

She *did not* look away.

Staring at me and me staring at her, our eyes locked, fixed; lost in each other.

Bree interrupted our private moment by taking her plate into the back and walking through the view we had of each other. It was as if someone cut off my oxygen. As I sat there, practically gasping for breath, Lainey pushed herself away from the table, gathered her coat and belongings, and walked out the door not glancing back at me once. Fran was hot on her trail.

"What are you bloody doing, mate?" Dylan's voice asked next to me.

"Drinking. Writing."

"You just eye-fucked that girl to death, Kade. You need to stop whatever is going on in that mind of yours."

"You just made it *so* much more tempting, brother," I said, laughing.

"Bloody hell, Kade. You're laughing. *You're laughing?* You're barmy, brother. I haven't seen you laugh in..." He looked at the table I had been staring at for the last hour and realization dawned across his expression.

Want to hear how deep my sickness runs? I did it again the next day and the next. Followed her and ended each night sitting at the same table watching her, delighted as hell a restraining order hadn't arrived for me yet.

On the third night, the brandy slid across the top of my table and her eyes fluttered down to mine. "A sketchy black truck has been seen everywhere I've been for the past three days. Intense steel-grey eyes staring me down and peeking in my windows. You're the worst stalker I've ever met. What are you going to do now? Ask me to help you find your lost puppy? Offer me some candy and shove me in your truck? Or will it be something subtler, like asking me if your napkin smells like chloroform as you grab me from behind? Or wait, maybe you'll just sit here and stare at me menacingly and pet your imaginary cat while collecting strands of my hair to knit a sweater for yourself later."

"Wow. Don't hold yourself back. I really get under your skin, yeah? Kind of hate me, *huh*?"

"If I gave you *any* amount of thought in my head, I probably would."

I choked down the mouthful of brandy and almost spit it out all over the front of my laptop. "Are you always this witty? Or should I be afraid? And I haven't peeked in your window since the mop dance. My heart wouldn't be able to handle it again, although I do find myself listening to that same damn song every night. And I can't knit...yet."

Then, for the first time since seeing her in the diner, she smiled at me. "You should be terrified, actually. You never know when that little stalking plan of yours will backfire and I show up everywhere *you are*, like a crazy woman with zero self-esteem." She leaned over the table, hands laid out flat across the wood top, "I'd keep repeating in a high pitched voice...that we were made for each other...that I couldn't bring myself to shower after being so near you. You'd find me stealing your clothes and wearing them just to have your scent all over my body. Maybe I'd crawl into your window at night and slip under your bed and poke you every so often so you couldn't sleep."

"I will definitely be leaving the alarm off tonight," I said, chuckling.

"Why?"

"Because I like the thought of you under me in bed," I stated.

"No, Kade. Why are you following me?" She whispered.

Fuck. I had nothing to say to that. She would probably slap me if I told her I had trouble breathing when I wasn't near her.

"My TV is broke?" Cold harsh humor laced my tone. I really was *trying* to be funny and flirtatious, but I needed to work on the lack I had of this talent.

She crossed her arms, "Try again."

"I like the view?"

"Well, *that's* not creepy at all," she said, dryly.

Laying my palms flat against the table, I just let go. *"Because Lainey, you somehow soothe the chaos that's inside me. You heal me."*

Chapter 7

Lainey

Kade had been at the bar every night for almost a week, staring at me so hard that I feared he might burst a blood vessel. I peeked out of the door in the bar's kitchen and watched him walk in. He was scanning the room, dark serious eyes searching. Was he looking for me? Was it fear that had my hackles up? Or was it excitement? I wanted to punch myself in my head for thinking it.

I mean his actions were incarceration worthy, but then what he said to me last night...it just...*touched me.* *Because, Lainey, you somehow soothe the chaos that's inside me. You heal me.*

You heal me.

You heal me.

"Let me guess. My brother is out there, yeah?" Dylan's voice rumbled behind me. He settled himself next to me and peeked beside me behind the door. The closeness of his arm to mine made me shiver and I moved away. When he realized what I'd done, his eyes widened, "Ah shit. You're scared of him? Damn, Lainey, is he scaring you? I swear Lainey; he's not a bad person. He's just not right in the head."

What the heck did that mean?

"We need to talk." Tears burned my eyes out of sheer frustration, and I ran. I ran down the hallway into his office, hoping he'd follow me so I could get some sort of answers. This too intense. His brother was vile towards me one minute, then the next, he was apologizing and following me around, being flirty in a weird way. I got that there was an attraction there. I mean Kade Grayson was glorious to look at. I now understood the idea of being attracted to someone at first sight, or whatever you wanted to call it. There was no denying something was there that drew us to acknowledge one another and to look at one another. I couldn't remember another time where I'd felt this instant attraction so strongly with somebody, and I saw it in him, the way he watched me, I saw that same strong pull in his eyes. *But he'd been following me.* Conveniently showing up in places I frequented, just watching and waiting. To say I was worried was the understatement of the century. I was ready to pull out my claws.

Dylan's serious face was in mine instantly, worry lines creasing his forehead, making him look so much older.

I paced back and forth in front of his desk, wringing my shirt in my hands. "Look, Dylan. I appreciate everything you have done for Bree and I, showing up here all messed up as we were, and letting us stay and work here, but you had to realize by now that I'm running from a really bad situation and I don't want to get myself mixed up in another one. So, please tell me what it is that is wrong with your brother."

Dylan's eyebrows rose with a sad expression, his shoulders slumped and he just seemed to give in. "Take the night off, Lainey. Go home and Google Kade Grayson. He's got his own damn *Wikipedia* page. You'll find everything that everybody thinks about him there. Once you read all the articles on what happened and what he did, then look up his books. His pen name is Cory Thomas."

I stood there staring at him. This whole town was bat-shit crazy, and the Graysons seemed to be the supreme rulers. Ever since we got here, I'd been waiting for someone to ask me to drink whatever weird Kool-Aid they were passing around. He couldn't just give me an explanation? I had to go on a freaking treasure hunt?

Slipping out the back door, I yanked on my coat as fast as I could. It was freezing outside, but thank God, I had less than a ten-minute walk to the trailer park.

I had no idea what I would find when I looked up Kade. What could possibly make an entire town fear him? What could possibly make a grown man choose a reclusive existence and have such a strong distaste of other human beings? And, why the hell would he take it out on me? Climbing the icy steps to my trailer, I was determined to find out.

Warming my hands around a steamy cup of freshly made coffee, I turned my computer on. Logging online, I immediately typed Kade Grayson into a search engine, and clicked on the first site. Not prepared for what I saw, my coffee cup fell from my hands, stinging a burn across my fingers and splashing down my legs. The cup shattered into pieces across the crappy linoleum of the trailer and echoed itself in my ears.

Saint Benedict's High School Massacre.

England.
School shooting.
1998.

A sixteen-year-old student killed a total of twenty-eight of his fellow students and three teachers.

Oh my God.

Oh my God. Oh my God. Oh my God.

My eyes scanned through the sickening photographs of the school. The crowds of screaming students, close-ups of crying teachers, zoomed in pictures of bullet holes in the windows of the classroom, and a terrifying black and white grainy video surveillance still shot of a lone gunman walking the hallway of the school, a duffle bag full of firearms hung from his shoulder. At the end of first period, each one of those guns would be emptied of bullets.

A shuddering fear gripped me as my eyes scoured the pictures. My tears fell and my stomach rolled with each new photograph. My cold trembling fingers covered my mouth and my chest tingled, as I scrolled through the pictures of each dead student. The beautiful innocent faces of each *dead* student.

Dead students.

Photographs of the three teachers, and their families that would *never see them again.*

The question whispered in my mind like the wind, slow at first, then picking up speed and howling through my skull. Was Kade a sick sadistic killer? Kade murdered those children. *How can he do such a thing?* My God...no wonder people said he was the devil. Why wasn't he in prison? Was it because he was a juvenile when he murdered a classroom full of innocent kids? Through the blur of tears, I finally found my answers.

Kade Grayson, sixteen-year-old high school junior was the only survivor in the entire junior class, although severely wounded. The gunman, sixteen-year-old high school junior, Thomas McKadley, committed suicide after the attacks by a gunshot wound to the head. In addition to the shootings, the disturbing and extensively planned attack involved propane tanks converted to bombs placed at each exit of the school, and two explosive devices rigged in a car and eight under the stands of the gymnasium.

Oh, my God.

Kade.

What do I even do with that? What do you do? How do you get over that? Fucking hell. That was just like Columbine. How...how do you live from there? Oh God. Sixteen? Severely wounded? Watched his entire class slaughtered.

How do you go on?

My chest tightened and my throat thickened with knots I couldn't swallow. A thick sheen of guilt and sweat covered my skin. I assumed Kade was a killer, just as he assumed I was a stripper. Kade was a man who lived through horror, real life horror. Of course, he would be untrusting and full of hate and rage. That's a fucking given when people are trying to kill you. You don't get over that. You never get over that; it scars you.

How did he live through that? How did he deal with it?

I googled Cory Thomas next, just like Dylan told me to, with tears stinging my eyes and racing down my cheeks. Websites upon websites, fan sites, fan forums, blogs, reading groups, Facebook pages and fan-fiction; it was an endless supply of people who loved this obviously incredible reclusive author. His readers loved him. *That is how he dealt with it, he wrote about it.*

I clicked on his list of books; there were hundreds of them. *Hundreds.*

All he did was write. All he did was hide from the world and write.

His latest book, *Behind Green Doors,* was independently published just the day before. There was a crazed buzz about it. Reviews and comments in forums spoke about it being his best work to date, a mixture of erotic horror, and thriller with a love story twisted inside of it. I downloaded it to my eReader, then cleaned up my mess of coffee, made a new cup and crawled into a ball on the couch. Wanting. Needing to climb into the mind of this man, this man who had seen mayhem first hand and had tried his best to live with it. I knew all too well how scary and real his nightmares might be. Trying to wipe away the last of my tears, my raw eyes strained to see my eReader.

Two beautiful green eyes graced the cover of the eBook, floating in darkness. I hadn't read a horror book in ages. I swiped the page and stopped on his dedication page, spilling my coffee for the second time in my lap.

For the mysterious green-eyed waitress
She is now my favorite flavor

What the fuck? What the fucking FUCK? I stood up, dropped my eReader and paced the room, coffee still dripping off my shirt. He made me lose two fucking cups of coffee. WHAT. THE. FUCK.

I was going to need an entire bottle of wine to read the rest of this shit.

I changed my clothes. Again. My body was shaking, worse than it normally did. I was livid. I was shocked. I was...I was smiling. Why the FUCK was I smiling? This was bad. This had BAD written *all the fuck over it.* This...this is just a morbid filled ice cream cone dipped in psycho flavored sprinkles. My mind was racing, from pictures of the murders he witnessed as a sixteen-year-old boy, to the erotic violently sensual way he kissed me, to the lone man sitting in a diner, bloody and devoid of any expression, emotionally detached from the rest of the world. The room was literally spinning around me, pulling me under, and panic was pumping straight adrenaline through my veins.

Picking up my eReader, I tried again, taking a deep breath and counting backwards from twenty. I scanned the words on the device until my eyes blurred from tears...and my heart broke from...no, *for* Kade.

I can clearly remember the first time I met her. Those brilliant green eyes hiding all her secrets, keeping them from me... Like a wrecking ball, she came in, crumbling my walls into dust... She was as broken as I was...I could see some sort of pain in those green depths, some sort of mirrored knowledge that the world sucked. And, I thought to myself...finally...finally someone on my side of the fishbowl. I wanted to know what haunted her and hold hands in the darkness...together...

Blood. Gore. More blood and gore. By the fourth chapter, I was sure the male main character was a fucking serial killer.

As soon as my lips touched hers, her smile wandered its way to my mouth. I loved the softness of her lips, the warmth of her tongue, the way she moved her mouth over mine, her body leaned closer against me. "You make me smile when your lips are on mine, like I'm borrowing your happiness, like it's wiping off on me. Maybe I'm just stealing it, I don't know. All I know is that it gives me a calmness, a happiness I never thought I could feel...you give me a reason..."

She was mine, and no other's. Only my lips could kiss hers. Only my hands could hold hers. Only my body could sink deep inside her between those smooth ivory thighs...And only she could tame the beast I was. Only she could quench the thirst I hungered after, and coax the monster inside me to be a man again, if only a broken one...

More carnage. An eerily true to life decapitation scene from an accident, and wait...by chapter twenty, I believed the female character might have been the serial killer. This book...this book was dragging me to the dark dungeon of my own psyche where I did not wish to linger. Holy crap, I just got mindfucked. The book ended with a cliffhanger that made me scream. Like literally, scream. Out loud. His words were like liquid poetry, emotion dripping thickly off of every single sentence. It made my heart thunder in my chest and ache for the characters. They were written so close in likeness to both Kade and me, right down to the way my hands trembled and twisted napkins when I got nervous, to the destructive and angry way he tugged on his hair. The scenes of carnage, the gruesomely horrific violence, were so real and terrifying that I found myself gripping the edges of the couch cushions with anxiety.

Is that why the people in this town think he's the devil? Because he writes horror-fiction? That's absurd.

Rubbing my eyes, I looked at the clock on the wall; it was eleven. I read his words, his book, straight through for seven hours. Rifling through my drawers, I changed into a pair of jeans and a turtleneck to go back to the bar. Every sound I heard had me wondering if someone was outside the trailer, every howl of the wind had me hearing voices of people I never wanted to see again, and I didn't want to be alone. Kade Grayson was one talented writer, because I was still feeling the effects of the complete terror of his book.

After locking up the trailer, I silently made my way through the park, staying on the road with eyes wide open. No matter where you might have met up with your nightmares in your past, you could always find new ones on cold dark country roads. Relief swept through me when I had the bar in my view. The neon lights of the shaking ass sign were like a beacon of safety to me, but I still had a strange gnawing fear in the back of my head. It was probably from reading the horror story, alone...but I just couldn't shake the thoughts that someone was right behind me, reaching out their hand to grab me in the darkness of the night. You know that fear...that something is there just beyond your sight, waiting...watching you.

When my feet hit the asphalt of the parking area, I ran to the door of the bar and stumbled in, breathless and shaking. I could brush it off as being out of shape and cold, but truth was, I was dead scared. Because Kade Grayson wasn't the only one who'd lived through a real-life horror and I remembered all too well what those hands that spring from the blackness of the dead of night felt like around my throat.

The bar was practically empty. Cynthia (aka Sin Dee) was on stage, surrounded by four men raptly watching her spin herself around the pole, and for the briefest of moments, I envied her sexuality, her lack of inhibitions and her confidence in her beauty. I would love at least one night in my life to feel *that free* about my body and myself.

Dylan, Bree, Fran, and Natalie, another dancer, sat around a table in the middle of the bar, deep in some sort of discussion. Natalie was still dressed in her thong and a sparkly bikini top, and Fran didn't seem to own the ability to lift his eyes off her breasts. Good, maybe he'll ask her out and leave me alone with my coffee.

Kade sat in his normal booth. Back to the wall, facing the whole bar nearest to the back door, and now I completely understood why. He would always need to see the whole of a room, always need to be nearest to an exit, *just in case*. Kade Grayson had a whole new personality to me now, and I understood it. God, I *understood him*.

Immersed, consumed in whatever he was writing, I took advantage of his distraction to study him raptly. Leaning forward, the chiseled features of his face illuminated by the glow of his computer screen, his fingers danced quickly over the keys. He looked a mess. Hair tousled, falling darkly across his forehead, tight gray shirt, a simple cotton one, clung to his body, demonstrating his powerful chest and hard solid muscular arms. A smear of ketchup covered his cheek from the half-eaten hamburger lying on the dish next to his laptop. I found myself drawn in, in front of him, softly wiping the smear from his cheek. "*Shit,*" he whispered, looking up with wide eyes.

"Nope. Just ketchup," I whispered, feeling every beat of my heart as it banged hard against my chest. I couldn't believe I had touched him. Quickly, I wiped my fingers on a napkin, then balled it up tightly and squeezed it spastically in my hand. "I'm sorry." I gave him a watery smile and tried to hold back my tears, because I could still see the death and chaos around him. He wore it heavily on his face and in the tightness in his eyes. Like a soldier just home from war.

Slowly putting his drink to his lips, he took a long pull of his beer, his eyes never leaving mine.

Swallowing, he placed his drink down and snapped shut his laptop, ceasing the screen's glow against his skin. With only the flickering flame from the small candle on the table, it made his features look even more menacing and colder than ever before. His eyes were so light they seemed colorless. His hard angular face, chiseled as if from stone, tilted to the side in question.

"That was something a friend would do, no?" he whispered. Softly. Dangerously. Chilling me. His gaze dropped to my lips and it felt as soft as a touch.

I cleared my throat trying to get my breath back. "Why don't you come and sit with us? Have a bit of normal conversation, *friend.*"

His right eyebrow shot up. "I'm not *normal,*" he said, trying to provoke me, crossing his thick arms over his chest as if he was waiting for my rebuttal.

Leaning forward, I placed my face a few inches in front of his and whispered, "Then redefine what normal is, Kade." Being so close to him, I noticed the slight widening of the whites of his eyes, making his grey irises more brilliant than they already were. His pupils dilated completely, leaving me staring at complete black pools of desire. I swear I saw a layer of sweat burst out across his forehead.

A chuckle fumbled unevenly past his lips, and his head tilted to one side to look at the table I had invited him to sit at. "I appreciate your invitation, but I believe that every time that *Fran* of yours speaks to me, he's actively trying to annihilate every last one of my brain cells."

He was teasing me.

"Well, considering the average intelligence level of the people, and let's say the chairs and crumpled up napkins there, I believe you'd fit in perfectly with any conversation we could throw at you. Now, get up and stop your whining."

His smile...his smile almost killed me. Arrow right to the heart, with a stampede of fluttering butterflies exploding from it. That man was breathtaking when he smiled. And that dimple, *holy divots of smooth skin everywhere*, I could have fallen right into it and lived a happy life there for the rest of my days.

Sliding himself out of his chair, he stood up tall, and stretched. I was captivated by the way his shirt stretched and clung to the muscles of his arms and back. I was well aware that I was the one that looked like the obsessed stalker then, so I stepped away and tried to rub the sight of him from my eyes.

Walking side by side, we made our way across the bar to where everyone was seated.

"Here she is, just ask her," Bree slurred, smiling at me. "Who is the Karaoke Queen of Manhattan?" Crap. Bree was drunk. And telling everybody exactly where we were running from. Perfect.

I sat down across from her, leaving open the chair that faced the entrance to the bar for Kade to sit in. His face looked ashen, his entire demeanor screamed uncomfortable, and guilt quickly overwhelmed me. Catching his glance, I offered him an encouraging smile and he sat down and slid the seat closer to the table. The expression of everyone was astonishing to me. Dylan was giddy with happiness that his brother was there, but Fran was sneering like an ass. Bree was plainly drunk, and Natalie practically shoved her breasts in his lap.

"Bree was just telling us a little secret about you," Fran broke the silence. "She swears that your Karaoke skills are unsurpassable." Need I tell you that my stomach dropped for a bit, wondering what secret she could have drunkenly let loose?

"Ugh. My brother loved karaoke and he used to drag me to bars when we were younger to sing. It's no big deal. How did you guys get on this subject," I asked, watching Bree. Her eyes were closed and I knew she was thinking about Michael.

"Oh, I didn't know you had a brother," Fran said, scanning his eyes back and forth from Kade to me, and back again.

"Well, he's deceased, so I don't usually talk about him," I explained.

"Oh, I'm sorry. How did that happen?" Fran prodded.

Why do people think it's okay to ask that question? The answers are just for their own morbid curiosity and it hurts the person whom they're asking.

"They said it was suicide. Any other inappropriate questions you'd like to ask?" I said, offering an uncomfortable laugh.

Just like always, death kills the conversation. Four sets of silent staring eyes were on me, all except for Kade. No, what Kade did affected me the most, a simple brush of the back of his hand over mine under the table that took hold of all of my senses completely. My insides fluttered. Now that I knew about Kade's tragic past, I understood why we'd felt drawn together. People who have seen real life monsters up close will never feel understood by people who haven't. What those people don't understand, is that we still see those monsters, everyday. They will never understand how tragedy makes you bitter and spiteful, and how it always keeps its claws around your neck, ready to suffocate you.

"Um…what we were saying was that Dylan should have some karaoke on nights when us girls aren't dancing to get more people to come out to the bar. That's all," Natalie said. "I'm sorry about your brother, *hon.*"

Bree laid her head on Dylan's shoulder and kept quiet.

"Hey, they have a Karaoke bar in town. I should close the bar tomorrow night and then we could all hear this bird sing," Dylan teased, pointing to me.

Bree's face lit up, "I'm in."

Natalie smiled, "I'm in for a day off and going out, but I have to see if I could get a sitter for the little monsters."

Fran searched my face for my answer and I just shrugged, "Sounds fun." I turned my head towards Kade, "Want to come with us and watch me embarrass everybody?"

Again, his smiled crushed me.

"I still say the location is the problem with this bar, Dylan. There's nothing around here but the trailer park. What made you open up this place here anyway?" Fran asked.

My eyes caught the way Dylan looked at Kade, the same way Michael used to look at me after we'd bicker about something, and then he'd stick up for me in front of my mother, "Because I needed to be near my family. And this is the closest I've been allowed to get."

"Pardon me," Kade murmured, quietly pushing his chair back and walking off into the back hallway. Dylan ran his hands over his face, and gave me a pained stare. Curling his arms over his head, he cursed under his breath, "*Bloody hell. Lainey you just had him smiling and I go and ruin it with my mouth.*"

"Excuse me, I'll be right back," I said and walked into the back hallway, finding Kade in Dylan's office looking out the back window. "You okay?" I asked, as I walked up behind him.

"Yep." He snapped, rubbing his hand over the back of his neck. When I stood in front of him, he growled. "Okay, listen. I don't do talking and shit."

"Kade, shut up. I just asked if you were okay. You said you were, far be it from me to tell you otherwise. Your brother is just speaking the truth. If you don't like it, change it. And you *are* coming with us tomorrow night. You scare the shit out of the townies and I'll make their ears bleed."

I don't think he could have stopped himself from laughing, but I know he tried. A delicious smiled danced across his lips, "What I'm hearing is that, now you think we'd make a great team."

"So, you're admitting to hearing things, *Mr. Grayson*?"

Kade hung his head and laughed. When he looked back up at me, I saw the laughter reach his eyes. "Friends, huh?" The stress and tension that tightened his face eased away gradually.

"We could try," I said, slowly smiling.

His steel eyes softened as they held mine. Hesitantly, he reached his hand to my face and lightly brushed the knuckles of his hand from the bottom of my chin to the back of my jaw. The touch sent fire across my skin and every last nerve ending in my body awakened and tingled with warmth. Both of us stood there, silently watching one another, slowly leaning closer to each other until his hand slid up and wrapped around the back of my neck, threading his fingers through the strands of my hair. My knees instantly weakened and all my senses heightened with almost painful acuity. His scent of worn leather and whatever soap he used surrounded me, making me want to gulp deeply into his essence. The sounds of his close heavy breathing had my heart pounding as if it were surround sound. Everything seemed clear and just *more*.

"Lainey! Lainey?" Fran's voice called from the hallway.

Neither of us moved.

The pressure of his hand gripped at my neck tighter and a slow devilish smile appeared on his lips.

"Lainey?" Fran's voice continued to call.

Kade shifted and pressed his body against mine, thudding my back against the door of the office, clicking it closed. The hand tangled in my hair tightened more and his other slipped softly along the side of my waist, under the hem of my shirt and skidded hot fingertips along the surface of my skin. Leaning his face into the curve of my neck, he inhaled deeply, and I was instantly gasping for breath from his closeness. "I think someone wants you," he whispered, chuckling softly against my skin.

"Yes, I hear him," I whispered back, not caring at all.

"I wasn't talking about Fran." He growled, pressing his warm lips against my neck. *Oh, hell, it just got hot in here.*

Reluctantly stepping away, his hands released me, his eyes so intense, stared down into mine. "I don't know how to start this, I've never done *this*...," he whispered.

"Kade, I think you just did."

His eyes stayed fixed on mine as he smiled. Fran's voice was closer now, just on the other side of the door and Kade moved past me to open it. His hand brushed over my hip, along the curve of my waist to the front of my belly, and lingered just below my navel. I thudded my head against the wall as the strongest surge of lust exploded through my entire being. My soul wanted a piece of that man.

"Lainey? Are you okay?" Fran's voice shattered through our bubble, interrupting our moment. He walked through the door purposefully, looked at Kade and narrowed his eyes, then turned to glare at me. "Dylan is closing early tonight, everybody seems to have left. I'll drive you home now," he said, chancing another glance towards Kade. "To make sure you get home safe."

Kade's eyes never left mine. "Go," he said, "I'll see you tomorrow night with my pitchfork and horns."

"Goodnight, Kade," I said as I slipped out of the room, leaving him alone. I went back to the trailer that night with a very buzzed Bree, but I wore a smile plastered to my face. I was glad to soothe someone again, *to heal someone again.*

*   *   *   *

As I applied the tiniest bit of mascara to my lashes and the thinnest layer of gloss over my lips, I relayed all the facts I'd discovered about Kade's past to Bree. "That's the worst thing I've every heard, Lainey. Lord, no wonder he's such a hard guy to get along with. Did you tell him anything about what you've been through?"

"No, Kade doesn't know that I know, so there's no need to tell him about my past. And I won't, so please don't say anything to Dylan in your pillow talk."

"Girl. My pillow talk *will not* have you in it, not to worry," she said kissing me on my temple and winking at me as she looked into my reflection in the mirror we were sharing. She slathered on a thick layer of dark shiny lipstick and puckered her lips, blowing a kiss into the air, and then leaned all the way against the surface of the mirror. "How is it possible that it's the dead of winter and I have more freckles on my face? Skin cancer? Look at them. Do they look abnormal?"

Scanning her beautiful skin, I counted five very normal freckles across the bridge of her perfect nose. "Stop. You still only have five freckles. Your freckles *are* freckles, and you're beautiful."

"And you," she said turning to face me, "are actually putting make-up on your face. I know damn well it's not for Fran. What gives?"

I stared at her blankly.

"Holy crap, *you like Kade.*"

"No. Yes. No."

"You can't fix him, Sam," she whispered. "He's not broken and bleeding. It's something inside his mind, babe."

"I didn't say I wanted to fix him..."

Bree sucked in her cheeks. "Really? You're standing in front of a mirror putting *lip-gloss on* and I can see in your head, *I can see it...*"

The slamming of the trailer door and hooting alerted us to Dylan and Fran's arrival. Grabbing our coats, we followed their voices and found them lounging on one of the couches in a deep conversation about the healthy effects of drinking red wine as opposed to beer. Fran was going off on one of his tangents, stopped, looked me up and down, smiled and said, "You look nice tonight," and continued his rant.

Nice. Isn't *that* the adjective every woman wants to hear?

Fran's rant took us all the way through the drive into town to a huge bar called *Shenanigans*, where a decent sized crowd sat drinking and listening to people horribly singing Karaoke. I pointed Dylan to the empty booth closest to the exit. "Let's sit back here."

Natalie waved to us from the bar and skipped over with a round of beer in her arms and winked, "First round is on me! And I ordered chips and dip; it's so delicious here. *So good.*"

Fran attacked poor Natalie with *another enthralling* conversation, explaining what the rest of us had heard him drone on about for the entire car ride there, how healthier a glass of red wine is for your body. Dylan laughed and shook his head as Natalie sat listening closely to everything Fran hit her with.

After another round, I was bored out of my mind listening to Fran and Natalie telling me what I needed to do to live a healthier lifestyle, and Bree looked about ready to stick a fork in one of their eyes. In one large gulp, I drained my beer in front of the both of them and slammed my bottle down against the table hard. When the chips and dip arrived, it just got worse. As soon as Fran tasted the chips and dip, he would not shut up about it. Would. Not. Shut. Up. Maybe it was just me. Maybe I was losing my patience and easily irritated. I looked at Dylan and Bree who both wore the same expression as I did. No, it was all Fran.

"Lainey, you have to try this sauce," he moaned, through a mouth full of chips.

It's dip, not sauce. I took a chip because I was starving, but I didn't feel like dipping into a huge bucket of dip where everybody was double dipping their saliva. Ugh.

"Lainey, just dip it in the sauce. This sauce is delicious. You have to try it. Dip it in the sauce. Just dip it in the sauce," he pushed.

What the hell kind of sauce fetish owns this moron? "Jesus, Mary, and Jerome...I don't want to just dip it in the sauce," I said calmly. I wanted to slam my fist into the stupid bowl of chips to shut him up, but instead, I sat cool and composed, plotting how I was going to get him and Natalie together, so he would leave me the hell alone. I grabbed Dylan's beer and downed the rest of his as he sat back *beerless*, and laughed at me.

When I looked up, my heart nearly surged out of my chest. Kade had arrived and was walking his way over from the door. While it was true that, everyone seemed to turn to look at him with some sort of fear, I just looked at him with awe, knowing how strong he must be to go against his comfort zone, *and* he was drop dead gorgeous. Dressed casually in a worn pair of jeans and a beaten to hell leather jacket, he looked the part of a dangerous, reckless, and completely out of control man. It made my cheeks flush, and it made my insides heat, knowing that he came here because I asked him to.

"Hey," I said, sliding over in the booth to make room for him.

"Hey," he mumbled back, smoky grey eyes blazing at me through thick dark lashes. Leaning in slowly towards me, he tentatively brushed his hand against my forearm. Bringing his face closer to mine, he whispered, "Stunning."

Holding steady eye contact with him, my breath faltered, and what felt like a goddamn inferno surged through my body, slapping me in between my legs with such a forceful heat that I suddenly believed in self-combustion.

"Okay, ladies and gents. This next round is on me. What is everyone having?" Fran shouted out across the table. "Kade, my man. You have to try the sauce, it's outstanding."

Everyone ordered a beer, but Fran came back five minutes later with a beer for everyone and a glass of red wine for me, and a glass of red for him.

"Please tell me you did not just get me a wine on purpose," I said.

Fran winked at me from across the table, "It's a wonderful year. Have a sip."

"Oh, my God, I'm about to lose it," I muttered, and before I could say anything else, Fran interrupted me with more of his *tactful* conversation skills.

"So, Kade. It must be very gratifying to be such an accomplished and famous writer. You must have a plethora of women adoring you and throwing themselves at you. I bet you chew them up and spit them out, eh?" Fran asked, clearly trying to alert me to his presumptions about Kade's promiscuity. I knew, because he smirked at me after his pointed asinine question.

"Not if they taste good," Kade deadpanned, and then he slid his beer over to me, grabbed my glass of wine, and took a sip. "Most of them don't taste very well, mind you, but, once in a while...Once in a while, you find someone that you taste and it changes the way the rest of them do, and no one seems as sweet or delicious." His eyes locked on mine.

Fran was speechless, for once. And Kade? Kade was sitting next to me, stealing the air from my lungs with his closeness and his words, and I just burst out laughing. You know, one of those nervous, psychotic sounding laughs that end with a snort. Bree fell into a fit of giggles next, followed by some chuckles from Dylan and Kade.

Fran looked around at the people who seemed to be staring at us, and his cheeks reddened, "Lainey, try to control yourself. People are looking over here."

"Oh, my God, Francis, stop." I downed the rest of my beer. "That beer was delicious, Kade, thank you. I think I want a cup of coffee now," I laughed.

"Lainey, we're at a bar, stop with the coffee. You've probably had more than enough caffeine today. I'll get you another glass of wine. No more caffeine; I watch your hands tremble enough. And you don't even like beer. It's like you don't know what's good for you."

"Francis," I threatened, "if you don't stop this inappropriate compulsion with my eating and drinking habits, I believe I might cause you great bodily harm with some form of male testicular torture," I said, laughing hard.

He scoffed. A little snort followed by a smirk and that nasty crinkle of his nose, which was always plastered on his face. "Are you *premenstrual* right now?" he asked in a low whisper, as if it were an appropriate question. "An over-emotional female prone to exaggeration does not suit your personality type. This sort of change in your personality is what I've been trying to explain to you. It's from too much caffeine."

"That is the most arrogant, condescending, male chauvinistic and patronizing *mansplaining* bullshit I have ever heard," I said.

Kade slammed his fists down on the table and his presence seemed to expand and crowd into my small space on the booth. Before he could say anything, I brushed the back my hand over his arm, just as he had done to me a few moments before to let him know I could handle the situation. He visibly relaxed and leaned back into the cushions of the bench we occupied. It kind of made me feel *beautiful*.

Next to Fran, Bree covered her face with her hands and Dylan's expression looked shocked. I stood up, flattened my shirt down and wiped my clammy hands on my pants. I gave Fran a measured stare, leaned over the table, and asked sweetly, "Do you think yourself as a man that's well endowed, Francis?"

He squirmed in his seat, and gave me a slight nod.

"Let me ask you then," I leaned in closer and licked my lips, trying to act as seductively as I could. "Can your penis reach your rectum?"

Slowly, a flirtatious smile emerged on his face; he nodded and leaned his head closer to mine.

"Then go fuck yourself," I said evenly. Climbing behind Kade in the booth, I jumped off the seat, made my way to the bar, ordered another beer and a shot of whiskey, and stared down at my trembling fingers.

An icy cold beer and whiskey shot slid in front of me almost instantly.

"I'm taking you out of here," Kade's voice rumbled in my ear, fanning warm breath against my neck.

Gulping back my shot, I turned my head and looked up into his eyes, our faces so close, our lips mere inches apart. Slowly, his eyes trailed down to my mouth and he shifted his body to face me, "Come on, I'm in the mood for coffee." His dark features softened, his body slackened and relaxed against the edge of the bar as if he really felt comfortable next to me.

Drawing in a deep breath, I slid my gaze over to our table and heaviness settled over my chest when I locked eyes with Fran, then back to Kade. I had never dealt with any of this nonsense before. I'd never had two men at the same time vie for my attention (if that's what it was), but I did know what it was like to be with someone who tried to control you, and that, I didn't need. So, without any trepidation or fear, I followed Kade Grayson out of the bar with a wildly beating heart.

After I climbed into Kade's truck, I texted Bree to tell her I left. Shivering from the cold air, my teeth started to chatter and Kade looked at me questioningly. "You didn't go back to the table for your coat, and I didn't think to bring it to you when I asked you for coffee," he stated, the mist of his warm breath dissipating into the cold air of the front cab of his truck.

"Wasn't in my escape plan, no."

A slow sexy smile transformed on his lips as he unzipped his leather jacket and quickly yanked his arms from their sleeves and passed it to me.

Slipping the coat over my shoulders, I was hit with the intoxicating smell of Kade, a mixture of spices, man and thick, rich worn leather. Twisting the key in the ignition, his truck rumbled to life. The cold leather seats beneath me vibrated, as a Metallica song blasted deafeningly from his speakers with James Hetfield's deep raspy voice singing *Whiskey in the Jar*. Pure, raw nostalgia surged through my veins, teenage angst, and memories flooded my mind.

"Sorry," he muttered, fumbling to turn his audio system off.

"Don't!" I yelped. "Don't shut it off. I love this song. I was obsessed with Metallica when I was younger."

"*You?* You listened to Metallica?" he laughed harshly, doubting my honesty.

I despised it when people didn't take my word for truth, and I hated when people doubted

154

me. So, I sang the words to him as the music played, *"...stand and deliver or the devil he may take you..."*

His eyebrows shot up, but he didn't respond at all. He quickly looked out his windows for any oncoming traffic and pulled out onto the dark road. His eyes found mine again and narrowed.

"...I took all of his money..."

His brow wrinkled.

"...It was a pretty penny..."

He bit down on his lip to keep from smiling. I sang louder.

When he finally let his smile free, I danced around the cab of the truck singing and playing air guitar, until the song ended and he clicked off the audio system.

Emptiness. It was thunderous.

With the sudden loss of the music, a heavy *white-noise-roaring* silence fell over my ears. It had a tangible weight to it and my shoulders felt its heavy burden. I hoped I hadn't push too far. I hoped that being myself for a minute with him wouldn't cause him any more damage. Shifting over, I quietly leaned my forehead against the cold window and glanced out at the darkness of the tall trees that rushed by us alongside the road. Kade must have been speeding, because the trees were blurring past my eyes too fast. I said nothing though. If he needed to drive this fast, I needed to let him. Besides, I was the mother of all lead-footers; nobody drove as fast as I did.

Pulling into a large parking area off the main road, he parked his truck in front of an all

155

night diner that sat in the middle of an empty highway. With both hands, he tightly clutched the steering wheel until his knuckles were white from lack of blood flow. The muscles of his arms tightened and bulged, his back was rigid and his face stared straight out the windshield into the dark trees the grill of the truck was pointing towards. He had turned the engine off, so the temperature inside the cab of the truck was dropping fast and I could once again see the mist of his breath. "How do you do that?" he whispered, coldly.

Unbuckling my seatbelt, I shifted my body around to face him, "Do what?"

"Act comfortable around me," he said, as his head turned and his intense eyes collided with mine.

Pulling the handle of the door, I pushed it open and climbed out. Standing in the open door of his truck with the dome light on, I looked at him dead in the face. "I'm never comfortable with anybody, Kade. Ever. I just deal with whatever situation I'm in the best way I know how."

Slamming the door, I walked around the truck towards the front entrance of the diner, practically dragging his enormous jacket on the ground. Kade's door echoed mine, and instantly, he was in front of me blocking my way, his body so close to mine, but not once...not once touching me. *And, I wanted him too; I wanted him to touch me.* Leaning his face closer to mine, daring me to look up at him, I did. Pain was evident in his features;

confusion, struggle, and heartache were embedded in his skin. My heart broke for him.

"How?" he asked, leaning closer.

"Easy," I smiled, hoping to lessen his tension with humor. "You just gotta find your happy place, Kade. Mine is with Tatum Channing and a bottle of rum."

Caught off guard, his smile lit up the night, "Tatum Channing, huh?"

"Yes, please," I smiled, walking into the diner, melting with the warmth of the air that hit me as soon as we stepped foot inside.

Without speaking, we both headed for the first booth by the exit. If he noticed, he didn't say anything. He just sat down, back against the wall, eyes scanning the handful of customers that had ventured out just as we did. I could see the tension in his rigid posture and the tightness in his jaw as he surveyed the layout of the building, and I understood, more than he would ever know, I understood. When his gaze landed on mine, his tension seemed to slacken some, but not completely and I understood that too, I was just glad to notice that I helped in some sort of relief for his coiled body.

The waitress, an older lady with an impressive grey head of hair swept up into a 1960s beehive hairstyle, leaned her knee against the cushion of my seat and snapped a wad of gum in her mouth, "Hey, kids. What can I getcha?"

"Two coffees," Kade mumbled, "and I need a cheeseburger deluxe." He looked at me shrugging,

"Sorry, I'm hungry. Would you like to eat anything?"

"Actually, a cheeseburger deluxe sounds like heaven, so make that two," I smiled at the waitress. His eyes continuously scanned the room as the waitress walked away. Then after about three sweeps, his eyes met with mine again. He muttered another apology about being hungry, and held his eyes in a steady unwavering stare with mine.

"Don't be sorry. I am going to destroy that cheeseburger with my soul, I'm so damn hungry," I laughed.

Two huge mugs of steaming coffee were placed in front of us and he smiled tightly into the dark liquid as he poured in milk. "So what's the story with you and Francis?"

Sipping at my coffee, I rolled my eyes, "There's no story. I explained to him weeks ago, and I seem to have to remind him daily that I don't want a relationship with him. He has a hard time listening."

"He's about as fun as a funeral. And he's a big dick," he stated, trying to hide his small smile behind his coffee. "Dating him must be mind-blowing," he said dryly.

"You know what they say, having a small dick is the leading cause of acting like a big one," I quipped. He laughed at me and his smile was exhilarating, making me want to hear more. "And we're not dating. Dating sucks. Relationships suck. There are too many creepers out there."

"Creepers?"

"Yes," I said, smiling and winking. "There are all different kinds of creepers too. Let's see," I said, tapping my finger against my lips. "There's the touchy feely, hands-on creeper, the boob-gawking-mouth-drooler creep, the dirty talker creep, oh, or the fetish dude creeper, who stares at your feet during whole conversations. The dominant creeper who likes to victimize, is the worst in my book. There's the creepy geek freak, who talks Vulcan or quotes Star Wars facts during sex, or the dirty old man creeper. Can't forget the married creep or the cat guy creeper, or the creep your friend set you up with. There are so many," I laughed. "My favorite is the online creeper."

"Online creeper?" he asked, chuckling.

"Yeah. You know, the guy you meet online with an affinity for sending photos of his penis with every contact. For some strange reason, they love sharing pictures of their dicks publicly, like they are trying to promote them, make them famous or something. It's the equivalent of being a flasher in an overcoat on a train platform. And they're always trying to *sex-message* you some God-awful picture of themselves next to a can of soda to boast their size."

Kade's shoulders were shaking from his laughter, "What the hell is a sex-message?"

"It's one of those sex messages that you constantly get from people. *Hi. I am so-and-so and I just saw your profile and think you are kind and lovable. I want to be your friend and share my life with you. Here is a photo of me*, blah, blah, blah. *Do you have any naked pics?*" I sipped at my coffee, enjoying the warmth of it. "I'm dead serious, Kade. Just look at sites like Twitter, Instagram, and Tumblr, you'll realize the internet is a veritable sausage fest. Everybody is showing off their dicks these days. Creepers."

Laughing, Kade asked, "And what kind of creep was Fran?"

"Oh, he was the creep your friend sets you up with, touchy feely, *and* the cat creep all rolled into one."

"Must be hard pickings around here for you ladies to lock your ball and chains on someone, if all the eligible men are as *creepy* as Francis is," Kade said, reaching for a napkin.

I drew in a deep breath, blew it out dramatically and laughed, "Why do *all* women constantly get dragged into the same stereotypical group when someone is talking about relationships, and women *needing* to be married, like it's a universal constant? Not every woman wants to lock a ball and chain on somebody. It's like saying that all men actually do think with their dicks."

Our plates of food were placed in front of us, the smell of delicious greasy diner burger hit my nose like a freight train, and I moaned out loud.

Kade eyes snapped to mine, and a shiver ran down my spine. I just stared like an idiot back at him, holding my burger in both hands above my plate.

"But, men do. Take that moan, for instance. That had me thinking of you spread out over this table in nothing but a pair of black lace panties and your legs wrapped around my neck with those old white Converse still on your feet." His eyes pierced me and he shrugged his shoulders and smirked.

I froze at the thought, with my mouth just about to take a bite of my burger. "Subtle. Kade. Very subtle. I should give you a taste of your own medicine and go all *Harry-Met-Sally* on you."

A few minutes passed by as we both watched each other and ate, listening to the sounds of the kitchen and the wind whipping against the thick glass of the window next to us.

"Tell me about your brother," Kade whispered, low and cautious.

"What would you like to know?"

"Everything, anything. I don't know."

Staring down at my hands, I began unconsciously folding a napkin and playing with its creases. "Michael was my best friend. He was brilliant, a doctor, funny, and was unbeatable at playing pranks on people. Part of me is still holding onto the small hope that everything that happened was a cruel prank, and he'll just pop up from behind the bushes somewhere laughing his ass off."

A faint smile tugged at his lips. "I think that's everybody's default setting on death. Everybody hopes it was just a big sick joke. But, think about it, why would you want a person you love to be that cruel to you?"

"I wouldn't care. I'd just give anything for one more of our talks," I whispered. "Are you and Dylan very close?"

Glancing up at him, I noticed his face was twisted in grief. His brows creased in the middle of his forehead and he rubbed the back of his neck, "I'm not close with anyone."

"Not even Morgan?"

"Least of all Morgan."

The waitress leaned across our table, then gathered our emptied plates and poured us more coffee.

"Bree mentioned you both lived in Manhattan. Must have been culture shock coming all the way up here from a big city."

"Probably just as big as coming here from England. When did your family come to the states?"

He cleared his throat, clearly uncomfortable with the direction of the conversation. "I was seventeen." His expression darkened and I could visibly see his chest tightening. "So what was it like living in a big city growing up?" he said, struggling to think of anything else to talk about.

"My father always worked, and my mother was always busy, so my brother and I pretty much had the entire city as a playroom," I tried to explain without giving too much information about any personal subjects.

Slipping the check over the table, the waitress winked at me and walked away. Kade grabbed for the check, and I reached into my purse for some cash. When I tried grabbing the check from him to see what to put in, he practically bared his teeth at me and snarled. I watched him leave a hundred dollar bill on the table and he placed his hand on the small of my back and led me to the door.

"So, what's your story then, Lainey?"

"I don't have any stories you're going to want to hear, Kade. Do *you* have stories *you* want to talk about? Or you want to make this evening light and unheartbreaking?"

His lips curled up playfully, "Oh Lainey, I have tons of stories..." he said as we climbed into his truck and started the engine. "But my story? Let's see...my past is heinously horrid. Born with extremely powerful, yet flawed super human powers, I accidently melted my mother into a heaping pile of goo as soon as I fell from her womb. The guilt was unbearable and drove me to wear a mask to hide my deadly grey eyes, deliberately living a life of solitude as I search the world for a cure for my *flaws*. Everyone thinks I'm not living up to my heroic potential and that I should work for the government, fighting America's villains, but the reality is that I'm just saving everyone from my hell." Kade had pulled out of the lot and the dark road was racing under the wheels, and the trees were a blur of tangled blackened branches blocking out the moonless sky. For miles, an awkward heavy silence hung in the air when his story finished, both of us knowing there was some strange truth to his tale. Turning into the trailer park, he slowed the truck down from warp speed, pulled into the dirt road next to the trailer, and turned off the engine.

"I googled you," I whispered.

His eyes nailed me to the seat. Vaporous breath escaped through his lips as his chest rose and fell faster and faster. His eyes flickered and searched my face maniacally; his breathing became more erratic, intense gasps of air. "Goodnight, Lainey," his voice croaked huskily.

I leaned forward and laid the palm of my hand over his chest. I felt him tense and strain beneath the tips of my fingers. His eyes searched mine, as my fingers felt for the beat of his heart, listening to it, feeling it as it slowly settled into its regular pace.

"Kade."

"Don't. Just go, please. I can feel you in my darkness, Lainey, and you're shining, lighting up my way. Please go. Leave me to my darkness," he smiled bitterly.

"Kade, I know the mess you're dealing with and how it makes you feel. More than you know."

"You don't know anything!" He screamed, nostrils flaring and red-faced. He goes hot and cold like the flip of a switch. On-flip-Off. Hot-flip-Cold. "Yes. I have the characteristics of a real person. Flesh, hair, bones, blood, whatever...but I have *nothing on the inside.* Empty, devoid of any emotion, dead. Like I did die that day, and only my body remains here. Maybe you could feel flesh and pulse, see my blood and bones and you think I'm just as human as you, but I'm not. I'm fucking empty. There is *nothing* inside me. Nothing but violent scenes and pleading echoes. Then I saw you, and something small flickered deep inside the dead dark recesses of my mind. I don't need some stupid little girl like you telling me how you *understand me*, when you never would be able to conceive the unthinkable shit I've lived through. Just fucking leave me here, Lainey. Walk the fuck out and leave me here."

"I don't want to leave you *there*, Kade. Nobody should be left *there*."

"So, what? You're going to try to save me, Lainey? Leave me alone. You have no idea who and what I am. Get the fuck out and go back to your little perfect bubble."

Ignoring his rouse, I dug into him, "I can see you're in pain."

"My pains are not apparent to the eye," he muttered.

"*What the fuck are you talking about*? They're as apparent as the nose on your damn face, because you wear them so proudly! You act as if you carry some contagious sickness with you, something that you actually threaten people with. Well, I'm not scared of you and your self-inflicted disease. Especially since I suffer from the same exact one, I just know how to live with it. The first time I saw you - you fucked me like a teenage virgin with your eyes, then when I asked you for your order, you acted like a misogynist. I know, Kade. How about we do this? Why don't you snap a little picture of me and then later tonight, when I leave the premises and you're all by your wonderful Wizard of Oz lonesome, you could creep in for some quality time with the still, mindless, silent picture. Or maybe, you could just acknowledge the fact that I might understand what you're going through and deal with the real life me, the one that you follow around."

Why the hell couldn't this shit be easy, because honestly, I just wanted to be the one that fucking broke through that wall and get to the good shit. There I said it. I wanted to be that one, the special one. Tag me a stupid emotional clichéd girl, but I wanted that man to look at me from between my legs, lick me utterly senseless and to make me forget my name.

"Get the fuck out."

"You need a hardcore fucking detox for assholism. Let's lay it all out, shall we? Something *horrific* happened to you. There is no doubt about that. You had innocent children, friends, classmates and teachers slaughtered in front of you. A teacher, whom you admired and loved, who had a husband and children at home, jumped the fuck in front of you while a madman was taking out his sociopathic crazy on you, to shield you and save your fucking life. You suffer from flashbacks, yes? *Medically,* that's called Post Traumatic Stress Disorder, and you can *heal.* Trust *me.* If you want to, you can deal with this, *deal with it, and I can help you.* But to bind yourself to your house, to leave your brother worried and missing you...You hide yourself off from the world, from a woman whom you can't take your eyes off of, and complain that life has whipped you hard. You don't know me, Kade. Maybe I've danced with the same monsters you have. I know it all. Let me help you."

He slammed his fists against the steering wheel, "GET THE FUCK OUT!"

166

Shaken, I did what he told me to do.

He peeled out of the driveway, kicking up dirt and rocks in his haste, and I didn't see him again.

Chapter 8
Kade

I spent five days locked inside my den.

Five days. A great portion of them were spent in the dark, lying face down on the couch with my face pressed into the cold leather cushions, wondering how long it would take for my depression to kill me.

Monday. Entire day, face down feigning the flu, or plague...maybe a bit of walking corpse syndrome. If I thought hard enough about it, I felt warm, but there was no one there to ask so, yeah, whatever. I ate nothing. There was a half empty bottle of brandy next to me, so at least there was some sort of consumption of something.

Tuesday. I Googled everything and anything on Post Traumatic Stress Disorder. Then I inserted myself back on the couch, trying to sink myself deeper into the cushions and springs. I paid $200 for a delivery of chicken soup from the diner. It was ice cold when it arrived.

Wednesday. I turned over on the couch, lay on my back and watched my ceiling fan oscillate around depressingly. Spinning, spinning, spinning...always in the same exact circles. Just. Like. Me.

I snapped the blades off.

Of course, *this is my life*, so I also sliced my arm open while exacting my rage on the innocent propellers of air. Tore my arm to shreds actually, making me have to use all those pathetic supplies

Lainey had me buy at the store weeks ago, because she worried about me getting an infection. The supplies weren't pathetic, I was.

Thursday. I was so angry that she was right. Everything she fucking said was right, which led me to punch a hole through the wall in the den.

Friday. I was back, face down on the couch. Groaning. I missed following her. I missed seeing her smile and hearing her snappy quick comebacks.

Life had made me really good at being a douche. Since I was sixteen, I'd been on a one-way track to self-destruction, mowing down everyone in my path. Then I met Lainey, who pulled me out of myself and made me feel normal for a few moments in my life, and I had *lost it* right in front of her.

She must have felt as if she was pulling my teeth out, trying to get me to make small talk at the diner. My brain was in a fog being so near her. The entirety of the night was spent with me talking myself from sliding my splayed fingers up the back of her neck, fisting them through that silky hair and pressing my lips to hers, savagely. What she said in my truck...how could she know the things inside me? Thinking that someone felt the same as me, understood me, made me want to fuck her and to over indulge myself in her flesh. The need overwhelmed me. There was an overbearing realness to her that lay heavy on my chest, and if I never saw her again, I swore I would succumb to its weight.

Thrumming softly into my ears, the raspy vocals and music of *Simple Kind of Man* by Shinedown, held back the phantasms of my horrors, and showed me only my bitter longing to listen to the cadence of Lainey's soft calm voice and taste the sweetness of her soft pink lips. No matter how badly it was going to hurt, I didn't want to be anywhere but with Lainey. Let her crush me. Let her destroy me. There wasn't much good left of me, but I wanted her to take every last bit.

In those green eyes, yelling at me, holding up that metaphorical mirror that showed me some of my actions against her, I knew I'd come undone. And she was fucking right; I couldn't do this anymore. I didn't want to. I knew the true impact of my trauma was me just shutting myself down, quitting life. I stayed up all night, thinking and rethinking if I should ever see her again. Questioning if I could be capable of some sort of *normal* to offer her. 'Redefine normal' was what she told me, such innocent, brilliant words. I stayed up throughout the entire next day and watched the sun sluggishly pass through the sky, as if it was toying with me and wasting and playing with my time.

Just to torment myself, when the sun finally set, I went to Dylan's bar.

One of the guys from the trailer park was giving himself an impromptu bachelor party, bringing along a rowdy crowd of cave dwellers that had my panic set to high alert.

I wanted to haul Lainey over my shoulder and carry her out of the crowd. The whole time I was watching her as I stood by the entrance, talking myself into going in, she didn't smile at all.

Not even once.

I clenched my jaw and stalked toward Dylan's office, slamming the door behind me, which caused Bree to fall flat on her ass, right off the desk where she was playing a full contact game of tonsil hockey with my brother. "Coitus Interruptus!" I screamed. "Stop and put your hands where I can see them."

Bree stumbled awkwardly to her feet and walked out giggling. "Hello to you too, Kade. *Coitus Interruptus*, that's hysterical."

Without a thought, I started wearing a hole into my brother's rug, as he stood there, hands on hips, waiting for me to talk. I felt like a cloud of smoke, just billowing into nothing. My lungs felt like they were tightening and drying out, and I couldn't inhale enough air. My throat was tight and dry when I finally spit out the words, "I want her."

"She's sort of crazy about me, mate. And personally, I don't think you'd ever stand a chance with your *flagrantly charming* demeanor," he chuckled.

"I want *Lainey*, you dolt." He was just *ridiculous* thinking I could want the blonde perky one. She was...well, *perky*.

"Kade, mate. I think the girl has been through enough hell, okay? Don't drag her through yours," Dylan replied.

"I can't stay away from her," I growled, raking my hand across my forehead and back through my hair.

He looked me dead in the eyes, "Try a bit harder, Kade. It's what you're best at."

I covered my face with my hands and then ripped them violently through my hair again. "I don't want to be best at that. I'm *sorry*, Dylan. I'm sorry for everything I've ever put you through."

"What about someone like Natalie?" He asked.

Jerking my head back, I gagged in his direction, almost literally vomiting on him. "She's *fuckable*, not datable. There's a huge difference. I'm tired of fucking women that I have to hide who I really am and what horror lives inside me. I want someone to know me, just *fucking understand me*, and God...Dylan, I can swear when she looks at me, I think maybe...I don't know, that maybe *she does*. The only *thing* I know right now, is that when she's near me, I don't think of the blood that's been spilled in a classroom, but the rush of pulse from the flush of her cheeks when I look at her."

"What's that even fucking mean?" He asked.

I ignored the question. "She said I had PTSD."

"You do, Kade, face up to it. Get fucking help. I miss my brother."

"I want her," I growled again, as if I was sporting to have a tantrum.

Dylan leaned forward, talking low, eyes shifting behind me to see the door. "You didn't see her when she first came here, mate. She could barely walk straight. Bree had a fat lip and a bruise across her face, but Lainey... Lainey needed a hospital and wouldn't go to one, and it didn't seem like it was because she was afraid of doctors, Kade. I think she's afraid of the police. I think something is wrong...the way Bree talks about her...did you know Bree and Lainey's brother were engaged..." he whispered. He pointed his finger at me. "I'm not going to let you hurt her, because the only reason Bree is here is because Lainey is here, and I'm not ready to give Bree up yet, mate."

"Dylan, don't go getting your silk panties in a twist, yeah? I know she has some sort of wooly situation she's hiding from, but I want her and I have no clue how to deal with any of these feelings. If anyone is going to be getting hurt, it's going to be me."

"You're a real dick sometimes. You're just going to bring her down," he whispered, shaking his head.

"Hey, I lived through attempted murder and a massacre, cut me some slack. Aren't I supposed to get like a 'get out of jail' card for it, or some sort of sympathy card?" I smiled pathetically.

His eyes widened from the carefree lightness of my plea, "Kade, you're cracking jokes about it? This girl is really changing you, isn't she?"

"She's so different. She doesn't have to get naked to get a man's attention. She just has to walk in a room, glide in with her watery movements, and when she speaks, it's of substance. You fucking want, no...*you need to listen*. She's profound. It's ruthless on my soul. She is a woman who still blushes when a man looks at her. She's not a child, you know she's lived some sort of difficult life and the mystery of her is breaking me. I want her to crack and break in my hands. I want to open her up and gut her."

"Never thought I'd see the day," my brother whispered, smiling.

"The memory of her taste has me crazy," I added. Every detail of that kiss was still felt; I could still smell her, feel her and taste her. God, thinking about it made my cock ache for her.

"Taste?" He asked.

"I fucking kissed her."

"So what do you want me to do?" He asked, leaning forward.

"Tell me I should try, and that I might be able to be good enough for someone..."

"Kade, man, that's every one's fear. But, if this woman is getting you to come out of your self, then I'm all for it, just don't hurt her. Stop scaring her and tell her everything. Talk to her, talk to me, talk to someone. Please try, because God, Kade, I bloody miss my brother. I *can* see it, you know, these past few months. This girl *is* changing you. She's bringing you back from the dead, Kade."

The thought brought me to my knees. Metaphorically, my brother would call me a pussy if I did that in front of him. Doesn't count that I had to strain to hold myself up with my arms. Doesn't matter, because he was right.

"And Kade?"

"Yeah?"

"Don't take this the wrong way, but when you talk about her and what she does to your insides, mate, it sounds a lot like falling in love with someone."

"I don't know if I'll be capable of love, ever. Or trust. I'm panicking from hearing all the noise outside in the bar and I'm counting heads and windows. In my head, I'm going through all the different scenarios of someone coming in with a gun and how I would get to her and how I could save her, how I'd save everyone."

"That's what you do? You count heads and windows and constantly plan escapes? Lainey kind of talked to me the other day about PTSD and coping mechanisms, but I didn't believe her fully. You never once let me help you. You never once let me in. I have no idea what you went through unless I read about it in the bloody paper."

"You remember the sort of day it was, don't you?" I whispered.

Dylan slumped against the wall heavily and nodded.

I ran my hand down my face and gave a dark chuckle. "It was one of those beautiful days, not average for Britain, strange it wasn't rainy. I was with Thomas before first hour in our little hiding spot, getting in our last drags off our Marlboros before we headed inside. Lizbeth had just gone in. She was always afraid of being late. She gave me a snog. I had no idea that it would be the last time I would ever kiss her."

My legs gave out and I just dropped down heavily to the floor. Dylan followed along and leaned his back up against his desk. I thoughtlessly played with the cuff of my jeans. "I had no idea that my world was going to shatter so completely when I stepped into that classroom. So many people asked me if there were any warning signs before it happened, any clue in the few minutes before when we were sneaking our smokes, but there were none, not then. The fucking warning signs had come all before throughout all the years and months I'd known him. I knew Thomas better than anyone did. I knew him better than those analysts who tried to profile him did, I knew him better than his parents, and teachers. I knew when I stepped foot in there what he was capable of. I just didn't choose to believe it."

Dylan thudded his head against the desk, eyes rising to the ceiling, "I can remember the gunshots. We thought someone lit fireworks off in the main hall. But they had us evacuating immediately after. I knew it was bad. I knew it was bad the minute all the classrooms were emptied but yours. And we saw the bullet holes as they blasted through the window."

I tried to even out my breathing, I didn't need a full on panic attack right there in front of Dylan. "Not even two minutes after he walked in, he was standing in front of the class aiming, his black duffel bag full of guns at his feet. I was the first one, did you know that?"

Dylan's face went ash.

"Over everyone's screams, he eloquently explained why he chose to fire on me first, two nonfatal shots. He said, and I'm quoting here, 'I need you to be able to watch it to the very end, Kade. You stay until the end, watch me kill everyone, then you get to die.'"

Shaking the visions from my head, I stood up. My palms were sweating and my head felt light. I needed to see Lainey. I needed to see her calm face. I lumbered to the door and stopped shy of the threshold, clamping my hands on the top of the doorframe. "Back then, my biggest problem was trying to talk Lizbeth into showing me her tits. It all changed when my best friend aimed that barrel of the gun at me, and pulled the trigger without blinking. He had a goddamn smile on his face, Dylan. I relive that scene everyday. I relive the entire scene of him picking off all of my friends one by one, shooting kids hiding under desks, hiding behind other dead kids, and...*oh God*, Mrs. Turner. He executed them all; the whole time laughing and bloody singing a sick twisted song, then came back to me. But, when I look at Lainey, for a minute, I can think of something else."

Leaving my brother to mull over my past on the floor of his office, I made my way into the bar to look for my obsession. Lainey was standing behind the bar pouring a beer. Bree said something to her and she laughed, smiled, eyes dancing. My God, she was pretty already, but when she smiled like that, she was the most beautiful woman I'd ever seen.

Chapter 9

Lainey

Fran graciously sat me down and broke the delicate news to me that our relationship was not proceeding at the speed he liked, and that we would be better suited as friends. *Valiantly* (you can't see me, but I'm laughing here) he expressed his *extreme* guilt for going home with Natalie the night I left to have coffee with Kade. He believed she was the speed–relationship wise-he needed. *Eh. Gotta give him props for honesty, right*? I was still wondering where in the world he got off thinking we were in a relationship when I blatantly told him I was NOT in one of *those* WITH HIM. Two make-out sessions does not a relationship make, this wasn't high school.

Natalie was completely nervous and stressed about how I might take the news. I hugged her and whispered a relieved thank you in her ear. I didn't think she understood, but she would when she orders a beer in front of him, or wants a coffee, or tries to spit gum out of the window of his moving smart car, or God forbid, forgets to recycle a can of soda. Mentally, I was high-fiving her with my vagina.

It had been five days since I went for coffee with Kade. Five days since I'd seen him, and five days since he followed me. Five days since I opened my big mouth to get him to talk to me. Five days of uncontrollable itchiness to jump in my car and hightail it out of here to find another hiding spot.

That night, there was a huge last minute bachelor party at the bar, which I wished I had known about in advance. Say, like when I was dressing for work, so I could have opted out of wearing the short denim skirt I had on. I wasn't comfortable with all the men that night, I was just afraid of unwanted touches and looks that I wasn't emotionally stable to deal with. Worse than the strangers was Fran, who was sitting in the corner, pounding back an insane amount of red wine, two whole bottles to be exact, and bothering the hell out of me about how '*soft the legs of my skin look*.' No, I didn't just say that backwards, it was an exact quote.

When Kade walked in from the back hallway, I was stunned. His eyes blinded me. His stare made my knees go weak. He looked angry, enraged, and murderous. There was a new bandage around his wrist, making me wonder what he did to himself. I knew I would never be able to save him, but it was ingrained in me to save, and I wanted to be able to so badly.

From the corner of the room, his eyes claimed me, all of me-my eyes, my neck, my legs...making me *feel like he was touching my skin*... The heat that spread over every inch of where his eyes looked had me dizzy, like an acute case of vertigo, and I wanted to spin in it, spiral out of control and drown in it. Sitting on a bar stool, I let my skirt ride a bit further up my legs to watch his eyes widen and his breath quicken. I was swept up in a frenzy. I wanted to make him look at me; I needed him to.

"I really need to talk to you," Fran slurred behind me, practically pinning me to the edge of the bar.

"Maybe later, Fran. I need to use the restroom," I lied, squeezing my way around him and rushing into the back hallway. Glancing back over my shoulder, I smiled at Kade, hoping he'd find his way to talk to me.

Locking myself in the stall, I heard the bathroom door open and footsteps squeak in. I opened the stall door thinking that Kade would be there, his face, smirking at me, but it wasn't. The muscles in my shoulders tightened when I stepped out to see Francis. Drunk on either the wine he was guzzling, or some sort of nontoxic environmentally safe fumes of maybe, I don't know, bacon grease or something. My thoughts were quick and precise. He had me cornered by the sheer luck of me thinking about another man, and I was going to need to fight him. "I think you're in the wrong bathroom," I said. He just laughed condescendingly, as if I should know better.

"I think I made a terrible mistake about us," he slurred, stepping forward. I sidestepped him, squeezing my body around him without ever touching him. When I was the one closer to the door, my shoulders slumped a bit with relief. "Please hear me out," he mumbled.

Before I could get out an answer, Fran's body catapulted onto me. His mouth was on mine, bitter wine breath, strong body order and I swear I smelled one of those old-fashioned evergreen car fresheners. I wouldn't have been surprised if he had one in his pocket. Revulsion quaked in my belly and I shoved him off me quickly. "Fran, don't make me have to kick your…"

With a loud thud, the bathroom door flew open and smashed up against the wall, splintering one of the white tiles with a web of cracks. Natalie stomped into the bathroom, hands on hips and her usually cheerful expression twisted into rage.

"What the fuck is this?" She screeched, looking from me to Fran, eyes narrowing. "Are you fucking kidding me? My kids asked to call you daddy!" *In five days, she let her kids meet him and want to call him DADDY?*

Fran's hands dropped from my arms, his pleas were whines and lies, and it made me sick to listen. I couldn't look at the hurt in Natalie's face. I couldn't take the heartbreak, because it was like looking in a mirror and I knew just how she felt.

I ran out of the bathroom, tears stinging my eyes for Natalie for having feelings for a jerk like Fran. Running down the hall, I slammed head first into a solid chest, and looked up into the stormiest eyes I'd ever seen. With my stomach twisted into knots, I swallowed thickly and sucked in a sharp breath. *Kade.*

"Lainey, what's wrong?" he asked, eyes narrowing. There was tightness in his jaw, the muscles flexed and clenched. His hands instantly cupped my face, big, thick, warm hands. I wanted to tell him everything. I wanted his lips on mine, because I wanted to matter and make a difference to someone, and I wanted to stop this lethal game of hide and seek I was playing. I just wanted to be Samantha Matthews again. Hell, I wanted to tell Kade that I *was* just like him.

Natalie stormed out of the bathroom, and pushed between Kade and me. "Don't worry, hon. I know that was all him. I hate him so much right now, because my kids were crazy about him. What am I going to tell them now?" She sighed heavily, and looked up at Kade as if she just realized he was standing there. "But," she purred like a cat, "Revenge is sweet." She winked and grabbed Kade by the hand and shoved him into Dylan's office. "Take out that cock, Kade, I want to dance on it," I heard her say as the door slammed shut.

Instantly, I was sick. Desperation ripped through me, and I wanted to bang on the door and throw her off him. Though, what right did I have to do that? Because he stared at me for a few weeks? Because he took me for a coffee when he saw Fran treating me like a child? I was nothing to him; I was just a goddamn waitress in a God forsaken strip bar in the middle of nowhere. And what was he to me? Nothing but my boss's brother who lived a tragically lonely life. There was nothing between us but a simple attraction. Nothing to put hope in.

Nothing.

Yanking off my apron and crumpling it up in my hands, I walked into the bar and threw it under the counter. Then I walked out the door and right home to the shitty little trailer I lived in. Heading straight for the bathroom, I rummaged through my bag, grabbed a bottle of sleeping pills, and swallowed two dry.

Tossing myself fully clothed on my bed, I grabbed my iPod and jammed my earbuds in my ears. Pressing play, I was instantly surrounded by the haunting voice of Amy Lee and the heavy rhythms of *Bring Me To Life* by Evanescence, and waited until the magic of my pills worked. The night chilled my bones as small drafts of the cold winter winds drifted through that old tin trailer. I wrapped myself in a soft fleece blanket to keep myself warm and pretended I was lying in Kade Grayson's arms. Sleep lumbered slowly over my body as I thought how preposterous of a fantasy it was. I had enough scars on my body from the last man that held me in his arms, raised stains that read like Braille across my flesh, so I shouldn't desire another violent one. However, he wasn't the same man as the last; he was a far better one, were the last thoughts before sleep took hold of my mind. I didn't wake up until the next morning.

Armed with an entire pot of coffee, I walked through the dense evergreens that crowded this little part of the world, until I reached the bar. An early morning slideshow of images flashed through my imagination of the carnage and chaotic state of mess the bar must be in, and I cringed, hoping there were latex gloves I could use to clean. Darker images clawed at the back of my brain, juxtaposing themselves against the chaos, thoughts I didn't want to be thinking, despite the clarity of them. Twisted white sheets, guttural moans and whimpers of two lovers; I didn't want to visualize them, but visions of Kade and Natalie wrapped around each other were screaming in my mind.

Dylan already had the front door unlocked, and was standing in the middle of the barroom holding a mop in one hand, a bucket in the other, wearing a sheepish smile across his lips. "Morning, love. Where did you get off to last night?"

I wanted to grab the filthy mop out of his hands and sanitize it, but instead, I just slid my jacket off, hung it over a stool and started collecting the strange clothes and *debris* that was strewn around the bar. Feathered boas. Tassles. *A riding crop.* I completely passed over picking up the dirty looking G-strings. "Ugh. I hand a run in with an extremely drunk Francis and an angry Natalie, so I thought it better if I just left. Sorry."

"No worries. Did Kade get to see you?"

"I bumped into him in the hallway last night, but I didn't speak with him. Natalie needed him for something, I think."

A strange smile played at the corner of his lips, "He was looking for you most of the night. He slept on the couch in my office."

All I could think about was scrubbing the bar with bleach, so I shrugged my shoulders and held up all the costumes I collected to ask, "Where should I put all this stuff?"

"Just throw it in my office on the floor, or in my closet. It all needs to be cleaned," he murmured, pushing the mop along the floor, trying to hide his smile from my eyes. Shit. *Didn't he just say that Kade was asleep on the couch in there?*

Maybe he had lost it, drank too much of the Kool-Aid around here. I walked over to the entrance of the hallway and turned to face him. He was staring at me with a stupid knowing smile on his face. What it knew was beyond me. Maybe Dylan wanted me to walk in on Kade in some precarious position. Slowly, I backed into the hallway and made my way to the door of his office.

I was about to throw all the crap on the floor and run when I heard Fran's voice in the barroom talking with Dylan, asking him if he'd seen me.

Crap. Now it was between hearing Fran's excuses for drunkenly attacking me in the bathroom, opposed to sneaking past Kade asleep on the couch.

Kade. Fran. Kade. Fran.

All right, deep breath, *there was no way I wanted to see Fran and listen to his whining and begging.* In a rush of glittery costumes and feathered freaking boas, I dashed through the office door and searched for the nearest hiding spot. It was either under Dylan's desk where I sure as shit couldn't fit, or in his coat closet. Closet it was. I didn't even look to see if Kade was asleep on the couch.

Diving in, glittery sequins and all, I yanked the door shut behind me. Total darkness consumed me and a lone hanger swung against the rod and whacked me in the eye. "SON OF A..." I grabbed for the door handle, and it wouldn't budge.

Oh, just wonderful. I was locked in.

"Lainey? Lainey?" Fran's muted voice called from the hallway. His footsteps clopped heavily against the floorboards and moved throughout the room. "Oh, Kade, hey. Have you seen Lainey?"

"No," Kade's rumbly voice replied from somewhere just outside the closet door.

"Dylan said she was just here," Fran pushed.

"Does it look like she's in here? Go check the bathroom," Kade rumbled. Fran's fast footfalls stomped down the hallway, the closet door swung open, and a blast of bright light hit my eyes. Kade's face came towards me like a ton of bricks.

"*No-no-no don't*...don't close the door..." I whispered loud as he stumbled in with a rush of air, slamming into me, causing my head to knock against more empty hangers that jangled amongst each other and clanged to the floor. "The door locks..."

"Now, that's a piece of information I wasn't aware of."

Awkward silence. From somewhere just above my head the tiniest puff of warm breath came.

"This...is...interesting," he chuckled.

"Why are you in here?" I hissed, realizing that because of the way Kade landed in the closet, he was now pressed up against me. Leaning back as far as I could, I pressed the palms of my hands against his chest to push him away. Except that I couldn't, because as soon as my fingertips touched the tightness of his chest, the gasp that came out of his mouth made my heart race and I had to resist the urge to pull him close and bury my face in his scent. Godfuckingdamnit! I was *not* going to turn into one of those women who threw themselves at a man who didn't want her.

"I wanted to see why you jumped in here," he whispered back. Strong thick fingers gripped my arms. "You smell good."

"That's cleaning supplies, jackass." It wasn't. I lied. I actually did smell good.

He gripped me tighter, and I wanted to run, run before I did something stupid, like kiss someone who didn't want to have anything to do with me. A warm hand slid slowly up my arm... *He had to stop playing with me. I was not a toy.* As I started to speak, I felt the tip of his nose softly trace the edge of my jaw. The smooth, moist heat of his lips moved down to my neck then back up trailing a path of fire to my ear. I needed to stop him. I needed to push him away, but I couldn't, because I was frozen.

And, of course, there was the little fact that I liked it. I sighed into the silent darkness.

"You left me with that creeper last night. I couldn't find you. I knocked on your trailer door almost all night and I just came back here to sleep," he whispered hotly in my ear.

"Creeper?" My stomach flipped. *He had looked for me*?

"Yeah, what's her name, Natalie, I think," he replied, pulling the warmth of his face away from mine. I could still feel his breath on my skin, but I couldn't make out any of his features. "She was one of those touchy feely, be my baby daddy, gold digging, online pussy showing creepers."

"I figured you'd enjoy her company," I laughed darkly.

"Seriously? Did you get dropped on your head as an infant?" he asked dryly.

"Yep, into a large puddle of glitter, glorious intelligence, and flawless awesomeness. What happened with you, did you get left in the mud?" I heard him chuckle. "Oh, God. Look, I didn't quite think it fully through. I just wanted to get away from Fran, so I went back home and went to sleep, had my earbuds in listening to music and I might have taken two sleeping pills."

Against my ear, I felt him take a deep breath and exhale slowly with the smallest tremor. "Didn't affect you one bit that I might have fucked Natalie, huh?" he asked.

"I didn't think about it. Why would I care? You threw me out of your car last week and I haven't seen you since," I said in a low voice.

"Okay, then. I'll just grab my phone here..." he whispered, and there was a loud thud as, what I believed was his elbow, whacked against the wall. A string of murmured curses hissed under his breath. Then, suddenly a bright light illuminated the small dark closet, reflecting the planes and angles of his face. "And I'll just call Dylan and tell him to tell Fran where you are."

"You wouldn't."

"Fuck yeah, I would. Or you could tell me how you really felt about the stripper and me." A smirk lit up his face. "You never know, Fran could go all caveman on you. Get all possessive, seeing you talk to me this close in a closet. Grab you right out of my arms."

I leaned my back against the wall and shrugged my hands in my front pockets. "He *could be* a bad ass tree hugger. Very dangerous. What if he grabs you instead of me? You might want to rethink this plan of yours."

Kade leaned in, smiling. "Yep. I bet he could be very scary to a few dust bunnies under a chair somewhere." Taking in a long breath, he sighed, "Tell me how you felt."

I laughed, and looked down shaking my head. We were getting too close to each other in here. "I've been to his place; he lives in harmony with his dust bunnies." I looked up as a dangerous flash of something flickered in his eyes.

"You've been to his place." He leaned away. He looked down at his phone, closed it, and then leaned quickly back into me, his lips whispering against my ear, hot breath tingling down my neck. "I hate thinking that he's been inside you. It makes me want to hurt him. And I'm sorry for being such a mean dick the other night."

My breath caught from his closeness, "He was never inside me."

A small movement and the phone illuminated the closet once again.

"Okay. So you didn't fuck him, and now you know I hate thinking you were. What did you think about me and Natalie?" He flicked the phone off again and total darkness engulfed us.

"I didn't like it."

Light flooded my eyes again. His eyes looked menacing, intense. "Why?" He raised the phone.

"What, are you twelve? You shut that phone off one more time; I'm going to kick you, Kade."

"How about you kiss me instead?" The tension thickened, the small space turned humid, hotter...slicker. Scents of cinnamon apples against worn leather saturated my senses.

"I don't think that would make me smile half as much as kicking you right now!"

"Seriously?" He flicked the phone off again. Darkness.

"Kade," I hissed smacking my hand against his chest. The light on the phone flickered on again and we both watched the phone tumble out of his hands and land amongst the clumps of boas and costumes at our feet.

"Tell me how you really felt," he said, eyes softening, face moving closer to mine. "I need to know," his warm breath fanned across my lips. Eyes so painfully, savagely grey that they looked lost and colorless, starving.

Fuck, his words made sweat break out on my skin. Primal. Heated. "Yeah, why is that?" The phone's light blinked out.

"I want you to hate the thought of it."

"Kade, I hated the thought of it. I hated it so much I didn't even want to know. I want to get out of this closet and away from you. Your mood swings are giving me whiplash."

"I didn't," he whispered, pulling me closer. "I didn't touch her. I ran out of there and looked for you. All I wanted was you."

For a few slow heartbeats, the only sound was our breathing, soft hot breaths against each other's skin.

"I read your book," I whispered.

His movements stilled for a moment. I feared he stopped breathing, yet just underneath the tips of my fingers, I felt the erratic acceleration of his heartbeat and I knew I had somehow affected him.

My hands closed over the material of his soft cotton shirt, fisting it in my fingers. I wanted him to know that I didn't want to let go. In the pitch-blackness, I had shaken off all my inhibitions, all my fears of not being good enough for someone.

"Dedicated to me," I whispered. Light fluttery touches, brushes of heat against my skin caused shivers that made my whole body tremble.

Thick heavy hands slid slowly up the flesh of my neck, rough fingertips sending shivers up my spine, both of us breathing loudly into each other. In the dark, my senses exploded. My pulse raced, my body melted into his. Powerful.

"Cliffhanger almost killed me. How does it end," I whispered against his lips.

"Comes out next month," he said, as warm lips brushed past mine.

"*How does it end*?" The tension coiled around us thickening, expanding, and absorbing us. In the darkness, it was a tangible smell, feel and taste. Our bodies were touching, pressed close together in the dark. I could feel him everywhere, leaning against my knees and thighs, his broad thick chest rising and falling heavily against mine.

"Brutally beautiful."

The gasp that escaped my lips caused my own breath to quicken. His hands lay on my collarbone, hot and heavy and I wanted more. I wanted to feel them slide across my skin, every last inch of me. This was so different, so different from how I'd ever felt with a man before. This was more than want, this was more than lust, this was...pure *need*.

"Fuck this. I'm not staying away from you for another second," Kade growled. Hot hands grabbed the back of my neck, our lips collided, and my legs just gave out from his touch. Kade groaned softly, low in his throat as his taste flooded into my mouth. I could have measured the moments in heartbeats, because in the deep darkness, our beating hearts was all I heard. Loud. Pounding. Rising. Twisting together.

Heavy lips opening mine, the wet swell of his tongue had me falling, falling into him. Tumbling gently at first. Then plummeting, pulse thundering in my ears, hands tangling in strands of hair, fingertips slipping...sliding. Our lips circled and nipped. His lips pulled at my bottom one, tugging and sucking. Our tongues slid against each other's, dancing and thrusting. The kiss made me dizzy. He drew me in closer, arms tightening around me, hands gripping flesh harder, and the erotic sounds of our whispered moans vibrated between our lips.

When our lips finally parted, we were both panting, tangled in each other's arms, fisting silken handfuls of one another's hair, holding on to each other like lovers. In the darkness everything outside just faded away, just us existing together, all the heartache and all the suffering gone in an instant, in his kiss.

I didn't want it to end.

A sudden rustle of the costumes below and Kade's body slid down mine, his fingers wrapping around the waistband of my pants, "I need you, Lain." His words tore an ache through my body that tingled through the muscles and flesh of the warmth in between my legs. I moaned faintly in approval, covering my hands on his, helping to slide down the material. Gently, with no light to help guide him, he unwrapped one leg out of my pants as his lips brushed my skin and a trail of wet fire was left from his tongue. His hands, warm and heavy, slid up the bare flesh of my thighs to cup my behind and squeezed with slick intense pressure. His hot breath fanned out across my thighs. "I've wanted a taste of you since the first time I saw you," he mumbled hotly against my skin, his lips and fingers reaching their goal and the long wet lick of his tongue sent me reeling, arching my body into his face. "Fuck, you're as smooth as silk. Wrap your leg over my shoulder," he whispered. Flinging my leg over his broad shoulder, his fingers reached deeper, his tongue dancing eights along my clit. *Oh my God, I can't believe we're doing this.* His faint silhouette knelt before me, my thigh against his face, his lips and tongue exquisitely torturing me. My hips rolled into his mouth and the pressure started immediately building, coiling tightly as his thick fingers moved rhythmically inside me. Sweet waves of aching heat skittered up my skin, over my belly and spread across my chest. My muscles tensed, tendons pulsed and vibrated. *He's going to make me come like this. He's going to make me come harder than I ever have before. I could feel it, the explosion riding me, pushing me, taking me.* I arched my back and jerked, shuddering against the heat of his mouth. Trembling and moaning, I melted back against the wall panting. To me, in that very instant, in the confines of the small dark closet, a Supernova was created, exploding with force under my skin, annihilating me, sending my thigh muscles into clenched quivering flesh. A tiny nip of his teeth and I moaned out in delicious agony. Shuddering, panting, I swore under my breath and arched my wet flesh up to him to take more. A future in this closet with Kade Grayson was all I wanted. "Kade, I think I just kind of fell in love with your tongue."

His lips smiled against the flesh of my thigh, wet fingers slid across smooth lips and dampened skin. "Then I can't wait to introduce you to the rest of my body."

Tugging him up by his hair, we heard the low murmur of voices and the shuffling of footsteps just outside the door. Bree's voice called out my name, as Kade slipped my undies and pant leg over my ankle, softly yanking them up my leg.

"You okay?" Kade whispered against my temple.

"If I say no, will you stay in here and introduce me to your other parts?"

Chuckling, lips brushing past my ear, "Fuck, Lainey. I want to taste you coming again. Next time, I'm going to bury myself in you and I want to hear my name on your lips when you come."

I was too stunned to realize he called out to Bree right after that, my body was still trembling and in between my thighs was a tingling throb that drummed the rhythm of Kade's name, and my panties were damp from the most intense orgasm I'd ever felt.

Blinding bright light made me squeeze my eyes shut as soon as the closet door swung open. Knowing giggles flooded from Bree's lips when she noticed how disheveled Kade and I looked, but thank God, she had the manners not to say anything. I leaned my back against the closet door, trying to adjust my eyes to the light, but my head still seemed foggy.

Dylan and Bree were explaining how they got rid of Fran; at least I think that's what they were saying. The only sounds that reached my ears were the recollections of Kade's heavy breathing and soft guttural moans. It took every ounce of restraint I had not to drag him back into the closet with me.

Kade's eyes were wide, too. He looked ravaged; stunned. His eyes locked on mine and I was utterly swept up in Kade, in his eyes, drowning, drowning, not hearing or seeing anyone else in the room. I wanted to drown in him. I wanted to feel every inch of that look against my skin. I wanted to touch every last part of him. I wanted to make him call out *my* name.

Standing there in the office with Bree and Dylan still talking about Fran, I felt faint, surreal.

Still feeling his kiss burn against my lips, I covered them with trembling fingers. His voice, deep and husky, still echoing in my mind. Nobody ever kissed me like that, with force, with need, with fucking power. Nobody ever paralyzed me with one single look. Some nameless undiscovered organ in my body had opened and Kade Grayson was pouring himself inside me, seeping into my flesh, my veins, my cells, taking over my body. I was torn between wanting him to and not.

This man pierced my soul with his eyes. I feared he was seeing too much in me, peeling open my skin to try to find all the secrets within. However, the truth still remained that I wanted his lips on me, I haven't been kissed well in ages. I hadn't felt wanted and excited about a man in forever. I knew I shouldn't want him. He was wrong for me. He was someone I could never be real with. Shit...I'd never be able to be real with anyone for the rest of my life, would I?

Bree and Dylan ended their sentences and walked out. I wondered vaguely what was said, but I was too Kade-induced to care.

"Kade?" I walked closer to him. The only response was his eyes following me. "Kade?" I whispered. "Talk to me."

"I can't control myself when I'm around you." He stepped closer to me, face leaning down into mine, hovering over me, "You don't make me crazy, you make me feel sane. Don't ask me to stay away from you. I've been doing that for too many weeks now. I feel like I've been stealing from myself something I've been starving to have. And it's you." Damp sweaty hands cupped my face, "What happened in that closet is going to happen again, and again, and a-fucking-gain, Lainey. It's never going to end." He pressed his cheek against mine, the stubble of his unshaven face sent prickles of heat across my skin. The hands cupping my face shifted, and slid over my breasts and down my stomach. "This, Lainey," he growled cupping in between my thigh, squeezing hard and releasing, "is mine. And, I'm yours. All of me. Destroy me, Lainey."

He shuffled backward, and walked out of the office, leaving me...breathless.

Oh, my God...I was smiling.

The Kade-coma didn't release me from its tight grasp until late afternoon. We spent the day cleaning, me demonstrating to everyone how to sterilize and scrub the hell out of things, and everyone moaning and groaning about me being an anal-retentive crazy clean freak. Well, everyone but Kade. Kade understood and scrubbed harder than I did, and I know this sounds sick, but it made my muscles clench and pool with want.

As night settled, and darkened the skies outside the bar windows, four men came in, a handful of regulars, and one of them, Bobby, dropped a few quarters into the old jukebox. Without looking, I could hear the familiar jingle jangle of the coins clinking against the sides of the metal as they slid in. It was so quiet in the bar that I heard the clicks of the buttons as his fingers chose the numbers to the songs, and soon after, the first guitar strums of *Paint It Black* by the *Rolling Stones* drifted eerily to my ears.

Bree, Dylan, Kade, and I, were sitting behind the bar on our small booth. Bree sat next to me, the smell of lemons, limes and thick dark beer erased the clean sent of disinfectant, and I missed its calming sterile scent. I'd been staring down at the little square napkin I'd been unknowingly folding into one of those origami animals and thinking about the heat of Kade's lips on mine, when I felt Bree shift to stand. She walked over to the group of four men as Dylan made his way to the other end of the bar. My stomach did a flip knowing Kade and I was alone at the table and just out of the view of everybody and my hands stilled their movements.

My heart rate sped up when the small cushion I sat on shifted under more weight next to me. The warmth of Kade's arm brushed against my skin and the slight touch made my body tremble. Leaning in closer, he brushed his knuckles along my jaw, immediately making my eyes meet his. So many thoughts were said between us in that stare, so many secrets were shared, so many strings were pulled that I lost myself a little drowning in those eyes.

"You're going to leave, aren't you?" he whispered.

"Why would you ask that?"

"You haven't looked at me all afternoon. Your eyes are constantly on the door, and you look ready to run...Please stay...I didn't mean to scare you before..." Intense.

"Kade, I'm not scared of you. There's just..."

An explosive gritty crack rocked through the bar, a bright flash of light and the sizzling sounds of showering sparks and broken glass shattered out across the room, landing at my feet, and the music died instantly.

Even if I had never heard a gunshot before, it was not one of those sounds that you could mistake this close, but I knew for sure with every heartbeat what it was. That explosive sound that could deafen for minutes after, the slow motion of events right after, as chaos prepared its introduction. My heart thudded hard and all my muscles tightened into fight mode. For a half of a second, the room stilled and everything was bathed in thick silence. The smell of burning wires and acid filled my nose.

"Now that I have all you redneck's attention, where can I find Samantha Matthews," the gritty voice said, and I felt it in every cell in my body. *This was it.* Game over. I'd been found. My muscles tensed. Would he kill me quickly or drag me back home and kill me slowly in front of a live audience?

I still wore the stains of my decisions in slight white scars and discoloring on my skin. The strong feelings that I once had for my husband were locked in a small hidden box, and once that gunshot rang out, once the knowledge that his heart still beat somewhere, the lid of that box popped right open. My past exploded like warfare before my eyes. The feelings that I once had of love and comfort were twisted into hate and fear.

Holding Kade's wide stare, anguish tore through me. God, please don't let him kill me in front of Kade. *Please*, don't do this to him again. I slid down onto the floor, crawled in front of the safe, and focused on turning the lock without being heard, or missing a damn number. Kade's eyes pleaded with me. His hands grabbed after me to stay. His body slid across mine to protect me. My heart surged in my chest. Tearing my gaze away from Kade, I focused on the lock to the safe.

"I'm gonna repeat the question one more time. Where the fuck is Samantha Matthews?" The voice wasn't familiar, the son-of-a-bitch must have paid someone to hunt me down. I dialed the lock to the safe. Right 12. Left 27... as Kade's tense muscles hovered over my body mumbling low, just above a breath, in one of those horror movie singsong whispers... *"2 exits. 5 windows. 4 customers. 1 waitress. 1 brother. 1 Lainey. 1 shooter. How many guns..."* His hands gripped the flesh on my arms protectively as my heart was pounding through my chest. *Oh, God, he was losing it.*

The safe's door bounced open and I grabbed for Dylan's gun. I knew it was there, and I knew it was usually loaded. All I had to do was click the magazine into place and pray the gunman didn't hear. Slipping the safety off, I tried to get out from under Kade's arms.

"Don't know anybody by the name of Samantha Matthews," Dylan's voice said. *Oh, God, Dylan shut the hell up.* I could see him at the other end of the bar, both hands raised, face probably looking into the end of the barrel of a gun, his fingers trembling.

"I'll just get her to come out then," the voice laughed dryly, as two more flashes of light and sound exploded from his gun.

Behind the bar, a mere ten feet from me, Dylan dropped instantly.

Jumping up, gun raised, I braced myself for impact. "Drop the gun," I said. From the corner of my eye, I saw George, one of the regulars standing next to Bobby, with his gun already raised right at the shooter's head.

I adjusted the aim of my gun a few inches to the right until it lined up flawlessly to the shooters forehead, knowing perfectly well George was about to pull his trigger. Another shot ripped through the bar and the shooter collapsed. Shit, it was *Deputy* George and *Deputy* Bobby, as a matter of fact, all four regulars were cops. The four men moved in sync, two surrounding the shooter's body, the other two going out to see who else was around.

Bree screamed Dylan's name, then mine. It was crushing to hear the primal sound of her heart breaking as she crawled to get to him. I recognized how scared and freaked she truly was. It was the same way when they told her about Michael. She looked at me then as she looked at me the day they found his body. *Please help me.* I didn't realize it until then that she'd fallen in love with Dylan. I nodded to her with watery eyes.

Kade reached Dylan first and slumped down mumbling next to him. Bree slid next to us hiccupping and sobbing. "He's still breathing. Please help him. I can't do this again. I can't. I can't live through another Michael, Sam." Her tears spilled, cascading waterfalls of sorrow. Desperation.

"Bree, get the car and bring me my bag. Olaes is there. Get Olaes. Bring it all," I said.

Kade was breathing heavily next to me, whispering, "Who the fuck is *Elias*? Is he a doctor?"

Dylan's eyes looked into mine; fear and surprise. "What? What's going...what the *fu*..." His eyes scanned his body, registering the blood. "Oh, God...oh, God...I don't want to die." His eyes shifted to Kade. "Kade, I...I don't want to die." Sweat started falling from his brow.

Tearing his shirt off, I scanned the wounds. Hunger and anger bubbled in my chest. Two bullets split through his skin. Slipping my hands beneath his back, I searched, no exit wound on his back, one '*through and through*' on his right arm. I was not worried about his arm, because it wasn't a life-threatening hit, but the one in his torso could be. *It could be.* The scent of fear and metal stung at my nose and the guttural sob that ripped from Kade's throat was like a steel vise that wrenched around my chest, squeezing so hard I gasped for breath. I had to stop them, to calm them before their panic spread like frost against glass, freezing and paralyzing them both. I had to stop them from making everything worse. My hand shot out to Kade. I laid my bloodied fingers against his cheek and his eyes snapped to mine. I've done this before. "It feels like you can't breathe, *but you can*. It feels like you'll never get through this, *but you will*." My own breathing regulated and I offered him an encouraging smile. "Kade," I said evenly. I slammed my hands down hard on both of Dylan's wounds, applying as mush pressure as I could. "Dylan is doing great. Let's keep him talking and thinking about other things and we're going to get him some help. *Trust me.*"

I could hear the men in the background of the bar. They had a cruiser and ambulance on the way. However, the hospital was at least a twenty-minute drive from there.

Dylan wasn't going to make that. My throat thickened as visions of granite headstones stood like soldiers in a field of dead pressed up against the sky. I pressed the weight of my body against his punctures, smiling...calmly...always show them calmness...always be the comforting voice in the middle of madness.

Bree was next to me in a flash of panting sobs and cold winds, holding my aid bag. She had the zipper open and a torn Olaes pack in her hand before I could even ask her.

"What...What...What is that?" Dylan was asking.

"This is a tourniquet that's going to save your life, sweetheart. This is called an Olaes Modular Bandage." *Calm him. Talk to him.* "It's named after a very brave soldier."

"I...I...don't want to...to die," Dylan pleaded. His words sank in my belly, chilling my bones.

"Not on my watch you won't," I answered, wrapping and pressing, sealing and praying. It wasn't even a battlefield. This was not his fault. We should have never stayed here. These people were innocent. Innocent and bleeding, spilling and splattering crimson sunsets across the floor.

Because of me.

Chapter 10
Kade

Someone shot the jukebox.

With a gun.

A gun.

Oh fuck. Oh fuck. I squeezed my eyes shut tight. *This isn't happening again. This can't be happening AGAIN!* Violent anger crashed in waves over me so powerfully that I couldn't see straight. I grabbed for Lainey blindly. I needed her behind me, away from the danger. I wasn't letting anyone hurt what was mine.

Mine?

That's what I thought, wasn't it? It was what I told her, wasn't it? When we got out of the closet, I grabbed her and called her mine like a Neanderthal.

I'd have to revisit this moment after the shitstorm passes. I needed to hide Lainey under me and protect her from being hit. But, she was crawling away. *Fuck, she was CRAWLING AWAY FROM ME!* Crawling towards the gunman's voice, towards Dylan standing with his hands raised at the far end of the bar, just crawling, slinking right into the danger on hands and knees. Panic gurgled, boiled frantically in the back of my throat. Then she stopped at the safe as I yanked on her leg, trying to place her body under mine. Shield her.

The gunman was talking again and my gag reflex started playing with me...*2 exits. 5 windows. 4 customers. 1 waitress. 1 brother. 1 Lainey. 1* *shooter. How many guns...Deputies at tables...*The walls were closing in around me. *I have to get Lainey and Dylan out of here alive.*

Two more gunshots rang out, slicing through the coiled fear of the room, and then my brother fell. Dylan just dropped to the ground, collapsing as if he'd fainted.

What the...?

Confusion muddled my brain. Did he faint? *He fainted, right? Please, God, just let him have fainted, let him just be a pussy and have fainted.* I crawled on my hands and knees for my brother. I tried to drag Lainey with me, yanked on her pant leg hard, but *she fucking stood up.* I felt the sob in my throat before it escaped my lips. I did not want to watch her die. I needed to get that gun away from her and kill whoever it was on the other side of the bar, before they shot Lainey, but she moved so quickly, she was out of my reach in a second.

With a noticed familiarity, Lainey clicked the magazine holding all the bullets into the gun, securing the fact it was fully loaded. *How the hell did she know how to do THAT?* Calmly, taking off the safety as she stood, she aimed it at the shooter. "Put. The. Gun. Down," the calmness in her voice had a razor-sharp edge. *Oh, God no. Don't shoot Lainey.*

One gunshot rang out in front of her and she didn't even flinch. Shoving the gun in the back of her pants, I could hear Bobby and George's voices calling out for backup and securing the building. Backing away, I crawled over to my brother, but I couldn't see him. All I saw was blood.

People ran around us, yelling and screaming, yet all I saw was the dark red blood that spread and seeped across the thin material of his shirt. Dylan was shot, and he was dying.

With a calmness that stopped my jittering heart, Lainey kneeled down and talked to Dylan. Her voice was steady and authoritative, yet I barely heard the words. I had no understanding of anything but my little brother had been shot, bleeding and in pain. She was suddenly wrapping him in some sort of bandage that suctioned down over the bullet holes while she spoke to him in even, gentle whispers.

"Kade," she said to me in that same methodic voice, laying her hand on my face. "Go get one of those men and have them help me put Dylan in my car."

I stood and stumbled. "But the ambulance…"

She grabbed my face in both her hands, the rusty smell of blood choked my airways. "Do it now. He doesn't have twenty extra minutes to wait." She spoke the words with a quiet calm brutality.

I grabbed George, the biggest and youngest one, and dragged him over as Lainey had Bobby calling the hospital straight and telling them that we'd be there in less than twenty minutes and then had a brief conversation that included a bunch of medical terms that no fucking waitress should know.

Carefully, George and I carried Dylan out and stopped in front of a freaking *Porsche*; engine running. Lainey was in front of us opening doors and jumped right into the driver's seat, banging the hood of the car for me to get Dylan in.

We gently laid him in the backseat. Bree climbed in after him, and I was shoved in by George and yanked by Lainey at the same time. I wasn't even right side up in the front passenger seat and she was already shifting the car into drive and slamming on the gas pedal.

She pulled out of the lot as if she knew what the fuck she was doing. She didn't stop accelerating as her eyes glanced over to mine. "Kade, seatbelt. And keep your eyes to the right for traffic. I'm not stopping unless I have to and I need directions once we hit town."

Her eyes snapped to the rearview mirror and with a soft voice continued to speak with Dylan, "I'm going to get you to the hospital fast. How are you feeling, buddy?"

"Fucking hurts," he coughed. His voice crept into my chest like cold dead hands on my heart, squeezing it tight.

Lainey pressed her foot down on the gas harder and asked, "Bree, how was that cough?"

"Clear," Bree answered back through a garbled sob.

Flipping the dome lights on, she asked, "Skin color."

"Perfect," Bree sighed.

"Awesome. You're doing great, Dylan. I'm going to drive with the lights on so Bree can watch you for any signs of stress, because she's a big scaredy-cat when it comes to hospitals and such, and I think she's a little in love with you so, I just want to make her feel better."

"Yeah, mate," he said. *She was just keeping him talking. She was keeping him breathing.* She was saving his life. She was saving my brother's life.

The dial on the speedometer hit 150 miles per hour, and kept going while my hands gripped the seat. *How fucking fast does this little car go?* The surge of adrenaline pumping through my veins helped me focus on Lainey's voice during the whole drive, grounding me.

"You know, Dylan, there's an ancient Chinese saying that goes, '*You can live with a man for forty years. You could share his house, his meals, and talk with him every day about his every secret. Then tie him up, and hold him over a volcano's edge, one that's about to erupt. And on that day, you will finally meet the man.*' You're one hell of a strong man, Dylan Grayson." She glanced over to me quickly, "And so is your brother."

"Feels like I'm...feels like I'm in the volcano. Burns."

"We're almost there, Dylan, and as soon as we get there, you'll get something for the pain okay?"

The first glimpse of light from the old gas station's neon sign took my breath away. It couldn't have taken Lainey more than eight minutes to get to the town's border. "Slow down up near that diner that we ate at. You're going to make a left and the hospital is about a mile up that road," I said, trying to match the calm tone of

Lainey's voice. "Dylan, do you remember when Old Lady Bitlermeyer drove straight through the old gas station's sign and she wouldn't let me help her out?"

"Yeah, mate. She....said you were....the angel of death, coming to take her soul," Dylan wheezed. Not even listening to his answers, I just kept him talking, just as Lainey did, until the bright lights of the hospital came into view. I couldn't believe she'd gotten him there alive. The surge of hope in my chest burned a thick knot of fire so hot I had trouble breathing.

As soon as Lainey stepped foot out of the car, she grabbed the first guy in a white coat, told them who we were, and started sprouting off words that I would be definitely questioning later. An entire trauma team rushed through the pressure plate doors rolling a gurney and slammed it up against the hood of the Porsche with a loud crunch. When they pulled my brother out of the car, his face was pale and he was soaked with sweat. Lainey ran to him. "Two gunshot wounds...Possible right subclavian artery, loss of blood stunted by pressure and trauma tourniquet. Possible lung damage...Shortness of breath and wheezing, not coughing up blood yet and still able to speak. There are two trauma tourniquets around both wounds."

Strapped down to the gurney, Dylan was whisked away, with Lainey and Bree on both sides of the nurses, running through the sliding doors of the ER. Slowly following behind, the bright white florescent lights made my eye sockets ache and my temples throb. I watched as they wheeled Dylan into a hallway and out of my sight.

The sliding doors closed behind me and the room seemed to blur and wobble. Black spots crowded the corners of my sight and the floor slipped up to meet me. Iciness seeped under my skin, spreading like an infectious virus throughout my body. *Please God, don't let him die. Please don't take him away from me.*

Lainey's beautiful face was the next thing I saw. Her hands were cool on my skin, bringing my eyes back into focus and her soft smooth lips against mine brought my thoughts back from the chaos of my hell. Pulling me into a seat, she put her trembling hands into mine and then she did something that nobody in this world had ever fucking done to me. She laid her silky head against my chest, as if I were some sort of *comfort to her*.

Her fucking head was on my chest and she was taking comfort in *me*.

Laying her head right over my heart.

All I could do was to stare down at her in wonder. Then I wrapped my arms around her so tightly that I feared I might suffocate her. We stayed there like that for hours. I could barely breathe the whole time, because I was overwhelmed with the flood of a thousand emotions that I had hidden myself from for over a decade. They all came rushing in, thickening in my throat, burning in my chest and quietly streaming from my eyes. I didn't care who or what Lainey was, I just wanted her completely. Never in my sick life did I ever give a bit of hope about finding a person who was compatible, who could find comfort in someone as fucking twisted as me.

Silence ate away at the hours as hope devoured my fears.

Together, with Lainey holding me up, we waited for word on Dylan.

Bree sat across from us, lost to some unnamed place, eyes saturated with tears.

We sat frozen, like empty glass jars, on the cracked leather benches of the hospital waiting room, ready to fall and shatter into sharp shards across the floor. The voices of the deputies drifted past my ears as they asked questions that I swore Lainey was not giving straight answers to. Somehow, filled Styrofoam cups of coffee appeared like magic in my hands. Bree began pacing after two hours and Lainey was the only person who could speak the scientific language those asinine doctors spoke each time they came out with updates.

I sat, unmoving; way past the hour when my coffee turned cold until a smooth outstretched hand touched my chin and lifted my head to meet with pale green eyes. "Dylan is doing well. He's in recovery right now. He's going to be fine." Her fingers squeezed my chin, almost painfully, "Do you hear me, Kade? He's fine." Her eyes filled with thick fat tears that fell from long lashes, and her lips smiled wide.

She saved my brother's life. Dylan is not dead.

I crushed her body against mine and sighed in relief, breathing her in. She trembled slightly in my arms and repeated her words softly, "He's fine."

We stayed throughout the early morning hours and the next day, until Dylan was able to have visitors and despite all of the tubes and machines, he made horrible jokes about seeing *the light* and getting kicked out of heaven before he could even step in. Seeing him laugh so soon after being shot was euphoric, like a kid at Christmas. The surgeons kept explaining to us how lucky he had been that the bullet in his chest hadn't pierced a lung and that the bandages Lainey used on his arm saved it from being amputated. They couldn't stop saying how Lainey saved his life, and she just nodded and smiled softly like it wasn't a big deal and sat in the corner of the room quietly.

I watched her battle her eyelids to stay open; the war was a fierce one that she almost lost a number of times. Exhaustion settled over her features, and I offered to drive her car back to the trailer so she could wash up and change. She had been sitting in the emergency room covered in my brother's blood. She had to get my brother's blood off her. I couldn't stand seeing her with so much blood all over her; I wanted to wash it off her myself, find her beautiful smooth skin beneath.

She didn't fight me on it, just stood up, kissed a sleeping Dylan on the forehead, spread a blanket over Bree who was fast asleep next to his hospital bed, and trudged out of the room. As soon as her ass was in the passenger seat, she passed out cold; I even had to buckle her in.

The drive back was silent; my thoughts though, were anything but. Nothing made sense to me. *Why hadn't she freaked out? How was she so calm? And how did she spread that calmness to me? How did she do everything she did? Why did she have those bandages? Did she have to take a CPR class because she was a waitress?* Shit, I wasn't stupid, I knew there was seriously more to it, I just wasn't ready to admit anything yet, but a waitress she was not. *And whose Porsche was this?*

I woke her softly as soon as I pulled into her driveway, but when she opened her eyes and looked past me, I knew something was wrong. Her eyes were full of tears and I snapped my head in the direction she'd been staring.

The door to her trailer was torn off the hinges, broken in two and thrown against the stairs, like a child's toy that had been long forgotten. Vile, demoralizing words had been painted in neon spray paint across the front of the tiny white trailer. *Bitch. Cunt. You're going to die.*

With no regard for her safety, Lainey was out of the car and rushed through the ransacked trailer. "Lainey, stop, it's too fucking dangerous!" I called after her.

She ran in anyway and I fumbled like a madman out of the car after her. Instantly, she had my brother's gun in her hands, and stepped through the open doorway, surveying the room, as you'd see a police officer do on a crime show.

Windows were shattered, broken in, as if someone had taken a baseball bat to them, and glistening shards of glass littered the rocky ground.

Running up the wooden steps, I stopped just inside the threshold of the doorway and watched Lainey sink to her knees, surrounded by the mess of debris that used to be her cozy little home. "Clear," she yelled out loud in a haunted voice, but I had a strange feeling she wasn't really talking to me.

Dirt and mud caked the furniture that was all bashed and battered across the floor. Piles of what smelled like *fucking shit* towered over her tabletop and across her walls written in thick red ketchup, or some sort of morbid looking sauce, were the words: *Peek-A-Boo-Samantha-I see you.* Deep beneath all of it was some rancid smell of decay. I gathered my arms around her kneeling form, as if in prayer, and lifted her off the repulsive floor. Cradling her in my arms, I carried her to the bedroom and sat her on the bed. "Pack a bag for yourself and Bree. Take anything that's important, I'm calling the police."

"NO!"

"Are you fucking serious right now? Look at your trailer!"

"I can't...get the police involved."

Sitting on her bed, I pulled her into my arms and held her, let the world fix its-fucking-self, my brain shut to autopilot and I brought her closer, nestling her against my chest. *I'll just take her home with me, protect her.*

After a few moments, she untangled herself from my arms and began rummaging through drawers, shoving clothes into a large duffel bag. "What hotels are near that hospital?"

"Come home with me," I whispered.

"Shut up, Kade."

"Fuck you, Lainey, or whoever the fuck you are. You think after all this shit that I'll let you out of my sight? Fuck you."

"This isn't a game! Just shut up. Just shut the fuck up!" She slung the duffel bag over her shoulder, grabbed what looked like a computer bag from under her bed, and rushed for the door.

Before she could get past me, I kicked the door closed, and backed her up against a wall filled with craters of broken plaster. Slamming my hands on the walls on both sides of her head, I wedged her against the wall and my body, ensuring the fact that she wasn't getting away. *She could fucking shoot me for all I cared.*

Grabbing hold of her face with a tight grip, I tried to make myself perfectly clear. "You are coming home with me."

Without warning, a slap hit my face that stung like a bitch, "Don't put me in a corner, Grayson, my fucking claws will come out."

My fingers tightened around her chin, making her eyes narrow in challenge.

Her hand shot out for another slap, but I caught it in my fist, tangled her fingers with mine and pressed my forehead to hers. I felt her rage, it rolled off her in strong waves, and I took it, crushing my body against her and covering her mouth with mine. What traitorous vessels our bodies are to fold into each other with violence, melt into each other in danger and anger. Her lips opened to mine and I slipped in, never wanting to leave the heat of her breath, but I had to, I did, just long enough to say, "You. Are. Staying. With. Me."

From one of her pockets the shrill electronic beeps of a cell phone screamed out. I pulled away from her, allowing her to take the call.

"Hey, Bree. Everything okay? Yeah, you were both sleeping and Kade drove me home."

She listened to the reply, eyes fixed on mine. I took the bags and started walking to the door to put them in the car.

"That's great. Yes. Yes. Okay." She gave a small sigh. "Listen, we can't stay at the trailer, someone broke into it...Yeah, it's bad, looks like something out of *Scarface*..." She started to explain, and then closed herself in the small bathroom to finish the rest of the conversation without me hearing, but I was out of the trailer anyway, getting ready to take her out of there.

The drive to my house was silent. She spent the ride worrying her lip and twisting her fingers around the hem of her coat. We spoke no words to each other until she was standing in my living room, eyes wide, looking about ready to puke.

"May I sit?" she asked in a small voice. "My legs are trembling."

"Yeah," I croaked, barely able to get the word out.

Lainey sank to the floor in one fluid movement, like a cascading waterfall. Running to her, I pulled her up, and tugged her over for a better place to sit. I stared at her as she sat, eyes closed on the couch, hands trembling. My brother's blood, caked all over her was revolting and contradictory to her smooth ivory skin. I traced a trail of crimson with my thumb, rubbing the smear from her cheek. Her eyes opened wide, taking in my closeness and my deeds. My fingers couldn't help but linger against her face.

Lifting her in my arms, I carried her into my master bathroom and placed her on the chaise lounge chair. I ran the bath and dumped a shitload of bubbly soap inside. I distinctly noticed a sheen of sweat covering her forehead and I swallowed hard. "I have to get that blood off you. I can't...I can't look at you covered in blood."

"I know," she whispered.

"I want you to stay here with me. You're not leaving my sight," I snapped.

"I can't get you involved in this, Kade. It's not your fight."

"You just can't leave what's happened here. My brother is in the fucking hospital so you can't leave him, and you can't take Bree away from him."

"Bree has nothing to do with any of this, Kade. She could stay here with him. Hell, I want her too."

"You can't leave me."

"Kade, please."

"I'm not letting you leave me. You don't want to either."

"Can you stop doing that crap? Just get out of my head and stay out. There's so much chaos in there, you might get hurt."

I swept the hair away from her neck, tucking it behind her ear and the pulse in her throat came into view, pounding fast under her skin. "It's because you're screaming your thoughts at me. And just so you fucking know, you WILL tell me who Samantha Matthews is and why my brother almost lost his life for her," I exploded.

That shut her up. Backing up, I walked out of the bathroom.

I shut the door quietly behind me, giving her the privacy that she deserved, even though all I wanted was to sink inside of her and forget about what happened in the last twenty-four hours. *I left her there for my bitter curiosity too, I won't lie, because now I had a name to search, Samantha Matthews from New York City.*

I sat at my desk and powered up my laptop, just as small pellets of icy rain began their assault at my window.

Chapter 11

Lainey

Kade Grayson was the most unbearable, arrogant and demanding man, I'd ever met. What was worse is that he was the only man ever to be able to get me really worked up, and I was like a damn piece of putty in his hands.

From right outside the bathroom windows, a loud roar of rain began crashing against the glass. Within seconds, the even louder roar of my own blood rushing through my ears drowned it out, as I thought about my options. *I needed to get away from here.* I needed to keep them safe. I had clamped my mouth shut when he told me I couldn't leave his sight, and tried my best to throw him a hard glare, but I was absolutely positive with the state of my bloody attire and my matted hair, I didn't look too fierce.

As the tub filled with steamy water and bubbles, the faint smell of cinnamon and apples drifted through the room.

That man bought the soap I used? Opening the large linen closet, I found a bottle of the body spray too. If it weren't the most heartwarming thing I'd ever felt, I'd think it was a little creepy. *But, no* I didn't find it creepy at all. Nope. I found it gave me a warm tingling feeling all over my body. I. Needed. An. Intervention.

Stepping back from the closet, I looked around the bathroom and found myself wondering if anybody ever actually used it. It was too clean, immaculate, and sterile; I loved it. Everything in the closet was in a perfect little neat row, labels facing forward, each item in size order and even the towels were all folded to the same thickness. A perfect textbook example of compulsive behaviors of a control freak who was trying to create order in their chaotic life. It was as if I'd found my OCD-soul mate.

Stripping off my bloodied clothes and stepping into the warm water, I scrubbed my skin of blood, then immediately emptied the tub, refilled it with clean water and laid back into its warmth. Groaning out loud, I covered my face with my hands. I couldn't think straight. I couldn't think past the fact that Dylan got shot because of me and that *everyone* saw me save him. *Kade knows I'm not a waitress now and as soon as I step foot out of this bathroom, the questions are going to come flying at me like mortar fire.*

The door suddenly swung open, making me gasp, and Kade's menacing presence filled up the doorway, *half freaking naked*. Oh, it gets better. Wait for it.

Wait for it...

Then he dove right into the tub.

He splashed through the bubbles and water in nothing but a pair of black slacks. My stomach fluttered, and my hands curled into tight fists as the splashes of the water hit me. Water and suds spilled over the lip of the tub, splatting and sloshing all over the tiles in loud wet thwacks. "Grayson, you are seriously crossing the line of my bathroom boundaries here. I'm...I'm not dressed!"

Grey eyes registering my state, scanned across the bubbles that I was trying desperately to hide under. But with the savage way he dove in, there wasn't much left to conceal myself with, and I saw his eyes widen and hunger took over reason. Slowly, a flush of heat crept across my naked chest, up my bare throat and onto my cheeks. My God, if I could bottle the way that man looked at me, I'd never feel unattractive again. It was an *indulgent* feeling, one I wanted to keep, sip at it, swirl it around my tongue for a while, and then swallow. Any sense of guilt or shame, fear or insecurity was absent, and all I felt was *beautiful*, as if I could stand up before him and be viewed as a priceless, one of a kind sculpture, perfect and unbreakable.

The way he looked at me made me forget the things I was upset over. *Whatever they were that I was just thinking about.*

The sight of him was gloriously perfect, how...how to describe what this man looked like? The muscles of his entire torso were clearly defined and they rippled as he moved towards me. His shoulders, thick and solid, his arms tight and sinewy, he was the perfect specimen of a male and I simply couldn't take my eyes from him.

"It was my turn to use *Google*," he whispered hoarsely, his wet hands reached my chin, lifting it to him.

"Did you know that there's a missing person's report on two women from New York City? One's name is Jennifer Coswell, and the other is Samantha Matthews. Jennifer is a nurse at *New York-Presbyterian University Hospital* and

Samantha, well Samantha Matthews is the fucking head trauma surgeon there," his nostrils flared. "And they're both wanted for questioning in some sort of suspicious circumstances."

I tried to pull away, but he savagely grabbed the back of my neck and held me there; his cold grey eyes frozen, waiting for answers. I couldn't find the right ones. I couldn't find the words that would tell him...anything. I just wanted to run, run so he wouldn't know me, the real me. "Well, I hope those two woman are okay. Because, sometimes I hear stories like that and wonder, maybe, if certain women are better off missing than being found. But I wouldn't know anything about them, because I'm Lainey Nevaeh, and I've never been anything but a waitress."

"If you keep piling more bullshit on your story, you're going to get buried in it. You have some sort of dark fucking secret that you think you can't tell me, and I want to know. I want to know you." Leaning in, his rough, unshaven chin scraped harshly against mine, "I want to know you." Wet lips slid over mine, and the hands that held me down tangled themselves tightly through the wet strands of my hair, tugging my face closer to his.

My eyes fluttered closed with the pull, and there was nothing in the room, nothing in the world, but his mouth on mine, and the sounds of the lapping water against the porcelain tub. Pressing the warm tip of his tongue across my lips, he parted them, dipping in, persuading me to give in, to lay me bare, know my secrets. "Let me in, Lainey."

Wet fingers slid down my neck as I leaned back to look at him. "Something dark haunts us all. What darkness haunts you at night, Kade? What do you squeeze your eyes closed to when the darkness bites against your back when you're alone at night? Because I was married to mine. I was daughter to mine, and I refused to look into the mirror and see it make me as dark as them, so I walked away from it all."

Reaching my hands up, I pulled a white towel that hung from a small brushed-nickel hook on the wall. As Kade thudded his head back against the corner of the tub, his eyes fluttered closed and I stood, wrapping the towel tightly around me.

"Please don't push me away. Let me know you," he whispered when I reached the door.

"How very fucking hypocritical of you, Kade. Weren't you just the one in your truck screaming for me to get out when I tried to get you to talk to me? Why did you push me away? Why do you push everyone away? Maybe you have things you don't know how to talk about, maybe you've seen things that you don't want to see again, maybe you can't even get the words to fumble out of your mouth. Whatever reason it is, Kade, you should understand that it's probably the same reason as mine."

"I can't trust anyone," he whispered, clipped.

"Me neither," I replied.

"I'm not comfortable around people," he snapped.

"Join the *fucking club*. We meet in the bar every Wednesday night at ten," I said, stomping out of the room and grabbing my bag of clothes. I tore it open and shoved a shirt over my head and a pair of yoga pants on without wasting my time searching for any under garments. I growled out loud when I looked down and realized my shirt was on backwards. *Screw it.* I left it on anyway.

Kade was storming out of the bathroom, soaking wet pants, slicked against his skin and dripping all over his rug. "Don't fucking walk away from me. I'm doing what you wanted. I've been fucking telling you everything!"

"BULLSHIT!" I screamed. "The lack of exposition from a fucking award winning writer astounds me," I yelled, barking out a hideous laugh at his expense. "You haven't told me anything. I found out everything by reading about you online, and you know what? It still doesn't scratch the surface, does it? Because an entire town of people hate you and fear you. That's not what would normally happen when someone goes through a tragedy like that. You did something that scares the hell out of everybody so much that even your own brother is afraid to push you to live!" His expression looked ashen, repulsed by the words I was saying, "What, Kade? Just say it! Scream at me to get the fuck out again! But don't expect me to tell all of my secrets to a total stranger, no matter how good he is at making me come with his mouth." I shot him a tight smile, and shoving my feet into my sneakers, I strode past him and out his bedroom door. *I couldn't believe I had just said that,* but I needed him to let it go. I needed to keep him away from all my problems, because it was safer.

There was a small staircase at the end of the corridor that I didn't remember Kade carrying me up when we first arrived, and I barreled down each step as the wood tapped and echoed my footfalls.

Kade caught me halfway down, grabbing my waist, "Samantha, stop. Please."

My knees weakened hearing the name I loved, the name I missed so much, fall from his lips. It brought me right to the edge though, right to the edge of losing it, not certain if I'd scream more or lash out in tears, so I bit down on my tongue to stop myself.

He stepped ahead of me, pulling me down against the hard surface of the stairs causing me to slam down on the side of my cheek. It wasn't painless, but it also didn't warrant a cry, but I knew I'd be bruised in the morning. He fiercely cupped my face to make me focus on him. I closed my eyes.

"*Don't* block me out." He pressed my body against the wall of the stairs, my head lightly thudding against the handrail. His wet pants seeped a cold dampness into my skin. "I want to saw off my own hand, just so that I could let you go, let you go to keep you safe from *my* mind, from my issues. But you, you're just like me, right? Something's wrong inside you too."

"Fuck you," I spat, pushing him off me. "You're still not saying anything to me, Kade. You are still regurgitating the same fucking bullshit, just a little more poetically."

Without effort, he lifted my body off the stairs, carrying me down the rest of the way into a darkened living area and tossed me on a large couch, pinning me down with his weight. The feel of him on top of me made me breathless and needy. Burying his face into the side of my neck, hot breath fanned against my skin, and open lips across my flesh.

"You're adorable when you're angry," he whispered, breathing heavily.

"Oh, really? Then get the hell off me, because I'm about to get gorgeous all over your ass."

His sudden kiss stunned me, and the heavy thundering of his heart against my chest made my lips open to him. Breathing in each other, lips drinking thirstily from each other, I couldn't stop. My body wanted him too much.

His arms slid around me, hands slipping over my stomach, closing over my breasts. Cupping me tightly through my shirt, catching my nipples between his fingers, he squeezed gently, making my breathing uneven. "You want to know it all, Samantha, I'll give it all to you," he whispered against my lips.

The pressure of his fingers tightened; the pinch bringing tears to my eyes as the little tease of pain surged though my chest and pooled as thick hot need in my belly. *Do you know what it's like to HAVE to continue breathing, dreaming, thinking, living, hating, needing, while the friends you once had are rotting deep below the dirt?*

What happened to me that day shattered my trust in the world; my belief in goodness and innocence. It was my introduction to what is truly evil. I didn't understand it at sixteen how I could have had a best mate, like a brother, do something so...so...heinous. It was NOT clear to me. He joked about it... I didn't know the right way to feel and the remorse, the guilt, the shame paralyzed me. IT. STILL. DOES. It wasn't like I got a bloody email from God that pleasantly said: *'Kade Grayson, I have looked over the situation with your best mate Thomas and his complete annihilation of innocent youth, and I'm just dropping a line to let you know I consider your knowledge of the subject, and your continued love for your childhood friend to show no guilt of association for the murders and I hereby drop all judgment against you. You're free to live with no regrets. You're hereby off the hook. You have a guaranteed full paid ticket into heaven when your time comes. Signed, God. Cheers.'"* The scruff of his unshaven face scraped sharply against my skin as he pulled away from me. A small moment of silence sliced through the air and the only sound that reached my ears was the heavy breaths we both took.

I wanted to cry for him. Brushing my knuckles past his cheek, I said, "That guilt and shame you have for surviving is going to destroy you, *it is destroying you.* It's like a lethal injection that you've given to yourself. You're fucking drowning in it. Guilt is like a fucking cancer, Kade. If you don't stop, it will creep and crawl into every crack and crevice of your soul and *kill you.*"

"I'm not guilty for surviving. I'm guilty *because I knew he was going to do it.* He joked about it. For fucking months, I didn't take him seriously, and I could have stopped it. Lainey, *he went for me first*, shooting both my fucking legs so I couldn't run, then picked off every single person in that room and made me watch and told me I should have listened to him. I could have stopped him. Then he blew a hole in my chest, and finished off anyone else that moved. I wasn't supposed to live."

"Kade," I whimpered, struggling to get up.

"No. No. No. Listen to me. You wanted to hear everything, know everything. I'm going to fucking give you everything," he hissed, hands gripped my face. "There will be no excuse for you not to trust in me. I'm giving you everything I am, right fucking now."

I tried to hold back my tears, but the words, the expression on his face, and God, the grip of his fingers just hurt so much.

"Their lives were over. Over. *All of them.* None of them would feel the warmth of the sunshine against their skin or get to look upon the shining stars in a midnight sky again. They wouldn't be graduating with me that next year, learning to drive or fall in love and marry. They would *never* have those things. Never. They would *NEVER*."

He pressed his lips softly against my bruised cheek, causing a small lick of pain. "School shootings are so breathtakingly evil. They carry such suffering that is so far beyond the imagination, so fucking inconceivable to any ordinary human thoughts that no one can ever understand. No one can understand why, and no one can understand me. Everybody thinks they could figure out why, but they can't, they never will. Thomas wasn't someone you could ever think would do such violence. He was popular and everybody loved him...He wasn't clamoring for acceptance or attention. He wasn't bullied, or gay, or too short, too fat, too dumb or awkward, not a juvenile delinquent, not a depressed or disgruntled teen, not anything they claimed his reasons might be. He was a fucking psychopath, sly and clever. Thomas was the most charming and well-mannered little psychopath you could have ever met. I have spent years, years, trying to put reasons to what he did. And there are *none.*

What he did in front of me re-wired my brain. I resorted to violence - lavish in it now, so I stay away from everything and everyone so it doesn't completely overthrow me. It's like I feel as if I can become *him.* Redemption for me is unthinkable, because I still grieve for my best friend, and the fact that I still miss him...is sick. Nobody ever understood me after. And everyone blamed me, accused me of planning it with him, encouraging him, creating a suicide pact with him. He left diaries and video journals telling whomever would listen that it was my fault for not stopping him. And he was right. I should have stopped him. And I shouldn't miss him."

I heard him swallow, felt it against my skin. He tangled his fingers through mine and tightened his grip. *I think he was using me for strength.* "I mean, I didn't understand any of it. School was supposed to be a safe place. My girlfriend, we had just started dating, she...she was shot with a sawed off shotgun which blew a hole in her chest the size of a baseball. It blew her fucking shirt right off her body. That was the first time I'd seen her without a shirt on. Do you know what that's like? To get to see the tits you been trying to see for two months with a bloody gaping hole between them. It was horrific.

Bodies were all around me. All I saw were limp bodies. Some moved sluggishly trying to escape, gasping for their lasts breath. I can still see them, in front of me, as if it was happening all over again. The sounds were inhuman. Cries. Pleas. Gasping rattles of blood through lungs. The sounds of boots sloshing through the thick puddles of the blood coated floor."

Kade laughed darkly, a choking sound that made my chest ache and I needed a break, a pause. A moment to help me deal with how fucked up everything was that he was saying, but he kept up. Anguish and savageness dripped off his words. "There were blast holes in the monitors of the computers in the back of the classroom and someone's sneaker, smeared with blood, covered a keyboard with a dangling mouse moving back and forth. Back and forth. I was left hollow inside; my insides...the things that made me *Kade*, never escaped that classroom. *He never made it out of that school alive.*"

Kade shifted off me and stood. The absence of his weight and tightness of the grasp he had on me, made my body throb with pain. He walked over to a stone fireplace and went about building a fire and as the first flames licked at the dry wood he had placed inside, the scent of pine and burning cedar filled the room. His muscular broad back, full of its hard ridges and tight muscles held a tattooed list that ran down his spine. A list of names, 32 of them, with Thomas' at the very bottom. Just as if he'd carried the weight of them on his shoulders and down his spine since that very day. My throat knotted and I jutted my chin out painfully to stop my tears from falling. Kade Grayson was not the kind of man that wanted anyone's pity, but I sure as hell wanted desperately to cry out loud and sob for the sixteen-year old boy who lived through that hell. As he turned back to face me, a log crackled in the fireplace and a burst of small sparks shot against the darkness of the room.

I folded my legs underneath my body and leaned further into the cushions of the couch, quickly wiping at the stream of tears rushing down my cheeks. "Have you ever spoken to anyone about this?" I asked.

He was gazing down at something on the floor, and I waited patiently until he lifted his head and pained pale eyes locked on mine. "No."

"But, you should. Talking through these..."

"Will do nothing," he snapped. "Don't. Please, don't."

"But you're telling me?"

His body collapsed on the couch next to me. "I think you're hiding demons too, Samantha Matthews. I want you to introduce me to all of them, because I think I finally found someone whose demons would play nice with my own. It's okay if I call you Samantha Matthews, right?"

I sat silent.

He leaned his head back and offered me a sad smile. *"Fine, I'll fucking continue giving you everything.* Shot after shot. Pop. Pop. Pop. Then clicks, like he didn't believe all the bullets were used, repeatedly pulling back the trigger in hopes that more bullets would tear through our flesh. I was so happy he was out of bullets...*but, no* I was wrong. The insanity didn't stop, because he had more fucking guns, with a hell of a lot more ammunition. He never even told me he was that angry. He just joked about it, so I thought it was just a morbid joke. I never even knew he had a gun. I never thought he was serious.

After the massacre, *I mean it was still surreal to me*, that word, massacre. How many people can say they've lived through a massacre? After the massacre, I became fascinated with blood, especially my own. How it ran through my body, what kept it pulsing through my veins, and the biggest question I could never find the answer to, was why my heart was strong enough to keep surging that blood through my bullet riddled body when my *fucking mind wasn't.* Why did I survive? I know I didn't *live* after the incident, but why the fuck did I survive?

I was hospitalized for weeks after, but all I remember was pain and news reporters, which in essence was the same monster, wasn't it? When I finally got released from the hospital, I spent the majority of my time locked inside my room repeatedly slicing open my skin with razorblades like it was a drug. Just to watch my blood flow, watch the choices it made...to clot or to run thickly down my arm in one long stream of crimson. I could feel the quickening of my blood as it thickened and pulsated through my veins. How many people can say they feel that?"

He ran his fingers through his hair, tugging its ends, and scratched at his scruffy face. With a corded neck and clenched jaw, he continued, "Finding me one day, hands bloodied and scarred, my mother dragged me to the hospital and they kept me there for evaluation and questioning.

Did I have blood lust?

Did I feel the need to hurt myself?

Did I feel aggressive towards anyone?

He was my best friend, how did I not know?

Was I in on the plan?

They listened to my fears. I didn't want to go outside. I always needed an escape plan...but to them, my fears weren't justified, and medicine was their answer to everything. They believed I was just as sick as Thomas was. Why do people always vilify the people they don't understand?

Then came the fucking *Lithium*. They said I was bipolar, manic, beyond repair. So they gave me mood-altering drugs for voices I did not hear and mania I did not feel. I had to have blood tests to closely monitor me and regulate the toxicity of the drugs in my bloodstream. Do you know what it's like on that? I threw up for a month straight and lost 25 pounds. You don't get high on it, nope -

but you can enjoy some other wonderful benefits, including, but not limited to shit like diarrhea, vomiting, numbness of the brain. God *that's fucking fun*, and oh yeah, this one's the best...permanent deadness. Now, the other shit they shoved down my throat got me high; I hated not being in control. I hated sleeping, nodding out like a fucking junky all the time, moody and irritable. Insatiable.

I was a normal fucking sixteen-year-old kid before this shit. I had seen horror movies, I was well read and smart, I knew what I could turn into because of this. I knew there might be a monster lurking somewhere inside me waiting to escape. And I waited and watched, wondering when the Mr. Hyde in me would introduce himself. Nightmares kept me up, drugs put me out, and my mind was so out of focus and narcotic-induced-comatose that I would sometimes forget my own damn name.

Psychotropic oval-shaped blue pills made me constipated, gave me a sharp case of palsy in my limbs, and kept me in various states of fear and madness. I wasn't crazy, but they were making me become it. I was a walking zombie, a twisted imitation of myself, damaged by violence and tragedy. They called me delusional and paranoid. They called me the *dead kid walking*. But when I didn't take the medications they offered me as my cure, I would still see the splashes of blood against my skin, still smell the gun powder, still hear the echoes of the bullets and laughter. I could still see those fucking pitch-black colorless eyes of my tormentor, my best friend, as he tried in vain to kill me.

The world was trying to change me, telling me I was broken and damaged inside. I decided I was better off on my own, where people wouldn't assume I was going to turn into the monster that attacked me, like it was a contagious disease.

I ceased to be a person, and instead, became a case fucking study in violence. I became mute, voiceless for months, not wanting to give them anything more than what they took from me. So I wrote in one of those composition notebooks. It was an outlet for my adolescent aggression, my violent thoughts... I was alone and learned to live with the gruesome imagery in my head, by writing. The doctors kept telling me that it was all in my head, but what they forgot was that it had been in front of me. All of it was laid out brutally for my eyes to see the last breaths of my classmates, for my skin to feel the warmth of their blood, for my ears to hear their cries and pleas, for my nose to smell gun powder and acidity of iron, for my soul to feel damaged beyond repair. This wasn't in my head, this wasn't in my fantasies, it was chillingly and viciously *real.*

I spent years building up walls around me to keep people out...If I go to my brother's, I have to sit in the back, near the exit, in view of everyone, where escape would be quick. The tension coils tightly in my body *all the time*, I'm constantly in a strained state, my muscles are always working against themselves. I never had to spend too long in a gym, because I get more of a workout just standing somewhere thinking."

The tips of Kade's fingers traced a soft line on my jaw. One lone tear quickly slipped over my lashes, then more followed, streaking sadness down my cheeks. He curled his right hand possessively around my throat while the other wiped away my tears. "Kade, I've seen nothing in you that show madness, only your very understandable anger. Bad therapy can mess up the rest of your existence if you allow one person whom you think holds a degree in something use their opinions to change you into the person they think you should be."

"Enough about me. Now," he breathed against my skin. "Now it's your turn, Samantha Matthews. I just laid my life out for you, so don't be scared, because there's nothing you could say that would make me think differently of you." The fingers at my throat stroked my skin and added pressure.

"Kade, I'm very happy with the person I was and the person I am. I accomplished more in my life at thirty-two than most people do in their entire lives. I'm not ashamed or guilty of anything I've ever done. There's nothing that I think I've done that I regret. Oh, yeah maybe one," I laughed bitterly. "I guess I didn't check my husband's pulse after I thought I killed him, because the sick son-of a bitch is still after me."

Chapter 12
Kade

"So what did you do to him? Fuck, Sam, you tried to kill him?"

Her skin blanched, turning bright alabaster white. "Nah, I used my mega brain power to make him self combust," she tried to joke, and then tears poured down her cheeks, because she knew it wasn't funny.

"What happened?" I asked. *Did she really try to kill her husband? Husband? She was married? She was a killer? Attempted murderer?*

"I stepped out of the train wreck. Battered and bruised, but free. It all started in a heartbeat when my world shifted right out from beneath me and everything I'd ever believed was one huge lie."

"*Fuck*, give me one night of truth. One fucking night of truth for the both of us, before you run for the rest of your life and I get left here wondering why I let you go."

Samantha opened her mouth, about to share something then closed it tightly. Averting her eyes to her hands, she shook her head in frustration. She wiped the stream of tears off her cheeks and struggled to find the words. Her pain was killing me. She sat in silence, and I thought to offer her a bit of space to gather her thoughts together, so I excused myself to change out of my wet pants and get us both a drink. Brandy was always my choice.

With heavy wet pants, I trudged back up the stairs and into my bedroom. Inside my mind, I could feel the pressure building, the not knowing what had happened in her past, and whom she was running from. The question that slammed around my brain like a damn pinball machine was if the person I was obsessing over, the one that made me calm, the one I didn't want to leave. Was she a cold blooded killer? Or was whatever she did justifiable? My mind raced, and the pressure came close to bursting through my gray matter and splattering it against the walls.

Struggling to peel my pants off, my anger took over and I ended up ripping them off and launching them across the room into the corner, where they landed with a loud wet splat then slid wetly down the wall. I yanked open my armoire so forcefully the inside drawer came flying out at me and landed on my foot, sending sharps spikes of pain across it. "Bloody-Motherfucker-Wank-Shanking-Bugger!"

Pinching my fingers over the bridge of my nose, I knew I had to calm myself; I needed to get back downstairs and try to talk to her. I couldn't be up in my bedroom having a goddamn episode.

Rummaging through the mess of clothes that had spilled all over the floor, I found a pair of boxer shorts and pulled them on, then ran for the brandy. Opening the plug, I took a long swig right from the canister trying to settle my anger, then with harshly clenched fingers, I poured us both a glass. The only image that came to mind to help calm myself was smashing both glasses against the wall while still in my hands. I wanted to see the blood that would drip from the wounds and feel the burn of pain. I itched to taste the coppery liquid when I placed my mouth against the broken skin, craved it.

The walls of the room felt heavy against my flesh, moving in, taunting to close around me and collapse upon my body, trapping me. Sounds became solid and tangible. My antique hand-forged wrought iron clock drummed its heavy ticks and tocks inside my temples. Outside the window, rain hissed and clanked against glass like bullets from the sky. Creaks and groans of the floorboards under the rug cracking and whining from my weight sent splinters of electric heat up through my legs. Every sound was somehow physically assaulting my senses, and my breathing accelerated along with the beating of my heart.

Desperately, I tried to focus on the image of Samantha, downstairs, trying to control my monster. I barely made it back down the steps without having an attack. All I had to do was see her.

When I walked back into the room, Samantha was standing in front of the fire, staring into the burning embers as if they held all of life's answers. For a moment, I stood quietly and watched her, wondering if I would ever really get to know her. Her pale ivory skin took on a golden glow in the firelight and I knew I would never again in my life see such a beautiful haunted woman. She raised her arms, twisting up the long dark locks of hair, and clasped them in her hands almost as if cradling her head from frustration. Her chest rose and fell slowly as she took in deep breaths, and I could do nothing to take my eyes from the curve of her breasts and the perfect contour of her hips. She was no cold-blooded killer. Someone hurt her and she needed to defend herself. A fierce wave of possessiveness washed over me and my mouth ran dry. I wanted to erase everyone she had ever loved, any man she had ever cared about, and take her all for myself. Obliterate every memory of anyone that had ever hurt her, and fill her mind with just me. Only me.

Would she even want me after all I had said? Would she take me for half the messed up person I was? Why did it feel like she understood me, as if she'd been touched by violence too?

There was no easy synopsis to give her for what I had gone through, but there was never an easy way to let people in when all you want to do is hide from the things that have hurt you. So, I understood her silence, her hesitation and her pain. I could have told her every little detail of my nightmare, but to what avail? I just wanted to give her some part of me, so she could give me a part of her, so she could trust me.

There are never any easy answers for the questions that came with violence. Thomas made a goddamn videotape of his farewell speech, his suicide note to the world, and left it in the front seat of his car blaming me for everything, making everyone who watched it believe it was all my fault, which was all bullshit. I'd never known he'd go to such bloody lengths to hurt people. Nevertheless, for the rest of my life, I would constantly fight battles with invisible demons because of him, and whatever triumph I accomplished thus far was little to me now, as I stood in front of this woman, because I wanted to be a man she could confide in, someone who is not so damaged. Something about her, standing in front of those flames made me have hope. That made me calm, like the cool misty rain that comes after the chaos of a hurricane.

There were things that I never wanted her to find out about me. There were things I'd done that I felt weak for doing, yet I did them out of feeling so helpless and so full of despair I saw no other options. *Did she feel as helpless in her situation to have had to use violence on someone she had once loved?*

There were things that changed in me so completely from that one day that reverberated into everything and everyone in my life. My life became one huge domino chain, piece by piece, smashing into each other, knocking one another down. I was nothing more than a flimsy house of cards and one strong gust of wind tore me down, blowing my cards to the ends of the earth.

The demons I faced were not only the nightmares from that day, but the faces of the people whom I let down every day after that, because I couldn't hold myself together. My mother, God, my mother found me when I slit my wrists almost to the bone. I will never forget her expression. I will never forget that horror, and I would never forgive myself for it.

I could remember that moment as if it were a mere minute before. My mother unscrewing the hinges of my bedroom door, so quietly that I had no idea what she had been doing until the door fell flat on the floor of my room.

Tears poured from my eyes that day, for the first time since the shooting, when I was shoved into the back of an ambulance. The expression on her face broke my heart. See, I didn't stop to think about how it would affect her; I just wanted to stop my own pain. The paramedics, if you could call them that, orderlies maybe, since they had no knowledge of anything medical, hauled me up and literally threw me into the back of an ambulance, and I bled all over the white sheets of the gurney I sat on since nobody thought to tend to my wounds. The whole ride, my mother got to watch in horror, my life bleeding out from my wrists. *I did that to her.*

At the hospital, I was restrained in a lovely white form-fitting jacket that wrapped my arms fully around my body and I was labeled *insane*.

The people I met in that hospital made everything worse for me, because I knew I wasn't like them. I was touched by violence. There was no chemical imbalance in my head, no malfunction in my cerebral cortex, but no one understood this... They all thought I was mad just like before. The other kids in that asylum were terrifying, constantly listening and arguing with the shouting voices they heard in their skulls.

Jesus told me to kill my dog!
Yes! He did!
My dog told me to kill my teacher!
Yes! I fancy the idea too!

243

An alien from the planet 971 in the Garfilplex Galaxy offered me a million shiny golden stars if I slit my wrists.

Pass me the razor!

You could see the madness and chaos when you looked in their bouncy nervous irises. That was where I learned to watch people, read the body language of everyone around me, learn their innermost thoughts and their next moves. You just needed to recognize the tightness in the skin around their eyes and the tension that coiled the muscles of their faces when they were about to have an episode, because their voices became too loud for them to handle. Or watch the corners of the lips of the nurses and the way they moved their fingers before deciding to inject you with syringes filled with brain-to-broccoli-induced-*crap*. I lived there for three months until my mother finally understood that I wasn't insane, packed Dylan and me up, and left the country.

Nothing had changed since I was that young boy. Now I was this award-winning novelist, with nothing...nothing but scary stories on paper. What was I truly doing, but glorifying murder and horror? Yet, how many fans did I have? Millions. So few of them have actually had their life in jeopardy, faced a near-death experience or been introduced to the real terror of violence. Their way of experiencing it is by being perpetually entertained by books and movies that safely portray it. If they only knew how it seeped into your cells and overwhelmed your psyche, I wonder if they would cease to partake. The truth is easy.

Once you felt violence, most people couldn't cope with it, they couldn't even push the words through their lips. It instantly freezes the images in your mind, and those images are indestructible. Then there are people like me, who have been touched by violence so deeply that they completely lose their soul to it.

"Are you okay, Kade?" Samantha's voice, as soft as a symphony, floated through my muddled mind.

I lowered the two glasses of brandy to the table, and sat down on the couch, eyes fixed on hers. I'd been hovering on the edge of humanity for far too long. I wanted to step away from that ledge and I wanted to love her. "Everything that happened...to me...is stained here," I whispered, touching my hand to my heart. "It will forever be in my heart, but what I want, Sam, is to move it over a little so I can fit you in there too."

Her cheeks bruised crimson and I felt a surge of power knowing I could make a grown woman blush so deeply. She was taking all the chaos that constantly swarmed by mind and calmed it, without ever trying to.

I needed her. Right then. Right there.
She was going to be mine.
I didn't want to let her go.

Chapter 13
Samantha

"Undress for me," he whispered, raking his teeth over his bottom lip. "Slowly."

He leaned back into the cushions of the couch, sliding his splayed fingers across the leather. "I want to know who Samantha Matthews is...unwrap every part of her for me."

The words blanketed me, wrapped me in warmth, tucking me in tight.

"I want to see all of you, Sam. Every scar." Leaning forward, his elbows pressed into his knees, his whispers tickled my ears, "Then I'm going to make you forget how you got each fucking one."

I was breathless as I looked at him, trembling, throbbing...he'd changed into a pair of black boxers and nothing more. My muscles ached to slide over him, and sheathed him in my warmth. I wanted to tell him everything, have him make me forget with his kisses and his words. And I could. I could forget everything in someone like Kade Grayson for just a little while.

But I'm terrified.

Shaking fingers grabbed the hem of my shirt, heat surged to my cheeks, and I paused.

"Who made you frightened to stand in front of a man naked, Sam? Who broke you?" He asked in whispers.

The questions made my cheeks burn hotter, and for a moment, I feared they would blister and peel; falling like broken feathers to the floor.

Squeezing my eyes tightly, I slowly raised the soft fabric of the shirt up over my stomach and my breasts. A cool breeze lapped across my bare skin causing it to prickle and tighten. I lifted the shirt over my head and let it fall quickly to the floor.

"Open your eyes," his voice demanded.

His stormy grey eyes glistened with appreciation as he slid his hand under the waistband of his shorts and placed his fist around his cock, "Samantha, you're fucking stunning." Below the silky material he wore, his fist started gently moving. "Now, give me a piece of your heart, Samantha. Tell me something."

The flames of the fireplace snapped and crackled behind me, the burn of its heat scorched my naked back, biting at my skin. The small bit of pain it brought gave me courage; *but his stare*, his stare made me forget my inhibitions. "The first time you kissed me in the trailer...it was the first time any man had ever called me beautiful," I whispered, as I watched him pull himself out of those silky shorts.

A single pearl of pre-cum rested on the head of his cock as his clenched hands glided over its thickness. My tongue craved a taste, as I watched the small opal bead tremble slightly and slide down the smooth edge of his tightened skin. My breathing changed, quickening, as the teardrop slowly dripped under his fingers and disappeared into the rhythmic movements of his tightly fisted hand. "I tried so hard to stay away from you, but I couldn't get you out my head. Every time I thought of you, I became more and more consumed, haunted by you. The harder I tried to forget about the things you said to me, watching you dance, and *fuck me*, that kiss, the more obsessed I became. I couldn't focus on anything else but you. I had no clue what you were doing to me; only that I needed you with such intensity that it terrified me. I found myself back at the bar watching you, like a junkie jonesing for my fix. You're more than just beautiful, Sam." His hands moved faster over his cock, his thumb rubbing its milky tears around its head.

I was speechless. *This was a scene in a rated-R movie, not something that happens to a woman like me in real life.* His words had me hurtling through space, sweeping past stars with the brightness of the moon dancing its shadows over my skin. My thumbs slipped under the waist of my pants and I gently guided them down my legs and stepped out. I wanted to be the starring actress in this movie.

Releasing himself, he leaned his hands on the edge of the couch and slowly stood. Paralyzed, I stayed in front of the fire and watched as he slowly closed the distance between us, stalking closer and closer, a hungry predator. The damp flesh between my legs ached with a nervous anticipation and suddenly he was on me, against me, my back thudding against the wall. He pressed his forehead to mine, and fixed his dark stare on me. "Beautiful is a pathetically weak word for what I'm seeing right now," he growled.

The coarseness of his fingertips trailed down the skin of my neck sending tingles of prickly gooseflesh along my body. His mouth touched me, two soft warm lips against the flesh of my neck and the lightest flick of his tongue. His chest heaved against mine. My heart raced as I leaned my back further against the cool wall. I could feel my pulse throbbing in every part of my body as his erection pressed against the flesh of my stomach. "I can't get your taste out of my head, Sam."

Rough thumbs grazed along my jaw. His lips nipped my flesh again and again, raspy breath, hot against my skin. When his lips finally tasted mine, his savory flavor went to my head, his smell, and his touch. I was drowning in his warmth. His hands tore through my hair, his lips urgent and hungry. Just like in my trailer, you didn't easily forget this kiss. I was a thirty-two-year old woman and I'd never been kissed like this before. Ever. Kade Grayson kissed the thoughts right out of my head, kissed my fears and anxiousness away, leaving me empty, and then poured himself in.

With his lips still on mine, he walked backwards until the back of his knees hit the couch. Then his hands slid over my ass and he pulled me down against his body until I sat straddling his legs. His hungry lips kissed warm wet trails down my neck and across my collarbone.

The scorching heat of his skin, bare, against mine had me panting. The strong grip he had on my flesh tightened as he pressed his tongue against one of my nipples. It swelled and hardened under his mouth. I could have wept with the need to melt myself over him.

My hips rolled against his lap and the smooth taut skin of his erection slid just under my warmth. He ground his hips with mine and it made me want to slide my wet aching flesh over his cock. My muscles ached to wrap themselves around it, and bury him deep within.

Teeth raked against my skin, and my eyes fluttered closed as I savored the nip. I held my breath until he nipped again and let out a small gasp as his hands pressed me closer and slipped down into the throbbing heat between my thighs.

My flesh wept for him, his fingers, and his tongue and then when I could take no more, he climbed over me, wrapping my legs around his waist. Gray eyes fixed on mine as he suspended his face over me, his erection lying heavily against wet flesh. He paused, hesitated for a moment, basking in the need, standing against the edge of what was about to happen. I swirled my hips against his. I could barely stand the emptiness that ached inside me and it made me want to beg for him.

Thick fingers grasped the back of my neck; lips hovered over mine, eyes locked. "I'm falling in love with you, Sam, and I'm going to let you destroy me."

In one slow brutal thrust, Kade buried himself in me and I was lost.

His gasp shook along my skin as he moved inside me with slow deliberation. Muscles and tendons tensed, jaw clenched tightly trying to control the brutality of our lust. I didn't want his restraint; I didn't want his control. *I wanted him.*

I arched my hips to his violently. The look of pleasure settled across his face, and his growl echoed against my ears. His movements quickened, tightened and hardened. Long savage thrusts, the thread and pull of fingers twisting in my hair, the slap of wet skin against skin, thighs soaked with lust, this tangled state of ecstasy was what they wrote books about. Tingling heat coiled in my thighs. The pressure of explosion throbbed along my insides, building and building, aching and aching.

Kade bit into the sweaty flesh of my neck and I moaned a guttural sound as the brutally beautiful pain pushed me over the edge. My body jerked as my muscles began clenching around him tightly.

"Oh, God, Sam..." he whispered fiercely as my muscles continued to clamp shut around him, and within moments his breath struggled in his throat as he stared into my eyes. "Look at me, Sam. Open your eyes and see me."

I hadn't realized they were closed, but they were squeezed so tightly they ached. His eyes looked at me with such need that it made my entire body tremble and shudder uncontrollably, as he continuously thrust himself inside me. Pale grey eyes held mine prisoner as he spilled himself inside me with long hard thrusts, making me come again almost violently. I had never held someone's gaze before through an orgasm. It was the most intense feeling in the world. It felt as if he was telling me something with his stare, spilling *more* than himself inside me. It was beautiful and dark, twisted and profound. I felt cherished, treasured, and as terrifying as it was; I felt as if this was where I belonged.

That night, over and over again we explored each other's bodies, tasted, touched, clawed, scratched, bit and kissed in the dark sanctuary of his home in *every room*. I had never spent a night with someone like that. I never spent a night with someone that made me feel like I was beautiful.

When his lips finally pulled away, spent, it was as if the earth had lost its sun and I curled beside him under the blankets tucking my knees up against him for warmth. His breathing evened out as he fell asleep and I lay watching the reflections of lights in the dim room, fading into blurry colors. It reminded me of how easily any emotion can fade and shift into something you never believed you could feel. In a blink of an eye, fear could turn to bravery, happiness could turn to disaster and hate could turn to love. Kade Grayson told me he was falling in love with me and that I would destroy him.

The suffocating sensations of hands around my neck made me crawl out of bed. I needed air, and I needed to think all these emotions through, because I wanted to stay in that bed with Kade, I did. I wanted my life to start over again with him, and have that Disney fucking fantasy, but let's keep it real. Love wasn't going to heal either one of us. I was not going to erase the events that took place in his life, just as he wouldn't be able to save me from mine.

Chapter 14
Kade

I knew I was far-gone when I woke to an empty bed, after a night of continuously shifting towards the warmth of her body in my sleep, a sleep without the sweat of nightmares, only to wake and find a cold empty spot where I hid my heart. She had it too, and I was intrigued with what she'd do with it. Crush it beneath her little white converse sneakers, or with her bare fucking hands? I didn't care too much how it was she crushed it, just as long as she did. Pain was just as good as pleasure, because it was *something*. In a blind frenzy, I dove head first through the tangle of sheets to find her.

She was beyond my ability to put what I felt into words.

Something other than the emptiness.

The hate.

And rage.

But my fucking bed was empty. Empty and cold.

Slipping on a pair of shorts, I stormed past the balcony ready to search the ends of the earth for that woman, but I noticed a small movement just outside. Pressing my hands against the cold glass, I could see her silhouette in the darkness, huddled up on one of the lounge chairs, as soft flakes of snow fluttered down around her.

The door creaked as I pulled it open and her head turned in my direction.

"Jesus—Lain...Sam...it's freezing out here. What the hell? You're so cold that you're shaking." I hovered over her and gather her small shivering body in my arms, "Bloody hell, Sam, you're fucking soaking wet."

Her body shook against me. Then trembling lips touched mine with such a hunger that I was instantly kissing her back, carrying her inside the warmth of the house and thrusting into her so violently, so dominantly that I was afraid I might have broken her. But her hands fisted my hair, clawed at my back and matched my thrusts, her body pressed against mine, encouraging me, begging me for more.

Being inside her wasn't like any of the empty fucks I'd had before, it was filled with some sort of overwhelming emotion that made me feel like I could breathe. Her pussy was flooded with thick pleasure; her moans were all the music I would ever need to hear. It was pure insanity, crazed hunger that drove me into her over and over again.

It felt...it felt like I had never had sex before. Yeah, yeah, I know how damn crazy that sounds, but...it was the first time the flesh beneath me came with heat, and scent. It was the first time I noticed the taste of someone, the touch that only she gave; the tingle that only her breath could cause on the surface of my skin. It was as if I'd been abstinent for years, alone in a dry uninhabited land, completely unaware of what sex really was.

It was the first time I cared about someone. It was the first time it was real for me. She was just as damaged and out of bounds as me. All I wanted was to seep into her skin, curl myself around her heart, disappear completely and escape into her body. To have her taste on my tongue forever, have her smell and touch drown me, and her face always in my sight.

I wanted to erase everything fucked up that had ever hurt her. I wanted to spill myself inside her and fill her with me, no one else. She clung to me, clawed into me, ravaged me just as I did her, and finally, as sleep crept over her body, I watched her. The repetitive thought of her walking out of my door looped over and over again in my mind. I knew she would leave. I also knew that whatever darkness that held her prisoner was not something she was going to go back to.

I watched her. For hours, I just lay and watched her.

I watched as the first rays of glistening sunlight fell against her skin, soaking it with a golden morning glow. Her inky black hair splayed chaotically across my pillows, her breathing light and even. She lay on her stomach, as the sun and shadows danced their way across the curves of her flesh, unknowing. She laid bare, save for the thick comforter she'd tucked her toes under in her slumber.

She shifted onto her back and a small sound, almost a sigh, passed her lips. Watching the light spill into the room, crawling up her skin, my cocked twitched to life. Hardened rose tipped nipples lay perfect atop her ivory breasts. Her raw beauty paralyzed me.

I watched her.

My tongue found its way to the perfect peaks, and she moaned quietly against me; so close to her smooth skin. Then, with the sunlight slowly brightening up the room, I noticed things I hadn't seen the night before.

Torrid heat flushed through my body, stinging my cheeks and burning my scalp as adrenaline slammed through my bloodstream. Violent images flipped through my mind, a flash slide show of horror and blood, and *Sam*.

"What the fuck is that?" I growled before I could stop myself.

"Kade?" she asked in a sleepy voice. She lifted her head off the pillows, wild dark hair spilling past her shoulders, and sat up, tucking her feet underneath her. "Kade? Is something wrong? Is it...is it Dylan?"

Fuck yeah there was something wrong. She had scars across her body; raised fucking ridges of flesh, a pale pink shade that matched the natural color of her lips. Yeah, there was something real fucking wrong, because some of those scars spelled out fucking words. *It was a fucking name.*

David.

I could feel the anger coiling tight, threatening to explode.

"Kade?" She was looking at me with those beautiful doe eyes, and then realized what I saw and clawed like an animal for the blankets to cover herself.

"No. Don't," I whispered, but she continued to scramble for the covers, pulling them out from under my body, tugging and yanking. "No! Don't fucking COVER YOURSELF!" I screamed. I tore the comforter off the bed and hurled it across the room, and there she sat, naked, alone on my bed with her arms wrapped around her body as if she could hide behind them.

"Who the fuck is David? Was that your husband?"

"Yes."

"Why would you do that to yourself? Why the fuck did you let him brand his fucking name on you?"

She laid her palms flat on the bed and shifted herself over to the edge, and turned her face away from me, "I wasn't conscious when he did it." Moving off the bed, her beautiful lithe form glided across the room and started dressing.

No. No. No, no-no-no-no-no.

All the air just sucked out of my lungs and I had no idea what I could have said. I probably should have said so many things, but didn't, nothing filled my mind but emptiness. I watched her cover my sanctuary with remorse.

"He had his own branding tool and a butane torch."

"I'm sorry, Sam. I shouldn't have yelled. I...I don't know what to say...I don't know anything and I want to know everything..."

"Coffee," she whimpered, standing there in just an oversized tee-shirt.

"Excuse me?"

"I need coffee. I go through serious withdrawals without it," she smiled then, but I knew she was humiliated, and it drained away part of my impulsive anger, *part of it*. I knew she was just buying time until she could get out of there and never have to explain anything to me.

So I made her coffee. Because, well, if Samantha Matthews, whoever she was asked me to build her a boat, I would have worked on that too. Placing my hand over my own scars, I tried to think of anything but someone branding her smooth skin. Smooth ivory skin that smelled like apples and cinnamon. Smooth ivory skin that tasted like sweet sugar and felt like soft cream melting under my hands.

That pussy whipped me real good last night. Now I'm hard again.

The coffee mugs clanked as I slid them over the uneven wood of the butcher-block table, and midway across she just reached out, grabbed the steamy hot cup, and brought it to her lips. After the first few sips the relief in her expression was priceless and her shoulders loosened as she leaned forward, resting her elbows on the table.

"Sam?"

"Yeah?"

"Please fill in some holes for me."

"Which ones?"

"All of them. Start with your childhood, I don't care. But I want to know everything about the woman that will destroy me when she fucking walks out of my life," I clipped. *Damn, I was being a dick.* But, it hurt like hell and I wanted to fight with

258

her, sick twisted me, wanted her to ball up her fists and hit me.

She only offered me a tight smile.

That just made me angrier.

"Think those words are going to get me to fight with you? Think I'm going to fuel your rage, stoke the fire, Kade?" Then she leaned over and kissed me on my fucking lips; warm wet lips that tasted like the richest delicious coffee.

"I, ah...I didn't have much of a childhood," she began, sitting back down on her chair. "My father was the best neurosurgeon in Manhattan, my mother a socialite. They had no time for my brother and me, so we played in the hospital while my father worked and my mother did charity work. I grew up in a very sterile environment."

I leaned back in my chair, my anger bubbling just under my skin, yet surprisingly restrained. "Go on," I whispered, taking a sip of my coffee. It tasted better from her lips.

"I was better known for my brains, freaky bookish ways or just being the nerd sitting quietly in the corner. I was obsessed with taking things apart and putting them back together. Breaking and fixing. I was different, so different from everyone else that surrounded me, and I knew it too, deep inside that, I wasn't like everybody else. Instead of playing with dolls, I read my father's medical books and my brother and I snuck peeks at the cadavers. It's crazy to say really. And being that my father wanted my brother and me to follow in his footsteps, he let us view surgeries standing alongside the med students. Everything was always hidden from my mother though. My mother," she chuckled, darkly. "My mother and I didn't get along."

"Why not?" I asked, intrigued that someone couldn't get along with her.

"I was a reminder to my mother of her regrets and the heavy amount of wrinkles that her life delivered to her so unexpectedly. I was never going to be the gorgeous New York City socialite she always strived for me to be. There was not one ounce of sex-tape-diva in me at all. She tried to raise me to be a prim and proper wannabe-heiress. Frilly skirts, patent leather shoes, nails perfectly manicured and skinned tanned to a bronze. But my father raised me to use my brain. I was so against everything my mother wanted me to do, because it wasn't me. I was the Goth girl in the corner, listening to heavy metal music, smoking cigarettes and cutting class to read in the hospital's student library. I didn't want to be anything but a doctor. I wanted to be in the middle of it all." She sipped again at her coffee, placed the mug down, and absently stroked the rim.

"Sneaking into the morgue, or watching the doctors and nurses care for patients was thrilling to me, powerful. It became my obsession, and best of all, completely forbidden by my mother. Later, I would understand her reasoning for wanting me to abstain from the clinical detachment of medicine, but by then, it was too late to learn more from her, since injecting herself with the world's largest dose of morphine was of more importance to her. When my mother died, I was a girl interrupted. I no longer had to hide my addiction to saving people; I no longer had to hide my mother-disapproved freak-side bookish ways. I dove into my freakish nature, along with my brother and father to bury the truth about my life-taking, family stealing, morally corrupt, vain mother, and for the first time in my life, I got to be me."

"Wait, whoa. Your mother's deceased?" I asked.

"Yep. Her suicide letter was written on a neon pink post-it note...she blamed her death on my father's lack of attention, and the hate she had for her life as a mother and wife, and nothing more."

Silence overtook the room as she quietly stared into her coffee. Her brows pulled elegantly together and she leaned back and sighed heavily, "Anyway, I realized I had something special to give to the world and I fucking did it. I took pre-med college classes when I was still in high school. They put me in the accelerated program in a medical charter school and I started medical school when I was just nineteen. After med-school, I ah...I wanted to start helping people...I was exceptional at what I did; it was all I knew. So I did my doctoral program and my residency where I thought I'd see the most trauma, where I was needed the most, you know."

"In the city?" I guessed.

"No," she said swallowing nervously, one hand cupped around her coffee and the other twisting the bottom of her shirt. "I was a Medical Corps Officer in the 82 division of the US army. I spent six years there. What should have been my residency years doing rounds in a sterilized hospital with holier than thou doctors making me guess what was wrong with patients, I spent in the bowels of Afghanistan, where real life hell was being played out. Where I learned to be a real trauma surgeon. Where it mattered."

Holy fucking hell.

Anger bubbled over, and I jumped to my feet, fisting my hair in my hands. "Fuck, Sam. Fuck, Sam. FUCK!" *God, seriously? What the fuck? Can there be more shit to make me want her more? Can there be more shit to make me fall in love with her faster?*

"What about you, Kade?" She asked, ignoring my outburst. "What was your childhood like?"

"Normal," I barked, kicking over the garbage bin and sailing it across the room. "I was a jackass, my best friend was a dick and all we ever did was to try to get laid, and then he turned into a mass murderer. I never did anything remotely worthy of mentioning in the presence of someone who fought in wars or saved lives. You...you're like some sort of...of...I don't know, saint or something." I was yelling. Bitter words, twisted heart and devastation hooked its talons into my brain. Why was I becoming more and more enraged with how precious and moral she was? *Oh, the fucking answer was simple really, because when she leaves, she's going to take it all away from me.*

Her phone beeped and vibrated against the table like the ring at the end of a boxing match. She reached for it hesitantly and read the message.

Clearing her throat, she whispered softly, "Bree just messaged me that she's going to leave the hospital in about an hour. She wants to know if she could come here to wash and change. Says she smells like rotten meat. Deputy George will drive her..."

"Yeah, of course. She can't go back to that trailer and don't you mean Jennifer?" I snapped, trying hard not to lose it *completely*.

"Um...yeah." Her fingers deftly moved over the screen of her phone, then a moment after they stilled, it beeped and vibrated in her hands.

"Deputy George said the gunman had a rap sheet on him a mile long. They are linking the incident up with a bunch of highway robberies and suspicious missing person's reports from the city, but they don't believe we have anything to do with why it happened. Your brother was just in the wrong place at the wrong time." She typed something else quickly and placed the phone down in front of her, exchanging it with her cup of coffee.

"Stop talking about other shit! Tell me about the *fucking scars*. Tell me about David," I fumed.

"You're way too angry to talk about this," she said, rising off her seat.

She moved in front of me, her knees touching mine. I slid my chair back automatically, giving her room. Then...then once again, she did something in-fucking-credible to me. She straddled

263

her legs over my lap, wrapped them around the chair, threw her arms around my neck and fucking hugged me.

She. HUGGED. Me. I hadn't had someone hug me since I was sixteen.

For a minute, my arms awkwardly flailed at my sides, hugs were foreign territory for me. "You're just trying to get out of talking to me, and this is making me even angrier."

Her lips pressed against my forehead, long silky hair fell around our faces like a dark thick curtain, closing us in. The slow circular swirl of her hips over mine, the liquid motions from the muscles of her thighs and the delicious heat between them had me fighting to hold onto my anger.

Then one of the hands that had been holding my enraged expression, trying to calm it into a smile, slid slowly down into the warmth between those thighs. *Fuuuck me, I forgot she was only wearing that tee shirt.* The most delicious sounds of fingers slipping through wet flesh made my world spin and saliva flooded my mouth.

"No. I'm not trying to avoid telling you about him. I just want whatever time we have left to be worth something, and not spend it on him. He's taken too much from me already," she whispered, tracing her tongue against my lips. The sensation sent all the blood in my body surging lower, pumping my heart faster and made my cock throb with anticipation.

"You're right, but I can't let it go. I want everything from you, everything, Sam. Give me something, Sam."

"David was the kind of man that could bewitch the rarest of butterflies to land in the palm of his hand, then tear their wings right from their bodies and laugh when they tried to fly away. No more talking, Kade. Not now, the anger rolling off you is so thick I can see it. Please. Please, just take me."

Her lips brushed against my neck, her hand still moved between her legs and the violent thoughts in my head were building. "You're not going to be able to handle me when I'm this angry, Sam. I'm not a nice lover like this. I'm harsh. Rough. Demanding. I'll fucking break you."

Her movements stilled, her eyes locked on mine, "I've been broken by lesser men than you, Kade Grayson. Being broken by a good man is something I haven't done. Break me, Kade. Trust in me enough to know you can."

The spark of craving in her green irises and the seal of her lips over mine was all it took. Grabbing her by her wrists, I yanked her off my lap and pulled her into the bedroom, flinging her on the bed. "Take off the shirt," I demanded.

With my hands blindly rummaging through my top drawer for something to tie her with, my eyes were fixed on the sheer velocity of her yanking the shirt over her head and flinging it across the room. Stalking to the bed, I pulled up her wrists and bound them to my bedframe with my tuxedo ties with half hitch knots. Pushing open her legs, I kneeled between them, feeling the heat of her pussy against my skin. "Am I scaring you?"

"No," she said demurely. Perfectly.

Threading my fingers through her hair, I pulled her face up to mine. "Fuck Ms. Matthews, you like being tied up don't you?"

"Probably as much as you do, Mr. Grayson."

"You liked being spanked, Ms. Matthews? Because I've wanted to see that perfect ivory backside of yours turn pink under my hand."

Her answer was to flip herself around and raise her ass in the air at me, arms stretched and crossed from the bound bowties. It was the sexiest thing I had ever seen.

My hands glided up her thighs, slid over the plump cheeks of her ass and my tongue followed behind. "Give me a word for you to escape from this," I whispered against her flesh.

"I don't need one, Kade. I trust you."

"Baby, give me a word so you can have the control."

"*Tuxedo*," she whispered.

The slap made her gasp. And there, on the right side of her ass was the beautiful pink hue of my handprint. Just one slap. One slap and I was breathless, in a frenzy to thrust inside her so deeply. Two more slaps and I caressed the soft pink spots as she panted for more.

Slowly, I dipped my fingers into her. "You're soaked, Samantha. Tell me what you need," I murmured. My fingers stroked in and out, faster and faster, "So fucking wet." I wanted to consume her.

"I need you," she whispered, pushing her hips to the rhythm of my fingers.

Thrusting my cock into her, she cried out in a loud moan, thighs quivering. With my fingers still wet from her, I eased two fingers into her ass.

Groaning, her hips began grinding into mine. *Holy shit, she liked it dirty.* Her muscles squeezed around my cock, they trembled and wept as I thrust into her again and again. "You feel so good, Sam." Harder and harder. Faster and faster. She took it all. She's played submissive before, and she's played it well. The thought broke me.

"Oh fuck," she gasped. "Don't stop, I'm going to..." She was constricting around me so hard I couldn't hold back, I didn't want to.

Clutching at her waist, I slammed my hips against her flesh and spilled myself inside her, both of us collapsing and panting onto the bed.

Easing my fingers and my cock out of her, I freed her from the bowties and gathered her in my arms. She giggled and tucked her body into mine, "We are both in desperate need of a shower. We smell like sex. Lots of sex."

Chuckling into her hair, I smiled, "Smells pretty delicious to me."

She slapped my ass hard, "Come on, Kade. Let's get one together."

Fuck if I was going to say no to that.

In the middle of us trying to get dressed, and more discussions of her childhood and avoidance of any David conversations, my damn doorbell rang and Bree, or rather Jennifer, stood outside my door with a coat covering a blood

267

streaked shirt.   It sobered up my extreme horniness immediately. Samantha pulled her through the front door and into my kitchen, shoving a cup of coffee into her hands. "I was just telling Kade about my childhood," she said seriously to Jennifer.

Jennifer stood there awkwardly. "Kade, this is Jen and I'm tonic," she laughed. I didn't and neither did *Jen*. She always tried to make the most awkward jokes to ease other people's discomfort. Even though it never worked, she never gave up trying to make people feel better. That said a lot about her character to me.

"Uh...so...How's Dylan this morning?" Sam asked.

"He's doing really well, no infections so far. In fact, he's even up and walking."

Relief swept over Samantha's face as she pulled her friend into my bathroom, bringing her duffel bag full of clothes.

Sitting in my leather recliner, I listened as the women spoke, sometimes in whispers and I tried desperately to keep my rage under control.

"Before I leave, I just want to change my look again, maybe go blonde this time, cut it short," Sam's voice explained.

"Where are you going to go, Sam? I just don't understand it? How did he find you? I don't get it. He looked dead," Jen whispered.

"I've been trying to wrap my brain around this all night and I can't figure out how he knew where I was, or how he is even still breathing," Sam whispered.

Hushed words whispered back, "Have you stopped to wonder if it might be your father?"

A few heart pounding beats of silence filled the room. *Her father? Her father wanted her dead too?*

"I...I don't want to believe that, Jen. My father," I heard her clear her throat and struggle for the right words. "It could be him, but, I'm not staying here to find out. It's only going to be a matter of time before someone else comes here to finish the job. I just want to leave so everyone here is safe."

"Do you want me to..."

"No!" Sam yelled. "You shouldn't have come with me in the first place. You need to stay here with Dylan and have a life." The shower turned on and I heard things being moved around. "And, I also need you to make sure Kade is okay. Make sure Dylan and Kade stay close, okay?"

I didn't listen to the rest of the conversation, because I didn't want to hear anymore. She just needed to stay here. I could keep her safe. She was going to fight me when walking out my door. Waiting inside the kitchen, drinking the rest of the coffee, I battled with my demons and with reasons to tell her to stay.

After thirty minutes, they walked out and we drove to the hospital in silence. Sam and I glanced at each other often, but no words were exchanged and it started to weigh heavily on my shoulders. She wanted to leave that night and I wanted to be inside her a million more times before she left.

The three of us made our way to the front desk and grabbed visitor's passes, and then waited for the elevator to take us to the sixth floor. When we stepped into the elevator, I couldn't help but stand close to her, touch her neck and skim my fingers through her soft silky hair. I fucking wished that Jen wasn't there, because I needed Samantha, right then. I needed her more than anything.

Jen eyeballed us weirdly. "Oh, my GOD! You two had sex didn't you? Holy shit, you had sex last night?"

Samantha's face instantly turned bright red. "Why would you think that?"

"Because you've got that *up all night fucking* look and the way you're eye fucking each other right now...you're both itching to have elevator love, right here." Then she broke out into a chorus of *Love in an Elevator* by Aerosmith. "Gah, just don't get hot and heavy in front of me. Sex in an elevator is just wrong on so many levels. Get it? So many *levels*?"

"Yes. Very...*punny*," I chuckled, stepping closer to Samantha. Screw it, Jen was right and I wanted my hands on her, *now*.

"Well, I usually *take steps to avoid elevators*, especially if someone like Kade Grayson is on the elevator. You might end up *getting the shaft*," Sam whispered giggling.

Oh, it's on. No one could play word games as well as I could. "Yes. Elevators aren't very fun. It's like being *trapped in a box*. Although I'd like to be trapped in *your box*, and I didn't hear you complaining about my *shaft* last night."

"Even though you think you're *pushing my buttons*...you will not get a *rise out of me*, Mr. Grayson. Now, stop all the elevator puns, they're *driving me up a wall*."

I was dead-ass laughing. I had to think of more puns quick. "You didn't mind when *my shaft* was *driving you up the wall* last night."

"Yes, I recall being in between a *cock and a hard place*," Sam quipped.

"Yep, the best damn *cock climber* I ever saw," I smiled.

"This is like pure *pun*ishment," she laughed.

"Well, I am the *pun*isher," I said, locking my eyes on hers.

"Yes, my ass still stings nicely," she smiled. *How the hell did that woman think I was going to let her walk out of my life?*

The elevator doors opened to Dylan's floor and both women exited, laughing. I had three thoughts as I watched her walk out. One, I needed a sandwich. Two, I wondered where the best hiding spot was in this hospital to fuck Samantha. And three, how the hell was I going to get her to stay in this town? I wanted her to be with me, no one else was going to have her. Period.

Creepy? Yes. Possessive? Absolutely. We all know I have issues. I. Don't. Care. What. You. Think. I wanted her. She was the only person in this world that I had ever met that made me think differently about things.

My brother was sitting in one of those reclining hospital chairs next to a window when we walked in. The luckiest man I knew. Who else gets shot twice in a bar fight, and the bullets hit nothing important? He looked great, too. The color was back in his face, his smile was bright and they were already feeding him solid food.

"I'm so sorry that I brought trouble with me," I heard Sam say to him as she sat softly on his bed.

"It was worth it, just to get to see my brother as much as I did, and to see him smile. I wish you'd stay." His eyes glanced at Jennifer, "Jen told me about everything, but I still wish you'd stay here."

"I can't, Dylan. I can't have any more people hurt."

Hearing her say the words so decisively tore at my insides. Pulling up a visitor's chair, I slumped into it and detached myself from the conversation, from the smiles and the laughter, from the world, wondering if any of this was worth fighting for.

I only registered a bit of information they discussed. Samantha wanted to change her appearance, dye her hair again, and they bickered over colors. Jennifer spoke a little about the shooter, and then there were some mentions about states like Montana and North Dakota. Then at some point, I couldn't even tell you when or how long after we got there, Sam and Jen went to get coffee in the cafeteria and I was left alone with my brother staring at me.

"Kade, mate. Don't let her go," he said.

"What?" I asked, waking up from my self-induced coma.

Dylan leaned forward, clenching his face in pain and repeated, "Don't let her go."

"What the fuck am I supposed to do?"

"Make her feel safe here. She can't go out there on her own," he whispered.

I laughed bitterly, "Actually, I think she can. She's probably the only woman I ever met who could take care of herself on the run for the rest of her life." I stood up, stretched and walked to the window. My rage lay just an inch below my surface.

"Do you care about her?" He asked.

"Bloody hell, yes," I replied. Bending down to face him, trying desperately to hold back my anger, I sneered, "She doesn't want to stay. End of story. I'm not a hero. I have no safety to offer her, I can't even think of anything, except tying her up and locking her in my bloody basement."

"Fine, Kade," he mumbled, as the girls walked back into the room. "I guess after she leaves, I won't be seeing you for another couple of years, huh? It was nice to have you bloody visiting."

Samantha handed me a warm cup of coffee, but I didn't even taste it. I just sat back down in the corner and hunkered down in my fictional thoughts, where I had more control over everything. It was easier to breathe that way.

After we left Dylan, I drove her to the store. The day had turned to night and the darkness of it lay heavily on my shoulders. "So how did you meet David?"

"Why?"

"I have the right to know," I snapped.

"Why?"

"Because I've already thrown my heart out for you. Already stripped my soul bare for you, so I want the same in return. I want to know the person who is going to destroy me completely!"

"Does it make you feel better yelling at me, driving faster, gripping the wheel, clenching your teeth?" She asked.

"No."

"Then fucking stop it. You got something to say to me, say it. Don't yell at me because of the situation I'm in when my hands are tied."

"Now, I'm fucking thinking of you tied up. Just tell me the story, no more games. You're leaving right? Tell me something more!"

She turned her head to look out the window. The disregard for my feelings and her looking away cut me deeply.

"David and I developed a tumultuous relationship over one too many glasses of champagne at one of my father's hospital parties and our affair was fast and furious. I looked at him through rose-colored glasses, complete with lens flares and animated floaty hearts. I loved him, I really did. The easiest thing in the world was falling in love with him. I fell in love so fast, head first, feet first, heart first, doesn't matter; it's so damn easy to fall. The hard part was where I landed in his life and how I needed to hold on to who I was. But I fell in love with a complete lie. I never really knew the person he was. Let's just say that he and Thomas would have been a great team."

The parking lot of the store was unusually crowded. I pulled into the only empty spot, stomped out of the truck and slammed the door as if I was throwing a tantrum. "We will finish this fucking conversation!" I snapped.

"Oh, wonderful. I can't wait to continue. You're so lovely to talk to about all my secrets. Just a real sensitive being, you are," she snapped back, storming into the store.

Pushing the cart through the store, she was like a *NASCAR* driver, and you know it has that one fucking wheel that spins around in madness on its own accord, tripping her up and calling attention to itself with its whines. But she was determined. She was determined to get all the fucking shit she needed to change her appearance and leave me.

Hair dye. Men's clothing. Baseball caps. Make-up. I wanted to vomit.

The one, yes one, check out line was at least 25 people long, all of them staring menacingly at the elderly woman holding up the line with a thick wad of coupons for her cat food and asking the cashier to read aloud to her about its nutritional value. A crying, wailing, screeching something-month old baby was in the arms of a harried snot-nosed teenager who bounced quickly back and forth on her flip-flops, even though it was not even twenty degrees outside.

"Why the fuck do you need this shit for?" I picked through the clothing and boots, and other crap in the cart. "This line is impossible. This is insane. Look at these people. They're all pathetic trash. I can't stay here anymore."

"Shut up, Kade!" She hissed poking her finger hard into my chest. "Maybe, maybe this is more about something other than you! Those walls you built up for yourself. You should have installed windows in them, just to get a chance to see there are other people in this world besides you! Maybe that woman needs the nutritional value for herself and not her damn cats because her fucking social security checks don't cover what she needs it to...that baby and that teenager? Well, you think she wants to be strapped with that crying kid, when babydaddy is out with his friends after he promised to make it all up to her? That kid is sick, Kade. Look in that baby's eyes, she has a very high fever...look how limp her body is, look at her nose flaring and listen to her wheezing breaths. She shows signs of pneumonia, Kade, and look how tired the mother is. God, she's just a baby herself." Again, she poked me with her finger, harder this time. "You think they're all here just to get in your way? Look at me...Kade...I'm here because I need to change the fucking way I look because there is someone who wants to see nothing more than me die, and I won't let him...you don't know these people's stories. They are not less important than you are. They have there own issues, Kade, everybody does and you can't know what these people's stories are, even though in your head you think you can automatically tell who and what people are. Are you absolutely 100% sure that your reality is the fucking real one? In your gloriously disordered mind, I was nothing but a stripper."

"I automatically hate. That's all I know..." I mumbled.

She leaned closer to me, smooth skin against my neck, "Last night, you told me you were falling in love with me...love doesn't grow well when it's surrounded by such hate. Stop hating everyone because of the fucked up choices Thomas made. Thomas was Thomas, nobody else is Thomas."

"But they could be. They could turn into a Thomas!" I barked.

She spun me around, tore the sleeve of my coat down, and lifted my shirt harshly up my back. "No, Kade! No! They could be a Leslie, a Gemma, a Henry, a Cory..." she listed the names of my friends who were killed, while gently touching their names with cool fingertips. "You're forgetting the innocent people and always remembering the wicked one."

I yanked my arm away from her, and shrugged my coat back on my shoulder. By now, the whole of the store was watching our fight. "My freedom was taken from me that day!"

"No, Kade, it wasn't. Your *security* was taken from you that day. Your freedom is the choice to let it happen every day since then. This is *your* life. You don't even watch it fly by. You closed your fucking eyes to it, until you saw some waitress with a nice rack. You want to love, Kade, so give up the shit that weighs you down and makes you hate. Let it go. I will fucking meet you half way. I let go of my baggage, if you let go of yours or we're going to hit each other with the heavy packages for the rest of our lives."

My fucking head started buzzing like a cloud of killer bees was circling me. The voices of the people around me sounded too loud, they moved around too strangely, and they watched me too cautiously. "That's a bloody joke, right? For the rest of our lives? You're leaving here; you're leaving me. So there's no meeting anyone half way, is there?" I shifted angrily away from her as the line moved and I started slamming down the items on the conveyer belt at the register.

She scrunched her eyebrows together and lay her hand on my chest, "You're angry because I'm leaving?" The question was asked with pure innocent astonishment. Fuck, she really didn't get it, did she?

"I told you. You're going to destroy me," I hissed behind clenched teeth, as the items beeped past the electronic register in the hands of the cashier.

Instantly, she closed the distance between our angry, coiled bodies, curled her hands tightly around the back of my neck and pulled me down to her lips. Like a lamb to its slaughter, I went.

"Kade..." she whispered against my lips.

"I know I'm being so fucking selfish right now, but Sam, I fucking need you in my life. Stay here with me. I swear I will never let him hurt you again. I'll help you get a job at the hospital here, we'll..."

"I'm not a surgeon anymore, I *can't be*; he made sure to take that away from me. You don't know." Her eyes filled will tears, but they didn't spill. She held them in, I knew not to waste any more on him.

"That will be $286.31," the cashier yelled between us.

Chapter 15

Samantha

I never thought about staying. My only clear *realistic* thoughts were getting away from where David knew I was; the very place where he sent someone to kill me. Sloppily, I might add. David usually did things methodically and cleverly, planned everything out perfectly. *He must be getting desperate.*

Kade wanted to know all about David. Nothing could beat the insane, head bashing, *crapslapping* experience that was *David*. He had left enough marks on my flesh, but what he did to my insides was damage that was beyond repairable, and telling Kade wouldn't change anything. If anything, it would get him angrier than he already was, and the man was a ticking time bomb. Detonating him would only get him hurt, really hurt. Me staying in this town would get him killed, because if David knew I had feelings for someone, it would be an invitation to annihilate him.

Taking my purchases into his master bathroom, I sealed my lips shut. The last thing I wanted was to see Kade hurt, and the last thing I wanted was Kade in trouble, and honestly, the very last thing I wanted was to leave him. I would have loved to see where this thing between us was going, because I had never felt this drawn to a person before. However, I had no choice.

With trembling fingers, I emptied my boxes of hair dye onto the counter and took a deep breath. I had never been a blonde before. Lifting my shirt over my arms and head, unclasping my bra and sliding off my jeans, I stayed in only underwear, not wanting to dye what little clothing I had left.

"What's the natural color of your hair?" Kade's husky voice whispered from the door. He stood shirtless and clean-shaven, both hands resting on the top of the doorframe, pained eyes fixed on mine. Dropping his hands heavily to his sides, the pale yellow decorative globes above the mirror danced dark shadows over the tense flushed skin of his face. His body was hard and strained, muscles tightened and hummed just under his smooth ridged skin.

"Dark reddish brown. Like copper," I whispered.

The soft bristle of the metallic teeth of his zipper took my gaze away from his eyes. Sliding his hand inside the unzipped denim, he slowly tugged out his thick erection, and stroked it.

Warmth pooled low in my belly, twisting into an ache and heavy wet heat between my thighs. My mouth flooded with moisture as I watched his hands move and his expression darken.

One thick hand clutched the base of his cock as the other slid along the top of his shaft, circled around the head and slid back down in slow deliberate strokes. I could hear his breathing change, almost thicken, as his eyes took me in and his body gave in to the sensations of his own hands.

My God, he was glorious to look at.

So glorious that my hands moved all on their own across my hips and right into the cotton fabric of my panties, trying to feed some of the ache. As soon as my fingers touched my damp flesh, I shuddered and lost myself in his slow even movements, matching them. What choices did I have, when the man standing before me touching himself, pleasuring himself at just the presence of me standing there? *He* was a fierce potent arousal.

"Take them off. I want to watch," he whispered hoarsely.

Wet fingertips slipped under the waistband of my panties and slid them down my legs, then flicking them into Kade's chest. My cheeks burned from his attention, but the rest of my body reveled in it, at how open and dirty it was. Pulling myself up onto the counter, I spread my knees wide and pressed my fingers into myself as he watched with eyes wide. Hearing the gasp and heaviness of his breathing, my thighs trembled with delicious anticipation and my hips began moving in a circular motion to meet the thrusts of my fingers.

Kade groaned softly, lips twitched in the faintest of smiles, as he continued to rub himself in long, hard, sensual strokes.

My free hand slid up my chest and captured a nipple in between my fingers, squeezing it tightly. Never in my life had I done this, never had I been so confident sexually, so sure. My own breaths struggled in my airways, speeding up with the surge of pleasure that my own fingers teased a delicious tension in between my legs and along the surface of the hardened flesh of my nipples.

Then he was moving.

A small gasp caught in my throat as he closed the distance between us, leaning the heat of his body against mine. The smell of him, the salty taste of his skin, and the warmth of his breath on my neck was pure sex, mixed with violent possessive need. Right there, then, that feeling should have terrified the hell out of me.

"I'm not letting you go," he croaked, quickening his strokes, pushing the head of his cock along the slickness of my fingers that continued to move deep inside my warmth.

"No?" I asked breathlessly.

"No, I'm not letting you go. Ever. Tell me you want to stay; tell me the truth," he growled, stilling his strokes. The head of his cock pressed slowly into the smooth wet flesh alongside my fingers, teasing me, making my belly tighten with hunger. Desire, lust so thick and real, engulfed me, pressing its thirsty claws against my flesh, squeezing the sweat from my pores.

The need crazed me. It was maddening, as frustration clawed between my thighs, my muscles aching for him to slam inside of me. "Yes! Kade, yes! I fucking love the way you touch me. I love the way you want to protect me, and my God, Kade *the way you look at me.* I love the way it's starting to feel between us, and if I stayed, then YES. Falling in love with you, Kade Grayson, would be quick, easy and so fucking lethal for both of us. You *can't* save me, Kade!"

"You're staying, because you could *save me*," he growled with a jagged whispered breath, sliding the head of his cock up and down my lips, making the ache savagely painful.

"He's going to kill me!" I screamed, slicing through our hot heavy breaths with the serrated icy blade of reality.

"No." His fingers dug deep into my flesh painfully, hard steel eyes fixed on mine. "*I am*," he hissed, as he thrust savagely into me, giving my body what it wept for.

Chapter 16
Kade

The accident was brutal, but it had to be. Only something so bloody and devastatingly violent could count as the finale of her life. I wanted to give her an elegant death, but I also needed it quick and untraceable, so my violent imagination was rendered useless. I sat on my knees at the side of the road, Jen and me crying as we watched Deputy George and Deputy Bobby carry out the body bag that held the woman I had just began falling in love with.

Sickly blue lights rotated dimly in circles, reflecting their eerie deathly presence across the blacktop. Fiery colored road flares burned brightly, sputtering out their warning sparks of danger, leaving a strange chemical taste in my mouth. The scent of burnt metal, charred rubber and gasoline stung at my nose and eyes, making it easier for me to cry. Slick black streams of oil poured out from the main road and into a small ditch that held floating debris. A small lilac ribbon sailed on the surface, slowly spiraling in the thick current. She wore that same little bow the first time I laid eyes on her.

I reached down to keep it as a souvenir. Thick congealed oil coated my fingertips.

You could barely even tell what make of car it was or what color it had been, but you knew that Samantha Matthews was inside. I made sure of it.

The frigid January air burrowed its way into my clothing, seeped through my flesh and sank heavily into my bones. Deeply breathing in a lungful of the icy air sobered my nervousness, and the tears stung like icicles biting at my cheeks. I felt not one shred of guilt for what I had done to her. There would never be any regret in my actions and reasoning. I fought hard not to let her in, but she somehow soaked my soul with hers, leaving bruises and fingerprints, scars and open gaping holes that I knew would never heal. I would bleed her now.

Everyone thinks that men are the stronger sex, that women are weaker, the uncontrollable emotional and defenseless of the two. It's a fucking lie, isn't it? The greatest lie of all mankind, because she gutted me, emptied me completely and I never even knew what had hit me. The only thing I knew was, I wasn't letting anyone have her. *No one would have her, no one but me.* She burrowed under my skin, saturating my muscles and tendons, penetrating my blood cells and she *became part of me.*

My life flashed forward. Like a blunt cut scene of some horror movie with no slow progression to its next images. I found myself sitting in the hospital waiting room, Jen by my side, pale with swollen eyes from a torrent of tears. A large handful of deputies stood like centurions by the entrance, waiting and watching.

Jen had identified what was left of the charred body and personal effects, and so had the deputies. Dental records were pulled, compared and determined that without a doubt, the driver of the car was indeed Samantha Matthews, age 32. The same exact person that went missing from New York City almost six months before under suspicious circumstances.

Once the accident occurred, and after her identification was made, authorities had placed a call to her next of kin. We then waited for her estranged husband, Doctor David Stanton, and her father, Doctor Michael Matthews to arrive.

And they did. They arrived in a flurry of demands, ego and rage. The deputies and our hospital staff did everything they could to ease the turmoil of the situation and prove the identification of the deceased.

Through it all, I sat, still, with Jen on the right side of me, replaying the bittersweet images and sensations of the last time I had slipped myself inside *my* Samantha. Even though I had taken her away from him forever, kept her safe from him forever, my insides hummed with unimaginable violence towards him. Her death was simply not enough.

From where I sat, fists clenched white around the arms of the chairs, muscles pulled tight holding me in place, and I could hear the shallow breaths he took. I could hear the brittle sounds of his voice saying her name and all I wanted, more than I had ever wanted anything before, was to witness every ounce of blood spill from his body. The needs of violence hummed through my veins, causing my blood to pound faster and shifted my heart up into my throat, and my soul into my mouth. My pulse throbbed savagely in my ears, blocking out his voice and flooding my mouth with saliva; I was literally salivating for his death. Foaming at the mouth like a rabid beast.

His flat black eyes fixated on mine and claiming his territory, he asked Jen who I was and why the fuck I was there for his personal family tragedy.

Blindly, Jen entwined her fingers with mine and placed a wet kiss on my lips, "This is Cory Thomas, my boyfriend," she sobbed. "Whatever happened between you and Samantha is over, so go fuck off now and leave me the hell alone or I will tell everyone you beat the hell out of her *and me* before she left your sorry ass."

David's brows furrowed and he turned his back on her, disregarding any other information she would give him. Brilliant, but it barely calmed my thirst to strangle his throat with my hands and feel his trachea crush under my fingertips. My fury blinded me with such an extreme corrosive feeling that my sight turned red, and all I could see was how much I wanted him dead too.

As I stood up to kill him, Jen yanked me by the arm back down into my seat. My insides raged with vengeance until she elbowed me in the gut, "Let's go make the arrangements for her body to be transported back to the city for her *father.*"

"Really? Do I look like his bloody personal assistant? I rather make arrangements for those two sick fucks to get buried."

"Kade," she sobbed into my shirt. "I can't do this, please she was my best friend."

So we made the arrangements.

We also attended her lavish funeral in Manhattan. Wall to wall socialites and the faculty of an entire hospital showed up. The most emotional part was the patients who had come to honor her memory. People she saved. I stayed for exactly eighteen minutes and left. It was too hard.

It was too hard not to completely lose my shit.

It was too hard not to kill David Stanton and that other bastard that she called a father.

I waited in the car for Jen and Dylan with Samantha's little ribbon clenched in my hand. I just sat there and people watched, wondering what sort of life Samantha Matthews had, living in the raw intensity of New York City. Yet, all I could focus on was wondering if I did the right thing. I wanted to fast forward to a time when I would have no doubts about my actions. This bloody mourning was making me doubt everything.

My eyes blinked and it was March, two months since the accident. Two months since I had heard her voice; brushed my fingers along her smooth flesh or feasted my eyes on hers.

Two whole months.

Two whole months of therapy. I promised her therapy. Every fucking single day. It was torture, but how could I say no and go back on my word. Samantha Matthews had given her life to me, so the least I could do was give her some psychoanalysis.

Deep psychoanalysis and nonstop writing for two months. Disgustingly enough, my first shower in a week was just taken and I think I lost at least twenty pounds.

My latest books both received awards; the two books about that waitress Lainey Neveah. The ceremony was a black tie affair tied in with a charity event for our sheriff's department and local hospital. I donated all the sales of the second book about Lainey to the charity. It was somewhere in the millions.

I still counted the exits and people, my coping mechanism for being outside in the world, as I sat in my tuxedo on the head dais. I had reached number 211 when I noticed her. *Number 212.*

Petite and curvy, dressed exquisitely in a simple black dress that fell gently off her shoulders to show the swell of her flawless ivory skin. Ginger colored hair pinned up in an elegant French twist, with one curled wisp that fell along the side of her face and down her slender neck.

The deputy sauntered over to where I was standing, the beauty gliding like an apparition next to him, and I could look nowhere else. My obsession began to hum and hiss inside my heart, cracking and snapping off the thick sheets of ice.

"Kade Grayson, I'd like you to meet Samantha *Tucseedo*. She's a great fan of your work. She's the new doc at the family clinic."

She took my breath away. Big, beautiful sage eyes and lips that I instantly wanted to sink into.

"Hello, Mr. Grayson. It's a pleasure to meet you," she said. A slow sexy smile and a strong smooth handshake were offered to me. I took both greedily, holding onto her hand a bit too long. In fact, I didn't let it go.

The band had struck up a soft ballad a few moments before and I leaned in holding my mouth to her ear, "Dance with me."

Her smile was earth shattering.

I pulled her to the dance floor and wrapped my arms around her more tightly than I should have. "You look so fucking beautiful, Sam."

"Take me somewhere, Kade."

"You certainly are pushy for someone who has just met me. How do you know you can trust me?" I teased.

"I have scars on my heart from you, Kade Grayson."

My gaze lingered on her skin and on how the soft lights cast themselves over the fullness of her breasts in the dress she wore. I trailed my fingertips along the ridge of her collarbone and spread them out across the swells of flesh, gently rubbing the hollow of her neck with the tip of one finger.

She was breathless when I wrapped my hands around her waist, pulled her across the dance floor and into one of the smaller back rooms. I lifted her up and sat her on the edge of a table, staring down at her. My hands slid up the skin of her thighs.

"Didn't your parents ever teach you not to go anywhere with strangers?"

"Mmmm," she moaned softly when my hands reached the heat of her inner thighs. "No, why, Mr. Grayson? What's wrong with strangers?"

The blush that crept slowly over her cheeks had my cock instantly twitching and throbbing to be inside her. "Strangers are bad. Bad things could happen," I whispered in her ear. "They could take advantage of you, tie you up, use you for..."

Her dress was pulled up and she wrapped her legs around my waist, pulling me closer with her legs, "That sounds promising..."

"Fuck, Sam. You don't have anything on under this dress?"

Her lips smiled wickedly against mine.

"Mmmm. You're such a dirty girl," I whispered.

"Oh, Kade, you have absolutely no idea how dirty I can get."

I brushed my lips against the soft skin of her neck. My God, the smell of cinnamon and apples made my dick harder than it ever was. I wanted to sink my teeth into her.

"What's with the strange last name?" I asked, unzipping my pants and throwing my jacket onto the table behind her.

Warm hands, hands I had only dreamt about touching me for the last two months, wrapped around my neck and pulled me in. "It's my safe word," she breathed against my mouth, gliding the heat of her body under mine.

Fuuuucck.

I slid inside her with a deliberately slow thrust, wanting to feel every inch of her that had

292

been hidden from me for two long months. "God, Sam. You feel like heaven around my cock," I whispered.

"God, I've missed you. Thank you for killing me, Kade," she whispered, moving her hips in circles.

"Thank you for letting me, Sam," I whispered back, feeling the first tremors of her muscles flutter around me.

I knew she would feel like she would never be free of him. She would tell me again and again how she felt safe with the temporary witness protection the sheriff's office offered, but I knew deep inside, she still feared he would show up behind her one day, and try to finish the job he started. She would always be looking over her shoulder.

If the case went federal, and the U.S. Marshalls got involved, she would be uprooted and hidden away from me forever, and I couldn't chance it. That was why I had gone straight to George and Bobby with what I knew. We needed to build a case while she was here, a case that was tight, so he could go to prison for a long time. I hated it. I hated that he was still breathing, and that he had somehow hurt her. I hoped that one day she would trust and love me enough to tell me everything.

There were still two brands of his name on her body. I planned on taking her to get tattoos over them, and I knew she would agree... I hated thinking his name was permanently etched onto her. It made me want to end his life every time I saw her naked.

But, could I actually take another's life?

How?

What would I become after?

Did it matter? I needed to protect what was *mine*.

And if he found her again...

I *would* end his life, because I knew there was so much more to the story than she was telling me, so much more he had done to her. And I would kill him for it. It was only a matter of time; only a matter of time until my *Hyde* came out and the part of me that was Thomas would come out and play. Doctor David Stanton has until then to breathe, and until then, she was mine, every brutally beautiful inch of her.

Epilogue-The Love Notes

Letters written between Kade and Samantha in their two months apart.

My Samantha,

It has only been a few hours and already I feel as if my life has been completely emptied of all color. I know we promised one another that we would try our best to be apart until our set time, but this is harder than I ever could have imagined. I'm living in the constant memory of your laughter, your voice, and the way your hands have no fear of moving over my face. I feel lost. Know that I will miss you each moment you are not beside me.

Kade

Kade,

Your words touch my heart in places I never knew existed. Please stay calm, and know that we will be together again soon. I keep finding myself counting down the days and hours until I get to see you again. I can't wait to crawl into bed alongside you and tuck myself against your warmth and know how safe you've made me. I also think back and remember clearly the two nights we spent together. The touches, the whispers, the fights, and the unimaginable pleasure. Thank you for showing me that, and for sharing with me a part of yourself. Thank you for those two amazing nights. I hope we can share two million more.

Sam

My Samantha,

The first day of my psychobabble bullshit sucked. It sucked balls so big I'm exhausted, both physically and mentally. Emotionally I'm just gutted. The only thing that got me through not twisting my hands around that doctor's throat was the picture you sent me last on my phone. I've stared at it for so long that each time I close my eyes your image is burned onto the back of my lids. It wards off the demons. I miss your voice, though. And your touch. And the cinnamon fucking apples. It's not the same when I spray that shit into the air. You are what makes it smell so mouthwatering.

                                        Kade

Dear Kade,

I know how much talking through all the pain in your life hurts. I know how it brings back the nightmares and invites over the demons, but I promise you, it will eventually help you to be able to sit in the same room with them and not even acknowledge their taunts, please trust in me. You need this, Kade. Not for me, not for us, but for Kade Grayson. I miss your voice too. Although I could have sworn that today, my first day at the clinic, someone who looked strikingly similar to you, brushed past me in the hallway of the waiting area and caused me to smile inappropriately at sick patients for the rest of the day. I miss you. But, seriously, how'd you get the note in my pocket?

Sam

Sam,

I have no idea who could have brushed past you in the hall-way, but I'm sure he absolutely loved your natural hair color and the way it probably makes your green eyes brighter than the sun.

This morning, Dylan came home and I brought him and Jen here to stay with me. I know you still worry, so I wanted you to feel safer. Dylan is doing phenomenal, as you probably have heard and he's been at two of my morning therapy sessions with me. It has helped, but not like seeing you again would. I feel as if I've let you hold my heart while we are apart, and it's a struggle to breathe.

P.S. Did you actually pay the maid to slip the note in my underwear drawer? Because the thought of you in my bedroom has me going crazy. Yeah, I'll stick with that thought and not a 55-year-old Ms. Silas rummaging through my boxers.

Kade

Kade,

A small red rose was left on my desk for me this morning. In the middle of this icy cold winter, a beautiful bright red rose. It made me want to kiss you so hard and with such passion, I needed to splash water on my face in the restroom. I can't wait to kiss you again.

P.S. I did not put anything in your drawers, because if I did go in your drawers, believe me you'd feel it.

Sam

Sam,

I dreamt about you last night; your fingertips sliding across my back in the dark of the night to wake me, the taste of your skin flooding my mouth. All I can think of is you, Sam. Touching you again. It's the only place where we exist in my head. The door is locked and we're tangled in a mess of sweat soaked sheets and your lips are whimpering my name. If I close my eyes right now, I can still see you, our first night together, standing in front of the fire with my body pressing into yours against the cool stones of the wall and the flames from the fireplace scorching its heat on our backs. Tonight, Sam, when you lay awake in your bed, touch yourself, baby. Touch yourself and think of me.   -Kade

Dirty Man,

I do, each night. Each night since I've been away from you I do. My hand slides over my skin and I pretend it's yours and when I come alone, I still call out your name. Want to see? Just check your email tonight. I sent you a little present

Your Dirty Girl

Dirty Girl,

This evening when I checked my email, I received an explicit video containing some extremely sexual things.

Please send more. A.S.A.P.

Kade

Kade,

It's midnight. The doors are all locked, your deputy friends have made me feel safe, but I can't sleep. I received your video message while I was in a meeting with the attorneys, and had to wait until now to watch it

I'm lying in bed thinking how I would love to yank on the buckle of your belt and slide the leather slowly through each loop. I can smell the leather too, right now. That's what you always smell like to me, rich, expensive worn leather. My fingers tingle to undo your buttons, and pull down your zipper, pulling your clothes down to the floor. Tasting you.

I miss your taste.

Sam

Sam,

This is killing me. Not being near you. Not touching you. Today was one of the worst sessions. Doctor BrainMasher made me sit through the videos of Thomas. Home videos of us. And, of course, his suicide journal. Dylan was with me. I lost it. I swear I think this is going to kill me and then I think about you. You and your calm voice, your snow-white skin, and the way it feels to be inside you. It's the only thing that holds me back from ripping off that motherfucking shrink's face off and have the rest of my sessions with his bloody skeleton face. Dylan didn't do so well, he puked. Send me a voicemail. Let me hear your voice again.

Kade

Kade,

A few more weeks. A few more weeks and we'll see each other again. I miss you.

Sam

Brutally Beautiful Playlist

Whiskey In The Jar – Metallica
Leaving Earth – Clint Mansell
(Mass Effect 3)
Simple Man – Shinedown
Paint It Black – The Rolling Stones
Raise Your Glass – Pink
Radioactive – Imagine Dragons

Acknowledgements

To my writing bestie Carol Ann Albright Eastman, thank you SO FUCKING MUCH for all the pep chats and awesome advice you've given me. *Especially all the lessons on the correct way to write crap.* May we meet one day for real, although I am sure we'd definitely get arrested. But, no worries, I happen to know a guy...

Thank you to all the talented writers that have touched my life in some way: Angelisa Stone, Deena Bright, and S. L. Jennings, you girls rock. And a huge thank you to Triple M Book Club – a place to honestly share all the angst I have for the books I read, and the once in a while dirty talk, minus the elephant penis picture. I'm still scarred from it.

The biggest thank you goes to my family. To my mother Rita who has been my loudest cheerleader since the day I was born. You made me feel like I could do anything in this world, and then let me. Thank you for letting me - *be me.*

To my husband, Danny, the one I could keep up all night with my ideas and characters, thank you for all the support and encouragement.

To my daughters, Hailey Grace and Emily Marie, thank you for all your crazy, and for all your laughter and silliness. I love you both so very much.

I could name a hundred different people who I want to thank, but this last acknowledgement is strictly for YOU, readers. Thank you. Thank you for believing in me and reading my stories. Thank you for contacting me, friending me, and supporting me. I love you all!

Books by Christine Zolendz

The Mad World Series
Paranormal Romance
Fall From Grace
Saving Grace
Scars and Songs

For more information about Christine Zolendz, please visit:

https://www.facebook.com/ChristineZol?rehl
https://www.facebook.com/christine.zolendz
http://christinezolendz.blogspot.com
https://twitter.com/ChristineZo
https://www.goodreads.com/author/show/64489
39.Christine_Zolendz

Preview of Cold-Blooded Beautiful
By Christine Zolendz

Chapter 1

Samantha

I had just finished my trauma ICU rounds, sneaking in a Snickers candy bar with the cool wall of the staff lounge against my back, when the overhead call came through for an incoming trauma. "Trauma One. Trauma One. ETA five minutes." Savoring the sweetness of my first mouth-watering bite, I learned the paramedics were in route, and there was a fifteen-year-old girl who was ejected from her family's car in a head-on collision, *with an 18-wheeler*, on the Henry Hudson Parkway. *God*, that made my stomach plunge, and the burning bits of chocolate-nougat-caramel bile teased the back of my throat. In this job, you never knew what was going to come through those emergency room doors: gunshot wounds, stabbings, motor vehicle collisions, but the worst was when any of them had anything to do with kids.

Shoving one more bite of candy into my mouth, I tossed the rest of the unfinished chocolate bar into the trash and rushed out, sprinting down the corridor. Icy blasts of sterilized air, mingled with the dark bitter smells of disinfectant and hospital food, permeated around me—through me.

I was running through a crowd of people, toward the trauma bay to scrub up when a stunningly gorgeous woman stepped in front of me, tripping me up and almost hurled me into the wall. She grabbed my arm with icy cold hands, and yanked me to a stop just before I landed.

"You know," she whispered in my ear, digging her perfectly manicured fingers into my skin. "He says my pussy is *perfect*. He calls me his 'Triple P.' *Perfect Piece of Pussy*."

Oh, crap. Did the Freud Squad lose another patient?

"Excuse me?" I laughed a bit out of breath, thinking she must have me confused with someone else. Either that, or someone left a bag of *nympho-crazy-women* open on the wrong floor of the hospital.

"Your husband," she explains. "After I ride him hard and fast, it's what he says, 'Triple P,' that's what he calls me." She smiled triumphantly through blood red lipstick and sashayed away on a pair of loud, deep-red clicking heals that were the exact shade that was smeared heavily across her lips.

"I believe you have the wrong person, Miss," I called after her, standing straighter, one hand dropping over my stomach.

The stunning woman pivoted on the balls of her feet, flinging a handful of golden bouncy curls over a shoulder as if she was starring in one of those perfect hair dye commercials. The hospital corridors spiraled out behind her; bright florescent lights casting blurs of bleeding rainbows inside my tired eyes. "Oh, I don't think so, Doctor *Samantha* Matthews. No, I don't think so at all. He, *David*, even showed me a picture of you."

She knew my name. *And my husband's.*

Was my I.D. badge showing?

No, it was inside my scrubs.

Behind the woman, at the other end of the hall over the loud hiss and clink of the emergency room doors, chaos erupted with the incoming rush of EMTs rolling in the injured girl, and for a moment, a brief one that *I still am so ashamed of*, I froze in complete and utter anguish. Rusty metallic smells hit my senses so forcefully I stumbled back a step, caught off guard. The blonde haired woman smiled widely and winked, and then my vision caught the body of the fifteen-year-old trauma patient rolling towards me, and I was on the move, trying my best to detach and store the hurt and anger for later. *That bleeding fifteen-year-old needed me more.* I barely had time to snap on a pair of latex gloves.

My stomach twisted, tightening every organ on its way up to my throat, filling it with a pool of vomit. I had to gag before swallowing it back down. *Detach. Just do your job. Focus, before your knees buckle.*

The patient flailed about on the gurney, covered from head to toe with blood as panting paramedics screamed the rundown of what had happened. Deep crimson gauze was wrapped around the patient's thigh, head, and midsection, and I had to work fast and stay sharp to try to save the child's life. *Dear God please, please help me save this child, let me forget about David for a minute, let me do my job.*

Removing the dressings, I started going through my checklist, barking out orders. Thankfully, *Samantha Matthews, the sideswiped wife,* disappeared, and Doctor Samantha Matthews, head trauma surgeon, took over.

Despite the thousands of hours of surgical training, horrifying years as a military surgeon overseas, and even all the brainwashing I endured in my early medical career, I still struggled with all of the human emotions that go along with harsh trauma. You don't get desensitized to it, not when it's a kid lying on the table, fighting for her life; anyone who tells you otherwise is lying. Yet, as I always do, I try my hardest to project confidence and grace, strength and complete control in front of my trauma team. Mentally, as my hands crawled along the poorly bandaged girl, I felt through her injuries with the tips of my fingers.

Holy shit, under the bandages the kid was ripped to shreds. It was as if her skin, the entirety of it, split down her center on impact; the stark white of her bones stood out against the angry red of her torn flesh. The deafening sound of my own pulse rushed through my ears, engulfing my entire universe into one focal pinpoint. Exact. Simple. Save the life.

I immediately shoved my index finger into her bloodiest laceration in her thigh, plugging up the source of the most lethal area of the hemorrhage.

"Let's secure an airway!" I turned my attention to one of the trauma nurses, "I need an IV, and an operating room...and get me two units of O-negative."

"Vitals!"

"Eighty-two over fifty-two! Heart rate one twenty!"

"Let's go. Let's go," I barked and within minutes, my trauma team flew into the operating room, rolling in the patient with my fingers still deep inside her leg. The child's femoral artery was completely severed. In a matter of minutes she could be dead; I needed to work fast.

My team worked like one fluid person, perfect and precise. No one noticed my bones were warring with gravity to move, or that my muscles were braided with thousand pound weights, trying to pull me through the floor.

Within a few hours, I meticulously repaired whatever damage I could; I dressed her wounds and said a tiny prayer for the girl in my head. Praising my flawless operating staff, I trudged out of the operating room and headed straight to scrub the mess of blood and fluids from my body.

Emotionally exhausted, I made my way back to my office where I'd left the small lamp on and the door wide open. The outside sky had turned almost black with the moonless night and only one street lamp shone through my small window.

I'd done my best to save that girl's life. She was finally in stable condition in ICU, after four intense hours of surgery, piecing her back together. But there was no more family for her to be comforted by; they were all down in the morgue. There wasn't even any family to inform of the surgery or condition of the patient. They all perished in the crash.

With my adrenaline rush depleted, my body crashed, and I collapsed heavily into the chair behind my desk. I was beyond exhausted, and I still had two hours left of my shift. Dropping my gaze, I noticed a stark white envelope lying in the middle of the desktop, my name written in bold red letters across the top. I could've left it there, unopened and untouched, and then my story would have been so very different, but I didn't. The tiny flip of a paper, a small tear in the flap, and life could change completely, endings and beginnings meshed together and formed circles like the little hamster wheels I never knew I ran in. My bones turned rubbery as I opened it, hesitantly and fumbling. Unfolding the letter that was hidden inside, written on elegant pale pink stationary, I leaned my head back against the cold leather of the chair and read the words that would change my entire *fucking* life.

Made in the USA
San Bernardino, CA
22 January 2014